'The story is exciting, charming and full of emotional

AN

Working in Partnership
with Dundee City Council

g,

uch

to

a,

ke

HAVE YOU EVER WONDERED HOW BOOKS ARE MADE?

UCLan Publishing is an award-winning independent publisher, specialising in Children's and Young Adult books. Based at The University of Central Lancashire, this Preston-based publisher teaches MA Publishing students how to become industry professionals using the content and resources from its business; students are included at every stage of the publishing process and credited for the work that they contribute.

The business doesn't just help publishing students though. UCLan Publishing has supported the employability and real-life work skills for the University's Illustration, Acting, Translation, Animation, Photography, Film & TV students and many more. This is the beauty of books and stories; they fuel many other creative industries! The MA Publishing students are able to get involved from day one with the business and they acquire a behind the scenes experience of what it is like to work for a such a reputable independent.

The MA course was awarded a Times Higher Award (2018) for Innovation in the Arts and the business, UCLan Publishing, was awarded Best Newcomer at the Independent Publishing Guild (2019) for the ethos of teaching publishing using a commercial publishing house. As the business continues to grow, so too does the student experience upon entering this dynamic Masters course.

www.uclanpublishing.com
www.uclanpublishing.com/courses/
uclanpublishing@uclan.ac.uk

A GATHERING STORM

TAMSIN MORI

Cover illustration by David Dean

With interior illustrations by Hannah Blackman-Kurz

uclanpublishing

A Gathering Storm is a uclanpublishing book

First published in Great Britain in 2022 by
uclanpublishing
University of Central Lancashire
Preston, PR1 2HE, UK

978-1-912979-73-8

1 3 5 7 9 10 8 6 4 2

Set in 10/16pt Kingfisher by Becky Chilcott.

A CIP catalogue record for this book is available from the British Library.

Printed and bound in Great Britain by Clays Ltd, Elcograf S.p.A.

For Callen, who weathers every storm
with grace and intelligence

One

THE GATHERING

THE sea was a shimmering net of sparkles, stretching as far as Stella could see. She trained her binoculars on the beach and searched slowly from one end to the other. Tiny waves lapped at the rocks, but otherwise there was no movement. Nobody down there. No sea witch stalking the shallows.

Tamar had claimed that the Haken wouldn't return for months, maybe years, but Tamar had been wrong before. Stella wanted to be sure. It had become her daily ritual – scan the beach whenever they passed this way – make sure nothing was creeping ashore.

"No sign of her," she said to her cloud.

Nimbus didn't seem that interested in being a lookout. He was zigzagging back and forth across the hillside, flinging brief bursts of rain in all directions. He looked like he was having fun.

"Uh uh! No, you don't!" said Stella, stepping back as he swooped towards her.

A flicker of white caught her eye and she brought the binoculars up again: a sailing boat, near the headland, its sails flapping as it tacked. Her heart contracted and she glanced quickly at Nimbus. He was firing rain vertically upwards, then swooping higher to catch it.

"Nimbus! People!"

Nimbus shot straight up in the air for a better view.

"Stop it! They'll see you. Act normal!"

He froze for a moment, then plummeted to the ground and tumbled down the grassy slope to hide behind her legs.

Stella let out an impatient puff. That was *not* normal. But at least down low, he wasn't so obvious.

She squinted through the binoculars. Out by the headland, the triangular white sail tightened to take the wind, and the boat turned again, out of the bay.

"I don't think they saw," she muttered.

Unless they had binoculars too?

Stella looked down at Nimbus. "If I say 'act normal', just *act normal*, okay? Like a *normal* cloud! Clouds don't go shooting around all over the place *or* hide behind people – not even their friends."

Nimbus glimmered cheerful yellow. It was hard to tell if he was agreeing, or just pleased to be her friend. Maybe both?

Stella shook her head and smiled. "Come on. We'd better get to Tamar's. We're meant to be there already."

'An early start', Tamar had said yesterday. But Grandpa had refused to let her leave without breakfast, and she hadn't wanted to skip checking the beach. That would be *just* their luck, if the one day she *didn't* check was the day the Haken returned ...

* * *

Tamar was rolling a fat wooden barrel across the flat stretch of grass in front of the croft. Her tufty white hair was sticking out in all directions and she was pink in the face. Four barrels already stood in a row outside the small cottage.

"Morning, Tamar!" called Stella.

"Ah, good, there you are. Give me a hand."

Stella hurried over and helped Tamar roll the barrel over to the others and tip it upright. She lifted the edge of the lid and caught a sweet smell – meadow flowers. The inside was padded with twists of hay.

Tamar took the lid from her and set it down, then picked up an armful of what looked like rolling pins. There was a large pile of them, waiting on the ground next to the barrels. She began standing the thick sticks on their ends inside the barrel.

"What are those?" said Stella.

"Rain sticks," said Tamar.

Stella picked up one of the sticks and ran her finger down the side. It was intricately carved with a spiral of leaves and birds and flowers. She shook it next to her ear, but it didn't make a sound.

"I thought rain sticks were meant to sound like rain?" said Stella.

"These ones are empty," said Tamar. "That's why I've got them. Charge them up, bring them back to the Gathering, swap them for the empties. There's heavy rain due. Good time to get these charged up."

"*Please* can I come with you?" pleaded Stella. "Please!"

Tamar had already told her several times that she wouldn't take her to the Gathering, but Stella was convinced she could wear her down eventually.

Tamar shook her head. "These things shouldn't be rushed. It's far too early for you to take the trials."

The trials – that's what they were working towards. A series of tests, to prove you were ready to be a full weather weaver, not just an apprentice.

"Not to take the trials," said Stella. "I know I'm not ready. I just want to *see* it all!"

The Gathering sounded amazing – weather weavers from all over the world trading stories and unusual weathers. It was basically like a massive party. A festival of weather weaving. Even if she couldn't join in yet, Stella *really* wanted to go.

"Please?" She smiled hopefully.

Tamar shook her head. "Trust me. It's not a good idea."

"But why?"

Tamar stroked her mouth and looked at Stella uncomfortably. "You're new to all this, and Nimbus is . . . unpredictable."

"He'll be on his best behaviour. I swear. You won't even know he's there."

Nimbus popped out of the last barrel, scattering hay. Tamar raised an eyebrow and looked doubtfully at him.

"I could be your helper?" said Stella. "Carry stuff, run errands . . ."

"Huh," grunted Tamar. "I don't see you helping with these rain sticks!"

Stella quickly picked up an armful of sticks and began slotting them into the barrel. *Be good, Nimbus!* she thought. *I think she's coming around.*

The ends of the rain sticks were smooth and solid. Stella frowned as something occurred to her: "How does the rain get in?"

"It doesn't," said Tamar. "Just the sound. Rain follows rain. The sound of it calls in any wild rain clouds in the area."

"Why would anyone use a rain stick when they could just tell their cloud to rain?"

Tamar rolled her eyes. "Not everybody *has* their own cloud, Stella. There are plenty of people who need rain, but don't have a cloud. Count yourself lucky."

Stella looked at Nimbus and smiled. *I do feel lucky.*

Nimbus fluffed himself up to full size and floated a bit higher – he'd obviously heard her thought.

"Alright, no need to get big-headed!" laughed Stella.

Tamar slotted the lid back into place and patted the top. "Good.

All set for this afternoon. Should be a good trade this year – I've heard there's a whole delegation coming from warmer climes. They love a bit of rain. A nice cold breeze always goes down well, too."

"Shall I go and whistle more winds, then?" said Stella, her eyes lighting up. Nimbus bounced in excitement.

"No." Tamar shook her head. "Nothing worth catching, this morning. We should have more luck this afternoon – the sentinels say there's a storm front coming in."

Stella squinted out at the row of huge clouds on the horizon – the sentinels – Tamar's early warning system. She still didn't quite understand how Tamar spoke to them, but they were always spot on about the weather.

Shame they're not as reliable about sea witches.

"I checked the beach," she said. "No sign of the Haken."

"You don't need to keep doing that," said Tamar. "I told you. It'll be ages before she's back."

Stella shrugged. It didn't hurt to look. "There was a boat," she said.

Tamar narrowed her eyes. "A boat?"

"Yep. It's gone now, though. It was just tacking."

"You two weren't *practising*, were you? They won't have seen anything unusual?"

Stella's heart gave a guilty skip.

The people on the boat wouldn't have seen – she was pretty sure. Even if they had, they wouldn't believe it. They'd just think their eyes were playing tricks on them.

Tamar might brain-fog them though, just to be sure . . .

Stella shook her head. "The boat was far away. Anyway, I told you, I was just checking the beach. We weren't practising."

"Good," said Tamar, frowning out at the sea. "Always pays to be careful."

"Can we practice lightning again today?" said Stella, rapidly changing the subject. "Nimbus is getting really good at it, now. Well, apart from his aim, but he's getting better."

Nimbus darkened and let out a heavy rumble, making Tamar jump. "Shoosh!" she scolded. "No! Being good at lightning doesn't mean you get to skip green. Verdure again, this morning. A weather weaver needs to know *every* colour. The full rainbow."

"But we're rubbish at growing stuff," groaned Stella. "You know we are."

"All the more reason to practice," said Tamar. "It just takes patience, that's all. And a good strong feeling of belonging."

Stella hadn't had any trouble with the first part of green weather magic – secrets of stone – she could hear stone stories almost as soon as she started listening. But growing plants? *That* wasn't so easy. She hadn't managed to grow a single one so far.

Stella huffed – lightning was much more fun.

"Chin up," said Tamar. "Just think how pleased your grandpa will be – you can give him a hand with his veg patch. This is one type of weather magic he can get on board with!"

True, thought Stella, with a sigh.

"Did you bring everything I asked for?" said Tamar.

Stella nodded. She propped her bag on the wooden bench by the front door and emptied out the things she'd brought from home: spare seeds from Grandpa's shed, a bottle of water, and a wooden dibber for making the holes.

"A dibber." Tamar picked it up and chuckled. "That man and his tools! You know you can just poke a hole with your finger?"

Stella took the dibber from Tamar and wrapped her hands round it – of course she knew that, but she was still going to use the dibber. It was a big deal, being lent one of Grandpa's tools. He was very protective of them. And he'd whittled it himself, so it was special.

Tamar picked up the packets of seeds and shuffled through them. "Black potatoes, kale, beans, courgettes. Lovely! He's given us a fine selection. All you need now is a well-rooted sense of belonging!"

Stella took a deep breath and closed her eyes. *Home. I'm home. I'm where I belong.*

She was sure she'd felt it properly once or twice this week – mostly when she wasn't expecting it. But she wasn't sure she could just conjure it up. She opened her eyes and squinted up at her cloud. "You up for giving it another go, Nimbus?"

Nimbus bobbed eagerly. He looked more confident than she felt.

Two

PUTTING DOWN ROOTS

"**G**ROW!" exclaimed Stella. "Why aren't you growing?!" She kicked her toe in the mud.

Not even one tiny seedling. Her patch of freshly dug earth remained stubbornly bare. The very opposite of verdure.

"Take a breath," said Tamar, without turning around, "and focus on feeling grounded. Settle into your boots. *Calm* concentration." She reached up to add another tie to the top of her bean poles.

The bed she'd started alongside Stella's was already a sprawling riot of vegetables – potato plants, fat neeps, towers of runner beans. "Might've known calm would be a problem," she muttered.

Stella snorted softly. *Rude,* she thought. *We can be calm!*

None of the other weather magic had been this hard; rain, sunshine, catching winds. They'd even mastered lightning, despite the accidents at the start . . .

Tamar raised her eyebrows: *Well?*

"I know!" Stella huffed. "Keep trying."

She looked around for her cloud.

Nimbus had retreated and was lurking behind Tamar's bean-pole wigwams, unsettled by her frustration.

Stella sighed. "I'm not cross with *you*, Nimbus. I'm just cross." She beckoned to him. "I'm sorry, okay? Let's try again."

She waited until he'd floated back to her, before crouching down again.

It can't be that hard. Plants grow even without magic!

She closed her eyes and pictured seeds. Sleeping in the dark. Waiting to be woken.

"We're going to wake them up, this time, Nimbus," she murmured. "Every single one. You ready? Autumn rain, really gentle, full of growing magic."

There was a light patter of water on soil as Nimbus began to rain.

"Good," Stella nodded. "Just like that."

She imagined the hidden seeds uncurling, with a big stretch and a yawn.

Do plants yawn? she wondered.

The patter of rain stopped and Stella opened one eye. Nimbus had paused in confusion. "Sorry, ignore me. Just keep doing what you were doing. Warm rain – a touch of sunshine, too. And try to imagine belonging in one place, always. Seeds like that."

She closed her eyes again and thought about Grandpa. Nothing made him happier than growing stuff – pottering about in his veg patch, watering this, tidying that, muttering soft words of encouragement.

"Home," she whispered, as Nimbus rained. "This is home. It's safe here, little seeds. You can grow. Put down roots."

The smell of wet earth rose around her, rich and brown.

"Smells promising," said Tamar. "Petrichor, that's called."

"Tamar! I can't listen *and* concentrate," Stella snapped.

Nimbus gave an impatient rumble.

Tamar held up her hands. "Fine, fine. I just thought you'd want to know – that smell, petrichor – means you're on the right track."

Stella squinted at the patch Nimbus had just watered. She frowned and crouched lower, until her nose was almost touching the earth.

One tiny, folded sprout of leaf, peeking out of the ground like a question mark.

"A SEEDLING!" She bounced to her feet in delight. "There's a seedling!"

"Well, don't shriek at it," said Tamar, coming over to look. "You'll scare it back into the ground!"

Nimbus darted back and forth across the square of earth, raining wild zigzags of dark stripes across the little plot. The water gathered in shallow puddles.

"Hey!" said Tamar. "You're not aiming to drown it either!"

Stella beckoned Nimbus away. He tumbled towards her and wrapped her in a damp cloud hug.

She grinned. "We did it, Nimbus! Our first seedling!"

Nimbus drifted over to the tiny plant and bounced up and down above it, willing it to get taller.

Tamar crouched down and inspected the tiny stub of green. She nodded. "Excellent. It'll get easier – you'll see. We'll have you growing prize-winning veg in no time. Your grandpa will doubtless approve of that!"

Stella smiled. Tamar and Grandpa might not see eye to eye on much, but since battling the sea witch, they seemed to have reached a truce.

* * *

Stella took the inland path back to Grandpa's. When she got to the crest of the hill, she shaded her eyes and scanned the horizon. No sign of the boat now. She felt something unwind in her chest. It was fine. Nobody had seen anything.

She scanned the coastline and imagined another boat sailing towards them. Four weeks to go. Four weeks until Mum and Dad came home; until she'd have to introduce them to Nimbus.

She gave him a nervous smile. *It'll be fine. Probably.*

She'd thought talking to Mum and Dad on the phone would make them feel closer, but it hadn't. It just made them feel further away.

Stella had *tried* to tell Mum about weather weaving, but Mum hadn't believed her: "I'm glad you're having fun, love. But I hope you're not in a total daydream? If Grandpa asks for help with anything, be sure to use your listening ears."

"I am! You're the one who's not listening!"

Nothing could convince Mum it wasn't all some made-up game.

Grandpa had taken the phone at that point and reassured Mum that Stella was no trouble at all, she was helping with the washing up, and no, she hadn't run out of socks.

Like *that* was important.

Then Dad started going on about house-hunting in Lerwick . . .

Lerwick was no good! It was a big town! There were too many people there – Nimbus would have to spend the whole time hiding. It was hard enough to get him to act normal for five minutes!

No. They'd have to stay here. Near Grandpa and Tamar. Grandpa would help convince them – he'd promised.

They'd understand when they met Nimbus.

Stella swallowed and looked seriously at the little cloud. "You'll have to be on *best* behaviour when they get here," she said. "No raining on anyone. And *definitely* no lightning."

Nimbus bobbed cheerfully, then bowled away down the hill towards Grandpa's. He always treated this final stretch like a race, which was hardly fair, given that he could fly. Away down the slope, Nimbus launched himself over the fence and floated up to settle smugly on the ridge of the roof.

"Yes! You win again," called Stella, with a smile.

She liked coming home by this route – the house looked friendlier from the back. The front always looked like it was scowling, but from here, you could see all the Grandpa bits – the veg patch, and the chicken run, and his shed.

The shed door banged open and Grandpa appeared, carrying a shovel and a net of straw. "You're back early!" he called, as she got closer.

"In time for lunch," said Stella. "That's what you said this morning."

Grandpa gave a curt nod, but Stella could tell he was pleased.

"Lunch isn't ready yet," he said, propping the shovel against the chicken coop. "Won't take long, though. I just need to warm the soup."

"We'll keep practising then," said Stella. She beckoned to Nimbus and he tumbled off the roof.

"Nothing dramatic, I hope?" said Grandpa. "If you're going to start whistling winds again, you'll need to let me get everything tied down this time."

"No, no more winds," said Stella. "We're on to verdure, now – growing plants."

"Sounds more my speed," said Grandpa. "I can give you some tips if you'd like?"

Stella smirked and shook her head. Grandpa trying to teach her weather magic – that'd be the day!

"I'm just saying – I've won prizes, you know," said Grandpa. "My onions took second place at the country show a few years ago. You're looking at an expert right here." He dusted his shoulder off, as though brushing away the competition.

"I think we'll be alright," said Stella. "Which beds need watering?"

Grandpa pursed his lips and looked critically at his vegetable patch. "All of them," he said. "But you can start with the rhubarb. That loves a good drenching."

* * *

Stella stacked the bowls and brought them to the sink. She and Grandpa had got a bit of a routine going now – he washed up after lunch and she washed up after supper.

"You heading back to Tamar's?" said Grandpa.

Stella nodded. "Yes."

"Here, I got you a treat," said Grandpa, opening the cupboard. "Pop this in your bag."

Stella hopped with joy at the sight of the shiny gold and red wrapper. "A caramel wafer! I love these!"

"Some things don't change, then," said Grandpa. "Picked them up over in Lerwick. It was your Mum's suggestion."

Stella took it and felt her earlier annoyance soften. *Mum.* Still organising, even from hundreds of miles away.

She glanced up at Nimbus. He'd settled in his favourite spot, on top of the dresser.

"Do you think . . . Mum and Dad will . . . *like* Nimbus?"

Grandpa glanced at her in surprise. "Of course! What's not to like?"

"It's just, they're *normal*."

Grandpa's jaw tightened. "So am I," he said.

It was still a sore point. Gran and Tamar had kept everything secret from him, because he was 'normal'.

"I don't mean normal is a *bad* thing," said Stella. "It'll just make it hard for them to understand. I did *tell* them about Nimbus, but they didn't believe me. Mum even called him my 'imaginary friend'."

Grandpa spread his hands. "You can hardly blame them. Whoever heard of a tame cloud? You just need to wait until they get here. There's no arguing with reality. They'll like him fine, when they get to know him."

Nimbus took that as his cue to tumble off the top of the dresser. Stella smiled.

Of course, they'll like you. How could they not?

The wind keened outside and Grandpa narrowed his eyes. "Don't like the sound of that. It's forecast to be fair this afternoon."

Stella shook her head. "There's a storm front coming in."

Grandpa stooped to peer out of the window and frowned. "It's definitely darkening up out there."

"Brilliant!"

Tamar would be delighted – all the winds they'd bottled so far were light playful things – nothing really *powerful*. Nimbus picked up on her excitement and began to circle impatiently.

Grandpa clashed the soup bowls together as he picked them up. "You know how I feel about you and storms."

"No, it's a *good* thing, Grandpa. Tamar's been hoping for some proper weather – stuff she can trade!"

Grandpa's mouth tightened and he shook his head.

"It's probably not a storm anyway," Stella backtracked. "More like a squall."

The wind moaned again, as though to contradict her, rattling the front door and sending a cold draft hissing underneath.

"You sure you don't fancy staying here? Keeping me company?" said Grandpa. "We could have hot chocolate . . ."

Stella shook her head. "The whole point about catching winds is you need good winds to catch!" Nimbus was nudging against the door now, eager to get started.

"Well, if you're going to insist on going out, wear your raincoat," said Grandpa. "And take the inland path. I don't want you anywhere near the cliffs."

Stella sighed – overprotective Grandpa was back.

"I'm serious! Promise me," he said. "People have been blown off the cliffs before – larger people than you!"

"Alright!" exclaimed Stella, throwing up her hands in surrender.

Grandpa still didn't get it. She could snatch a wind out of the sky now – faster than it could snatch her off a cliff. But there was no point in arguing. He'd just get all worried and stubborn, and want to keep her home.

The first spatter of rain rattled against the window, driven by a gust of wind. Stella lifted her yellow raincoat off the hook and Grandpa frowned anxiously.

"I'll be careful," she said. "I promise."

Three

A BRISTLY REUNION

THE morning sunshine had gone, blotted out by heavy grey clouds trailing curtains of downpour. Stella fixed her eyes on her own little cloud, squinting as the wind drove rain into her face. Nimbus flew down the hill, guiding the gust towards her.

As he came close, Stella reached up and pinched together her finger and thumb, snatching the wind out of the sky. She pushed her hand deep into the weather bag at her side and let go.

"Got you!"

She rolled the bag closed, trapping the wind inside, and grinned. Three storm gusts in the bag already and they weren't even halfway to the croft yet – Tamar was going to be so impressed.

She pushed back the yellow hood of her raincoat and wiped the rain out of her eyes. "That was ace, Nimbus! Well done!"

The little cloud fluffed himself up in pride.

Stella smiled. If the wind kept up like this, they'd have a full bag of storm gusts in no time. Nimbus rode each gust, guiding them towards her, and then she caught them – they'd figured that trick out all by themselves and mostly, it worked brilliantly.

"Just be careful, won't you?" she said. "If you think it's picking up into a gale, you know what to do?"

Nimbus dropped out of the sky and huddled low in the long grass.

"Exactly." Stella grinned.

Further up the hill, the bog cotton flickered and danced. She pointed. "Look, there's another. Go on then!"

Nimbus was off like a shot, speeding up the hill and curving up into the air as he met the edge of the gust.

"Six is the record to beat," called Stella.

* * *

Stella slipped the bag off her shoulder and handed it to Tamar. "Eight storm gusts!" she said. "Just on the way here! Nimbus was helping – we've really got the hang of it now."

Tamar nodded her approval. "Good work, you two," she said. "We'll have more bottles than I can carry!"

"What are you planning to trade them for?" said Stella.

"Sunshine," said Tamar. "Sahara sunshine, ideally. That jar you used against the Haken was my last one. Scalding sunshine is in short supply round these parts, so I always like to keep a jar or two—" She twitched as though she'd been stung, then closed her eyes tightly.

"Are you alright?" said Stella.

Tamar nodded sharply, then shaded her eyes and looked up at the sky. "Where's Nimbus got to?"

"He's right here," said Stella, though when she looked around, he wasn't immediately obvious. "Nimbus?"

The little cloud popped up from behind a low hump in the grass. He had an apricot tinge, which meant he was up to something – he'd probably been trying to sneak up on them.

"I want you to send him off magic gathering," said Tamar.

"What, now?"

"Yes. Right now! He needs to get properly charged up. Might be why you were struggling to grow anything this morning."

"Oh . . . okay," said Stella in disappointment. Not having Nimbus would make wind-catching tricky – it was a lot easier with his help, not to mention more fun.

"Far and wide – as much magic as he can carry," said Tamar. "Tell him to take his time."

Stella nodded. "Nimbus?"

The small cloud rose a little higher as though standing to attention.

"Magic gathering time! Until you're completely full, okay?"

Nimbus shrank a little in protest – catching winds was his favourite, too.

Don't worry – we'll catch more when you get back.

The small cloud swung from side to side, clearly reluctant, but Stella nodded firmly. "Go on! Tamar's orders."

Remember, we need to stay on her good side. Don't you want to go to the Gathering?

Nimbus swiftly turned and scooted away along the cliff path towards Grandpa's. Stella watched him go, a pang of separation tugging at her chest. It felt uncomfortable, now, when he wasn't around; a taut emptiness, as though her heart was a rubber band. Hopefully, he wouldn't take too long – he could usually find enough magic in an hour or two.

She turned to see Tamar looking in the opposite direction – towards the broch. Out on the horizon, a line of blue was opening in the grey sky – a very straight line, heading right for them.

"We've got company," said Tamar.

Stella's heart quickened. "The sea witch?!"

"No, no. Velda. She's on the council. Leader of the Ice Weavers."

Stella shaded her eyes and looked towards the horizon. *The council!* Tamar had told her about them – the oldest, wisest weather weavers – the ones in charge of the Gathering!

"So, she's really important?"

Tamar snorted softly. "You could say that," she said. "I wonder what she's after?"

* * *

Velda strode towards them down the path from the broch. She looked nothing like a weather weaver – not the way Stella had imagined them, anyway; a sharply tailored coat, wide legged trousers that swished as she walked, and a glossy swirl of hair that reminded Stella of ice cream. She looked like someone who was used to being in charge.

"Let me do the talking," said Tamar, buttoning up her cardigan.

Stella glanced down at the mud-caked knees of her trousers. If she'd known she was going to meet one of the council, she would have changed back at Grandpa's.

Too late now.

"Velda," said Tamar, nodding at the woman as she approached.

"Tamar. Always a pleasure. And who do we have here? A new apprentice?"

"Assistant."

Stella glanced at Tamar, feeling bruised. *Assistant?* Surely, she'd proved herself by now?

"Rain sticks!" said Velda, patting the top of the barrels. "How quaint. Nice that you're keeping the old traditions alive. Do they trade for much at the Gathering?"

"What do you want, Velda?"

Stella looked at Tamar in surprise. There was a distinctly prickly tone in her voice. She'd expected Tamar to be polite, given that Velda was someone important.

"Just checking up, making sure everything's in order. I want this year's Gathering to run like clockwork – no shocks or surprises."

Tamar's eyes narrowed. She looked as though she were trying to figure something out and coming to the wrong answer.

"The council are relying on me," continued Velda, "to ensure the smooth running of our sacred and time-honoured—"

"Spare me the speech and spit it out, Velda."

"I received word the sea witch had returned," said Velda briskly, unphased by Tamar's rude interruption. "It's not long now, 'til the first delegations arrive, so I want to be certain you have it in hand. We wouldn't want any . . . disruptions."

Tamar unknitted her eyebrows. "Ah. You can rest easy, then. I saw her off. She won't be back for a long time."

Stella nodded. That was one way of putting it. Though it wasn't Tamar who'd defeated the Haken, it was her – her and Nimbus.

"You're certain she isn't a threat?" said Velda.

Stella nodded again, the memory of it bright in her mind: pure power, flowing between her and Nimbus, igniting him with lightning. Terror, too – Stella didn't want to kill anyone, even a sea witch.

Velda looked at Stella and her eyes flashed. "Dangerous creatures, sea witches. I'm sure you were *very* glad of Tamar's protection?"

Stella looked at her, suddenly uncertain. It felt like a trick question.

"Very," she agreed.

Velda gave her a swift smile, as though they'd shared a private joke.

"Why don't you head inside, Stella?" said Tamar. "Count how many bottles we've got left."

Velda glanced up at the sky and dusted her hand from side to side. A small circle of blue opened directly above them, bathing the croft in bright sunshine. "There, that's better. Don't you think?"

This was next-level! Stella gave Tamar a wide-eyed look that meant: *Please! Let me stay*, but Tamar raised her eyebrows impatiently.

Stella gave a short sigh and headed for the front door.

If only Nimbus were here. *Then Tamar wouldn't have been able to call me an assistant!* She could have shown Velda some of their tricks. Nothing too flashy – maybe a bit of upwards rain.

No. A frost lace! That would be better – Velda *was* an Ice Weaver, after all.

Trust Tamar to make her send her cloud away at exactly the wrong moment.

"Stella," said Velda. "It is Stella, isn't it?"

Stella jumped and turned back towards the two weather weavers.

"Be a dear and put the kettle on?" said Velda. "Tamar and I have a lot to discuss – I may be here a while."

Tamar rolled her eyes and nodded. Stella smiled, her heart doing a little dance.

Velda was going to be here a while . . .

Maybe long enough for Nimbus to get back?

Inside, Stella filled the kettle and set it to boil, then quickly cleared the mess off the kitchen table. She picked the three nicest mugs from the cupboard and set them out neatly. *There.*

"We have big plans for this year's Gathering," said Velda, following Tamar inside. "You'll be pleased to hear that we're extending the opening hours of the market."

Tamar's face brightened. "Well, that *is* good news."

"Seemed sensible," said Velda. "Yell is hosting this year. There's always such a large turnout there."

Yell.

Stella knew the name. It was an island – one of the North Isles. She didn't remember ever having been there, but it wasn't far away.

If only I could go, too!

Tamar checked the cupboard, shook her head, then bustled down the corridor to the larder, muttering about shortbread.

The spikiness between Tamar and Velda seemed to have passed.

Stella busied herself drying the empty bottles on the drainer. They were going to need more of them, what with all the storm gusts she'd caught this morning.

"Leave that, for now," said Velda. "Come and have a seat. Keep me company."

Stella smiled shyly and sat down opposite Velda.

She couldn't quite believe it – a real life council member! Here, in Tamar's kitchen. It was hard not to stare. Up close, Velda looked almost unnaturally perfect. Her skin glistened and her hair glittered slightly when she moved.

Stella had imagined they'd all be old ladies, like Tamar, but Velda was much younger; probably about the same age as Mum, only *a lot* more glamorous.

"How long have you had *your* cloud, Stella?" said Velda.

The melody of the question was light and cheerful, but a doubt crept into Stella's chest. She bit her lips together as she tried to work out what to say.

Velda's face was friendly, matter-of-fact. "The council sees everything," she said, gesturing to the cloudy sky outside. "There are no secrets between weather weavers."

She's been watching us? Stella glanced out of the window with a shrinking feeling.

"So?" said Velda. "When did you catch your cloud?"

Four

V IS FOR VELDA

"I CAUGHT him, um, a while ago?" said Stella, evasively. She looked anxiously down the corridor, willing Tamar to come back.

Velda followed her gaze, then leant forwards and steepled her hands together. "And where is your cloud now?"

"Out," said Stella. "Collecting magic."

Velda nodded slowly.

"I understand you've been having trouble with *lightning*?"

"No," said Stella, shaking her head. "Not really. Only at the start."

Velda sucked in a sharp breath and sat back. "So, it's true!" she hissed. "An untamed thundercloud!"

"No!" protested Stella. "He's not untamed. He's really good. He doesn't do lightning at all, now. Not if I don't let him."

Velda stared at Stella, her mouth working like she was chewing on thistles. "Thunderclouds are *forbidden* to novices!" she burst out, finally. "It's against the law!"

Stella stiffened in shock. "Forbidden?" she said. "But . . ."

She glanced at the doorway. Tamar stood there, clutching a large biscuit tin, her face full of outrage.

"GET OUT!" barked Tamar, making Stella flinch.

But Velda didn't move. Her attention was fixed on Stella. "You don't have *any idea*, do you? Tamar hasn't told you!"

Tamar slammed down the biscuit tin, strode round the table and yanked the chair out from under Velda.

"I said OUT!"

Velda leapt to her feet, looking ruffled for the first time since she'd arrived. "You know the rules, Tamar. It's *dangerous*! Learning lightning is—"

"OUT OF MY HOUSE!" roared Tamar, sending Velda darting to the front door.

Velda opened the door, but turned to glare at Tamar. She was braver than most people – Stella had to give her that.

"You'd better not be training her, Tamar, not without an assessment. *You* know the risks better than anyone!"

"GET OUT!" Tamar raised both arms and the bottles on the

shelves behind her began to jangle. Two jars popped open. Hailstones the size of ping-pong balls fired out with a machine-gun rattle. They hit the ceiling and ricocheted towards Velda.

Stella dived under the table.

Velda rushed out and Tamar followed, the hail swarming around her like angry hornets.

Stella yanked a heavy blanket off one of the armchairs and pulled it over her head. All around her was the crack of hailstones hitting hard surfaces. None of them had hit her yet, but if they did, they would hurt.

Behind her, the jars of weather continued to rattle against one another. Stella glanced at the wall of shelves and her eyes widened. *If any more of those lids come off—*

Wrapping the blanket around her like a shield, she bolted for the front door. When she got outside, she pulled up short. Tamar stood with feet planted firmly and arms spread wide. Above her, the sky whirled with hail; sparks crackled and fizzed from her fingertips.

Wild lightning!

Up the hill, Velda was hurrying away.

Something smashed inside the croft and a gale shrieked out of the doorway, knocking Stella to her knees. Tamar pointed uphill and it tore after Velda, carrying a volley of hail with it.

Stella tensed as it reached the fleeing figure, but it met an invisible wall and bounced, with a noise like firecrackers.

Cloud cover, thought Stella, with relief. She didn't want to see what happened when hail that big actually hit someone.

Cloud cover or not, when the hail hit, Velda shot one last venomous look at Tamar, then broke into a run. She was soon out of sight.

Tamar stood rigid with fury, staring up the broch path, as though Velda might reappear at any moment. Hailstones orbited her, like icy comets. Stella shrank back against the wall, flinching as one of them skimmed her cheek.

Bright threads of lightning crackled above Tamar's head and the air fizzed, tangy with electricity. Stella edged away until she reached the far end of the croft and slid round the corner to safety.

This was not the Tamar she knew; she was out of control.

Even when the sea witch had threatened, Tamar had stayed calm . . .

Staying low, Stella crunched along the side path of the house. Better to have a building between them.

She took shelter between the back of the croft and the small shed, huddling into the corner as winds continued to shriek out of the croft.

Nimbus, I'm scared.

How far had he gone to gather magic?

A movement in the grey clouds above the headland caught Stella's attention, but it wasn't Nimbus. A patch of blue sky was opening up.

Velda was leaving.

A clear line was cleaving its way through the clouds, moving away, in a different direction than it had arrived – a huge V of blue, cutting through the grey.

Like she's signing her name on the sky, thought Stella, with a shiver, *or drawing an arrow, pointing right at me . . .*

Here she is! The law breaker. The girl with an untamed thundercloud.

But Nimbus wasn't untamed! Not anymore. And she'd only done what Tamar had said!

"There you are."

Stella jumped at the sound of Tamar's voice.

Tamar heaved a great sigh. Her clothes were rumpled and her hair floated around her head, full of static. She held out a hand to help Stella up.

Stella ignored it and pushed herself to her feet.

Tamar was meant to be calm, unflustered, practical – her mentor. It was *not* okay for her to lose her temper.

"You nearly *hit* me with that hail!"

"Good job you ducked," said Tamar.

Why couldn't she just say sorry?!

"You knew, didn't you?" accused Stella. "Why Velda was coming. Is that why you sent Nimbus away?"

"Visits from Velda are never good news," said Tamar. "It was just a precaution."

"So, it's true?" asked Stella. "Nimbus being a thundercloud, you teaching me lightning, it's all against the rules?"

"Pah! Rules are for fools," said Tamar. "Velda's a great believer in them. Especially when they're rules she's invented."

"What did she mean about 'an assessment'?"

Tamar pulled a face. "It's perfectly obvious that you two belong together. I don't need an assessment to tell me that!"

"Can't we just *do* the assessment? Then she'd see! Nimbus isn't dangerous."

Tamar snorted. "Do you want to give Nimbus up?"

"No!"

"Well, then," said Tamar. "Trust that I know what I'm doing."

"Won't we get in trouble?"

"Probably," said Tamar. "But that's nothing new."

Not for you, maybe, thought Stella.

What sort of trouble were they in? Did weather weavers have police? Would they get arrested?

"Velda won't try to take Nimbus away, will she?"

The storm smell fizzed in the air again and Stella took a nervous step backwards. She hitched the blanket higher around her shoulders.

"Sorry," said Tamar. "It just makes me so angry!"

"Take deep breaths," said Stella. "That's what you always tell me . . ."

Tamar glanced at Stella in amusement. "Good advice," she said. She took a long slow breath and blew it out, then raised her eyebrows. "Satisfied?"

Stella nodded.

"Velda will almost certainly try to take Nimbus," said Tamar, bluntly.

Stella's eyes widened and her scalp prickled with fear.

"Having said that, I don't think she'll try anything here," said Tamar. "So, I'll see you in the morning. For now, head home and wait for your cloud."

"What are you going to do?"

Tamar glared at the wake of blue sky, the fury still sharp in her eyes. "I'm going to ask a few questions, see what comes back on the wind. Then? We'll come up with a plan."

* * *

Stella took the cliff path home. No point in going the long way round – the sky was clearing and the wind had dropped completely. Velda had seen to that.

When she got to the lookout point above storm petrel beach, she rapidly scanned the rocky shoreline, looking for anything unusual – anything 'untoward', as Tamar would say. The waves lapped at the stony beach and a tern flitted high overhead.

No sea witch. Not today.

No boats, either.

A queasy feeling slithered into Stella's stomach.

The boat. This morning. That must have been Velda, watching them.

She wrapped her arms around herself and watched the waves. Maybe there were worse things in the world than sea witches?

Velda didn't *look* like a monster, but she wanted to take Nimbus.

And *she* had the whole council on her side.

Untamed!

Forbidden!

Dangerous!

The words kept playing round and round, on a loop in her head.

The image of Tamar crackled in her mind, lighting little fires of unease. Stella shuddered. The hail had been bad enough, but the wild lightning . . .

It reminded her of when she'd first learnt about the rainbow glass, for uncovering truths and intentions.

"What do you look like through the red one, Tamar?"

'Terrifying!"

For the first time, Stella could believe it.

Five

EVERY COLOUR OF
THE RAINBOW

STELLA hadn't slept well. The sea witch nightmare had come back. Only now, Velda was in it too – pointing down from the cliffs and yelling 'Forbidden!', as Stella swam desperately towards the shore.

But Nimbus was home. He'd turned up this morning, blotting out the light at the window until she'd opened it to let him in.

He was definitely fully-charged – unwilling to settle anywhere. Right now, he was bouncing back and forth between the backs of the two armchairs. There was a sharp tang of ozone in the air.

Grandpa raised his chin and sniffed. "Smells a bit . . . sparky, this morning?

"He's full of magic," said Stella. "That's all."

Was that all?

Maybe she shouldn't have told Nimbus about Velda. He'd been all fluffy and cheerful when he got back, but now he looked like he was twitching for a fight.

Grandpa glanced up at the scorch marks on the kitchen ceiling.

That was before! thought Stella. It had only been once. Before she even *knew* about wild lightning. Nimbus wouldn't do that now . . .

"He won't do lightning, Grandpa. Promise."

Grandpa pursed his lips. "Still, might be wise to take him outside for a run-about? Burn off some of that energy?"

* * *

Stella played out all sorts of scenes in her head as she walked to Tamar's. She hoped Tamar would be back to normal: being bossy, making plans, telling her not to worry. But the image of Tamar surrounded by lightning kept popping back into her head.

Tamar was bending over the vegetable patch when Stella arrived. She straightened up and clapped her hands together with a smile. "So! I've decided. I'm taking you both to the Gathering."

"What?! No!" exclaimed Stella.

Nimbus let out a shocking clap of thunder.

"Don't!" squeaked Stella. Nimbus immediately shaded to an apologetic lilac, but she shook her head crossly. "Go and keep a lookout. Somewhere up high."

Nimbus shot straight up in the air and Stella tried to calm her breathing.

It felt like Velda was stalking her; every flicker of the grass, every shadow that passed, made her heart leap. She didn't need Nimbus acting up, too.

Tamar was looking at her expectantly.

Stella shook her head. Yesterday, she would have been dancing at the prospect of going to the Gathering, but not now.

"Velda will be there."

"Exactly!" said Tamar. "The best tactic is to take the battle to her. Make it public."

"But she's on the council! In charge of the whole Gathering – that's what you said yesterday!"

"In charge of the *whole* Gathering," mimicked Tamar, in an annoying high-pitched voice. "She'd like to think so! No. Velda is just a chilly-hearted fear-monger, with an over-inflated opinion of herself. Worse than that, no one's challenging her lies."

"She was lying about thunderclouds being against the law?"

"No," said Tamar. "And that's why I'm taking you with me. We'll show them – you and Nimbus are no danger to anyone."

Stella glanced up at the little cloud, floating high overhead. She lowered her voice. "What's to stop her taking Nimbus?"

"Only newly paired novices are separated," explained Tamar with a sly smile. "But you *aren't* a novice any more. You're a fully trained apprentice!"

"*Fully* trained?" said Stella, in surprise.

"Near enough," said Tamar. She smiled grimly. "Velda may be in charge of the Gathering, but only while she has the council's support. She can't separate the pair of you if you're fully trained – she'd be breaking her own rules."

A small hope fluttered to life in Stella's chest. "You're sure?"

"Positive!" said Tamar, with a firm nod.

"The council won't let her take Nimbus?"

Tamar gave a sharkish smile. "Not a chance. You can *prove* you and Nimbus belong together! And Velda won't be able to do a thing about it."

"Prove it, how?"

"By taking the trials," said Tamar.

Stella gaped. "But I'm not ready! You know I'm not."

"I know nothing of the sort!" said Tamar. "I wanted to keep the pair of you hidden from Velda – that's the only reason I didn't want you parading around the Gathering. But it's a bit late for secrecy now."

Stella looked up. "Nimbus? You can come down now."

Nimbus pretended he hadn't heard her – probably annoyed he'd been sent away so abruptly. Anxiety twisted in Stella's chest. What if he pulled this sort of trick at the Gathering?

"Nimbus! Now!" It came out sharper than she meant it.

The small cloud plummeted, dropping a well-aimed spatter of freezing rain to make her yelp.

'Unpredictable', Tamar had called him, before. He was always unpredictable when he was full of magic. *And when I'm stressed out.* Knowing that didn't make her feel any better.

Stella wiped her face on her sleeve and frowned. "What if we fail the trials?"

"That's the beauty of it," said Tamar. "I don't need you to pass. Taking part is what's important. If the council let you enter, they're admitting you're fully trained!"

"But you said I need to learn every colour of weather magic first?"

Tamar crouched to inspect the little sprout of green in Stella's vegetable bed. It hadn't got any bigger since yesterday.

"It's still alive, and you grew it from seed," she said, nodding in approval. "That's a pass in my book. I'm ticking off green – and *that*, my girl, means you're ready." She stood up and spread her arms wide, making her cardigan fly out sideways. "I thought you'd be excited?"

Stella stooped to look at the tiny seedling. 'All of them grown to full size' – that was Tamar's instruction yesterday. "You're *sure* this counts?"

"Absolutely," said Tamar, with a slightly manic smile.

"Will they even let us in?"

Tamar nodded. "All we need is an invitation. We'll run through the whole rainbow this morning, then I'll send off for it."

Stella glanced at Nimbus. "But what if the council don't—"

"The council need to *wake up!*" snapped Tamar, making Stella jolt in alarm. Nimbus moved protectively towards her.

Tamar sighed. "What do you think my first cloud was?"

Realisation dawned. "A thundercloud?"

"Yes! And I wasn't a rarity – there used to be lots of us. You needn't think it's just thunderclouds either – she's banned all storms!"

Stella's mouth fell open. Beside her, Nimbus swelled with indignation.

"That's not even the worst of it," said Tamar. "You want to know her latest plan?"

Stella nodded hesitantly.

"All clouds are to be 'selected' for young novices. No prizes for guessing who's doing the selecting?"

"Velda?"

"And her band of 'assessors'. The arrogance! Thinks she knows better than the clouds themselves!" Tamar raised her eyebrows at Nimbus, who rumbled in disapproval. "Quite!" Tamar smiled at him. "Is he fully charged up?"

Stella nodded. "Practically fizzing."

"Perfect," said Tamar, rubbing her hands together. "In that case, let's do the test." She headed for the front door.

"What test?"

Tamar waved a hand dismissively. "Won't take long. It's to secure your invitation – prove you've learnt the full rainbow."

Stella heaved a small sigh.

She'd been looking forward to this moment. They'd done it! Learnt every colour of weather magic! So why did it feel like cheating?

She looked dubiously at the tiny seedling.

Is that really good enough?

Nimbus glittered anxiously and drifted closer until she could feel the chill of frost under her hand. Stella smoothed him gently.

She looked at the little cloud and determination slowly settled inside her.

"We have to do this, Nimbus," she said. "Whatever it takes. I'm not losing you. I know it's scary, but if we can fight a sea witch, we can do the trials. It is what we've been training for . . ."

Nimbus shivered the frost to the ground in a sparkling shower and shaded back to steely grey. He wasn't happy, but he *did* look determined.

Stella gave him an encouraging nod. "Are you with me?"

Nimbus leant against her leg, as though to say: *always*.

"I haven't got all day!" called Tamar, from inside.

* * *

"Where do we start?" said Stella. "Red?"

"Good grief, no!" said Tamar. "Why do you think warning signs are always red? The whole point is to avoid it! If you can be full of fury, but resist unleashing wild lightning, you've safely passed red."

Stella gave Tamar a deadpan look.

"Yes, I know! I know," blustered Tamar. "What can I tell you? Velda presses all my buttons. Anyway, we're testing *you*, not me." She waved a blank piece of paper in the air. "Orange first – Rain!"

Nimbus immediately swooped towards Tamar and drenched her with a torrent of rain. "Argh!" spluttered Tamar. "Pass! It's a pass."

Stella burst out laughing, but quickly quelled it when she saw Tamar's expression.

Stop, Nimbus!

"You did ask him to," she said, tossing Tamar a thirsty towel from by the sink and eyeing the test paper curiously – a broad orange stripe had appeared across the top.

Tamar towelled her face dry and grunted crossly. "Next time, aim for the test paper! And remember, you don't get marks for enthusiasm. *Control* is what you'll need to demonstrate."

Nimbus bobbed once. Anxiety fluttered in Stella's stomach, but she nodded. "Got it."

* * *

"Yellow is fine," said Tamar, inspecting the three bright stripes on the page. "Sunshine is easy enough and you've been calling summer winds since day one. Green is there, but it'll need a little practice."

More like a LOT, thought Stella, looking at the narrow green line on the page. She wasn't convinced their tiny beansprout actually counted as a pass. But at least Tamar wasn't pretending it was perfect.

"So, blue," said Tamar. "Velda's speciality. Fear, melancholy, isolation."

Stella sighed. She could do blue, but she didn't like it.

"Show me some snow!" said Tamar.

Stella closed her eyes and tried to conjure up the right thoughts.

The sea witch, creeping ashore.

Grandpa's face when he's missing Gran.

Mum and Dad, far away.

The feelings grew in Stella's chest, heavy and cold.

Above the table, Nimbus silently began to snow. A light dusting at first, then a tumble of fat flakes, falling onto the test page like feathers. Stella tried to hold the feeling steady, but it was hard. Snow whirled, faster and faster.

"Good, good," said Tamar, flapping it away. "That'll do fine."

Stella let out a great huff, blowing the awful thoughts away. "Why would *anyone* want to spend their time summoning those?"

"They're powerful," said Tamar. "A counter to most weathers – rain can be frozen, plants can die, winds can be filled with snow and hail. Ice has an answer to everything."

"Not lightning," said Stella, raising her eyebrows hopefully.

"No," said Tamar, grinning. "Controlled lightning. Purple. Most powerful of all the weathers. Are you ready?"

"What, in here?" said Stella, in alarm. She shook her head at Nimbus, in case he got any ideas.

"Control, remember?" said Tamar. "When you're ready?"

"I'd rather we do it outside."

Tamar shook her head. "Lightning hasn't been included in the trials since . . . well, since Velda's been in charge. I've no idea whether they'll make provisions for an outdoor skills trial, so you need to be able to do it anywhere. So, carefully now, I want you to get that cloud sparking. Let's see what you can do."

* * *

"I'm sorry about your table," said Stella, trudging up the hill after Tamar.

"My fault – I should have remembered he was freshly charged. Hard to make a small spark with a full tank of magic."

Stella swallowed. She had *said* they should do it outside. She glanced back to check Nimbus was still following.

"Otherwise, I'd say that was a roaring success!" said Tamar. "You've shown your colours. You're ready! If Velda tries to say otherwise, she'll be laughed off the council."

Stella smiled, confidence rising in her like bubbles. All they had to do was show up. Nimbus would be safe. And Velda wouldn't be able to say a word! She followed Tamar with a new skip in her step.

The Gathering! The Gathering! We're going to the Gathering!

She'd get to see the weather display and the market, and meet loads of different weather weavers. If it was even *half* as good as Tamar said, it was going to be *amazing*!

She'd assumed, from the direction Tamar had taken, that they were going to the broch, but when they reached the fork in the path, Tamar turned right.

"Where are we going?"

"To see your grandpa," said Tamar. "We need to have a little chat."

A prickle of worry scampered up Stella's neck and she trotted ahead of Tamar. "Why? What for?"

"I'll need his permission to take you to the Gathering," said Tamar.

Six

KNOTTY BUSINESS

"AND you've just decided this, have you?" said Grandpa. "Without consulting me."

"I'm consulting you now," said Tamar.

"*After* you've told her she can go?" said Grandpa.

Stella stepped between them, before Tamar could make it any worse. "Let me tell you about it, Grandpa," she said. "*Then* you can decide." She flashed a glance at Tamar, warning her not to say anything else.

Grandpa let out a huge puff, but let Stella pull him over to the kitchen table. He sat down heavily at the head of the table and Stella sat down next to him.

"It means I've completed my training, Grandpa," she said, willing him to be excited for her. "It means I get to go and meet all the other weather weavers."

"You haven't completed the training yet," contradicted Tamar, pulling out a chair down the far end.

Grandpa frowned in confusion.

"I haven't?" said Stella.

"No. You've completed practical skills – there's still theory to cover," said Tamar. She turned to Grandpa. "I think she's *capable* of it, as long as she works hard. Of course, if she doesn't have your support . . ."

"You *know* she does!" said Grandpa, his eyes flashing dangerously. "Always!"

"So, you agree then?" said Tamar, with a crocodile smile. "Stella *can* come to the Gathering."

Stella saw Grandpa's jaw set. She leant into his arm and gave him her sweetest smile. "Please, Grandpa?

Grandpa was outnumbered and he knew it. "What exactly is this Gathering?"

"It's amazing!" enthused Stella. "Weather weavers come here from all over the—"

"Stella," cautioned Grandpa. "I can well see how excited you are, but have you ever actually been to one of these Gatherings?"

Stella bit her lip.

"No," he said. "You haven't. So, let's hear what Tamar has

to say, shall we? Besides, I'm more interested in practicalities. Where is it? When? How much does it cost?"

Tamar nodded and relaxed. She clearly thought Grandpa's questions meant he was already on board with the plan.

She really doesn't know Grandpa at all, thought Stella anxiously.

"It's not far," said Tamar. "It's on the island of Yell. There's nothing to pay – Stella will come as my apprentice. There'll be accommodation and meals for her at the big house. And it's four days – a long weekend. You'll hardly notice we're gone."

"Gone!" said Grandpa.

Stella stiffened – there it was – she'd known it was coming.

"You needn't think you're going without me," he said.

Tamar recoiled. "You *can't* come!"

"That's the deal," said Grandpa, giving Tamar a level stare. "Take it or leave it."

"You're not a *weather weaver*!" said Tamar. "It's a gathering of *weather weavers*, not just any old fool who fancies tagging along."

Stella sucked in a breath. She glanced at Grandpa in alarm, but he was still staring at Tamar with the patience of a rock.

"If you want to take Stella, I'm coming too. That's the only way this is happening."

Tamar's face crinkled in exasperation. "There's nowhere for you to stay!" she spat. Even to Stella, it sounded like a pretty weak excuse.

"I can stay on the boat," said Grandpa. "In fact, it makes perfect sense – I'll take you up there in *Curlew* and then sleep aboard. You and Stella can stay in the house, as you said."

"Weather weaving is not your world," said Tamar. "If Stella's to succeed, she needs your *support*, not your interfering! You're just going to have to *trust* that this is the right thing for her."

"I trust Stella just fine," said Grandpa. "But let's be honest, you don't have the best track record when it comes to keeping her safe."

It wasn't very fair – the sea witch was hardly Tamar's fault – but for a split second, Tamar's face went slack with sadness, then her shoulders drooped.

Stella felt their plans slipping away like quicksand. Tamar didn't approve of Grandpa even *knowing* about weather weaving. She definitely wasn't going to bring him to the Gathering. But if he wouldn't let her go on her own, she wouldn't be able to take the trials. Then Velda might come back, and—

"Very well," said Tamar, nodding. "We'll all go."

"Really?" said Stella.

Tamar spread her hands in resignation and Grandpa smiled.

"When do we leave?" he said.

"End of this week," said Tamar. "Provided Stella can practice every day until then."

Grandpa nodded. "Sure. If she's up for that?"

Stella nodded enthusiastically.

Tamar pushed her chair back. "That's settled then." She hitched her bag onto her shoulder, gave Grandpa a sharp nod, and headed for the door. Stella made to follow, but Tamar shook her head. "We'll start in earnest tomorrow."

Stella stared at the door as it closed. *What just happened?*

Tamar had told Stella plenty of times: the Gathering was only for weather weavers. So, what was she planning? Brain-fog Grandpa when they got there? Try and lose him once they arrived? Maybe there were big beefy weather-wielding security guards who'd stop him at the gate?

Stella looked up at Nimbus, perched in his favourite spot, on top of the dresser.

We'll have to look out for him, Nimbus, she thought. *Stick together.*

She suddenly realised she was quite glad Grandpa was coming too.

Grandpa patted his hands on the table in a soft drumroll. "Do I take it we've got the afternoon to ourselves, then?" he said, with a smile.

"I guess so."

"Grand. In that case, I've something to show you," he said, pushing his chair back from the table. "Can't have you thinking Tamar's the only one with things to teach you!"

He went outside, then reappeared carrying a large right-angle, made of two planks of wood. It looked like an over-sized bookend.

"For you," he said, setting it on the table in front of her.

It had small metal loops and pulleys screwed onto the vertical side. On the flat base, there was a doorknob, another metal loop and a wooden cleat, like the ones on the boat.

"Thank you," said Stella. "Er . . . what is it?"

"A knot board," said Grandpa. "Everyone should know a few knots, whether you're a sailor, or not. It used to be your dad's."

Stella smiled, picturing Dad playing with it when he was small. She ran her fingertips over the smooth wooden cleat.

Grandpa pulled a length of cord from his pocket and looped it around the doorknob. In seconds it was secured with a neat knot.

Stella reached out and tugged the end. It wasn't going anywhere.

"Bowline, that one," said Grandpa. "Always handy. So, what do you say? Are you up for *learning the ropes*?" He grinned, delighted at his own joke.

Stella smiled back. "Show me again?"

Grandpa undid the knot and tied it again, slower this time. "Pull a loop towards you – that's the rabbit hole. This here's the rabbit," he said, flapping the tail end. "It pops up through the hole, goes round the tree, and back down the hole. Here, you try."

* * *

By the end of the afternoon, Stella had mastered a bowline, a clove hitch, and a figure of eight knot. Grandpa said she was halfway to being 'competent crew'.

Dad's going to be so pleased.

Though it was still early, Grandpa was already at the stove, browning saucermeat in a pan. Stella sidled up next to him and pinched a crispy bit off the edge of one of the little patties.

"Fingers out!" said Grandpa, swatting her away. "It's not ready yet. If you've had enough of knots, go and read a book or something."

Stella fetched *Shetland Myths and Magic* from her room and opened it on the kitchen table. A faint memory twinkled in the back of her head.

"Isn't one of these stories set on Yell?"

"The Tale of the Trowie Mound," said Grandpa. "Loads of Trows on Yell. You'll see." His eyes crinkled in a smile.

Stella couldn't quite tell if he was joking or not. Surely, Trows weren't real, were they? She narrowed her eyes at him. "Know lots of Trows, do you?"

"The good folk," said Grandpa, suddenly serious. "That's what they like to be called."

"It's not like there are any here now," said Stella.

"Ah, but you wouldn't know, would you?" said Grandpa. "They're not easily seen. Besides, a little respect never hurt anyone."

"Alright," said Stella. "Have you ever seen one of *the good folk*?"

Grandpa shook his head and smiled. "Never met one, personally. But I'm beginning to think anything's possible. I've always imagined I'd get along with them."

Unlikely. Grandpa didn't get on with anyone much. He was happiest in his own company. *And mine, now,* Stella conceded.

She flicked forward through the book until she found *The Tale of the Trowie Mound.* The first picture was of a small gnome-like man, sitting on a grassy tump. She remembered the story now – it was all about one Trow and his quest to find a fiddler willing to play at his birthday party.

She flicked forward to the last picture – a huge crowd of Trows, all dancing and drinking and stuffing themselves with food, while the fiddler played.

It *did* look like a good party, but she couldn't picture Grandpa in that scene. He wasn't one for parties, or dancing, or crowds of people.

"Why do you think you'd get on with the good folk?" she said. "It's not like you play the fiddle."

"That's just one story," he pointed out. "My mother was full of tales about them – hidden treasures and magic medicines, charms and curses. They're fine wee people, as long as you treat them with respect. And masterful at stonework!" He shrugged. "I suppose they'd have to be, living underground as they do."

That explained why Grandpa thought he'd get on with them. She pictured Grandpa discussing mortar mixes with a Trow and smothered a smile.

"And Great Gran said they live on Yell?"

Grandpa winked. "She grew up there, so she would know."

Stella still couldn't tell if Grandpa was playing with her or being serious. She looked down at the picture again.

It *might* be true, whether Grandpa believed it, or not. The sea witch had turned out to be real – why not Trows too?

Seven

TRAPPED IN THE BROCH

FOUR whole days they'd been practising for the trials and the more they practised, the more Stella didn't feel ready. Despite their best efforts, the vegetable bed remained bare, and Tamar *still* wasn't satisfied with their lightning.

She didn't see why they had to practice so hard, if passing wasn't important? But Tamar was insistent – she was worried about Stella's 'control'.

Like anyone could control a thundercloud when it didn't feel like listening...

Stella leant over the inner wall of the great stone tower

and looked down, her insides shrinking – it was a long way to the ground.

"Nimbus!" she called.

Us, us, us, the curved walls echoed.

Far below, she could see the sanctuary stone in the centre of the circular muddy floor. Even from up here, she could see the silver inlay of magic where Nimbus had mended it. Before, it had been a fairly plain-looking rock, but now it had star of silver at its heart.

"I hope you don't think we're done yet!"

Done yet, done yet, done yet . . .

Stella straightened up and looked out at the murky horizon. The sky glowered low, the air misty with mizzle, drifting and shifting in the breeze. The sea looked unfriendly – full of flinty shards of light; the waves choppy and dark.

No sea witch though, not today.

Stella's cheeks suddenly dotted with cold and she looked up to see Nimbus high above, dropping a steady column of snow, with annoying accuracy.

"There you are!"

At least it's not rain, this time.

Though thinking about it, that was odd. She squinted up at him. Usually, he turned peachy orange when he was messing about, but right now, he looked dead serious.

"Nimbus, what's up? Come here."

The little cloud drifted lower, snowing all the while, and came to rest on the wall. Silvery grey – a frightened cloud.

"What's got into you?" said Stella in concern. She hadn't seen him look this alarmed since—

A movement down on the rocks caught Stella's eye and her heart leapt into her throat. *The sea witch!*

She quickly crouched out of sight, her nerves jangling with fear. She leant forward and peeked out.

Not the sea witch.

Worse.

"It's Velda!" she whispered. "She's back. Nimbus, hide!"

Nimbus poured off the wall and flattened himself on the stone walkway.

"Stay down."

Stella peeked over again. Velda had reached the slate path now. Had she seen them?

Perhaps not. She was walking slowly – no sense of hurry – like someone out for a stroll. But the path only led to one place: the broch.

"I've changed my mind," hissed Stella. "You need to leave," Nimbus turned several shades darker and she reached out quickly to calm him. "She won't do anything to me. It's you she's after. *You!* You have to go – now!"

Nimbus gave a low rumble of disagreement and moved closer to her.

"Shh! Nimbus, please? I need to know you're safe. I'll come and find you when she's gone."

A soft scraping sound whispered up from below – Velda was

inside the broch. Stella moved furtively to peer over the inside wall. Velda was crouched next to the sanctuary stone, running a fingernail along the lines of silver.

"Now!" whispered Stella. "She won't see, if you leave now. Go to Tamar's. Hurry!"

Nimbus hesitated a moment longer, then rocketed over the wall. He sped away up the hill behind the broch, faster than the wind. Stella breathed a sigh of relief as he disappeared over the bluff.

"Stella? Are you up there?"

The voice sounded friendly, but Stella wasn't fooled. She looked over the wall to see Velda staring up at her. She was smiling.

"We need to talk," said Velda.

"We don't have anything to talk about," said Stella, and moved back, out of sight.

"I think we do . . ." called Velda. "I'm concerned for your safety." Her voice sounded hollow, echoing up out of the great stone tube of the broch.

Stella shivered and pulled her coat tighter. "You don't need to be. I'm fine."

Go away! Just go away! Leave us alone.

Nimbus was probably back at the croft by now. Would Tamar realise why? She wasn't sure if Tamar turning up here would be good, or really, really bad.

"I'm not your enemy, Stella," called Velda. "I'm worried for you, that's all. There's so much you don't know." Her voice sounded well-meaning; full of concern.

"I know you want to take Nimbus," accused Stella, looking over the edge.

Velda shook her head. "I'm not here to take your cloud, Stella," she said, spreading her hands wide.

"Tamar said—"

"Tamar hasn't told you everything. She's keeping secrets from you, Stella – spinning you lies."

Tamar wouldn't lie to her. Keep secrets, maybe, but not lie.

"Has she told you about the sea witch?"

The broch caught the high note at the end of the question.

Witch, witch, witch?

It was just a trick. A trick to make her listen. She shouldn't listen . . .

Stella scowled – she was trapped. But Nimbus would be safely back at Tamar's by now. And she didn't *think* Velda would hurt her. Velda wasn't like the sea witch. She had to follow rules . . .

Stella took a deep breath. "I'm coming down," she called. "But not to talk to you. I'm coming down, and then I'm going to leave."

Velda sat down on the sanctuary stone and gracefully crossed her legs.

Stella moved quietly to the doorway and cautiously began to make her way down the spiralling stone steps. The inside wall of the broch was punctured with small openings, letting light into the hidden staircase. Stella glanced down through the first one.

Velda hadn't moved, but she was watching.

Stella shivered and carried on down the shadowy stairs.

"How have you been getting along with your cloud?" said Velda, her tone light. "Does he *feel* like a good match for you?"

"Yes," said Stella. "Tamar says we're a perfect match."

"No more wild lightning?" said Velda. "Thunderclouds are hard to control." She drummed her nails lightly on the sanctuary stone and Stella swallowed. Maybe she'd realised it was Nimbus who broke it?

But they hadn't had any more accidents, since then. Nimbus was loads calmer, now.

"Tamar isn't someone *I'd* recommend, as a mentor," said Velda. "I'd go so far as to say: she's entirely reckless."

"No, she's not!" blurted Stella.

"A risk taker," continued Velda. "You must surely have noticed, by now? I'd guess she's been rushing your training? Encouraging *you* to take risks, too . . ."

Stella set her jaw.

Ignore her. Get to the bottom and leave. Go to Tamar's. Find Nimbus.

But it was hard to keep her mind on the plan, with Velda's words worming around inside her head. Tamar *was* a risk taker.

The sanctuary stone wouldn't have shattered if Tamar hadn't *insisted* they conjure lightning *inside* the broch. Stella hadn't been able to control it.

And now, with the trials? Yes – it did feel rushed.

But she wasn't about to admit any of that to Velda.

"*You* fought the sea witch, yes?" Velda's voice snaked its way up the stairs. "And Tamar saw nothing wrong with putting you in harm's way."

"That wasn't how it was!"

She'd chosen to stay – Tamar had needed her. It was the right thing to do.

"You might not have been so eager to fight, if you knew who the sea witch *once* was. Aren't you curious?"

It doesn't matter who she was, Stella told herself.

But the question had landed like a fish hook.

"Heather. That was her name," said Velda.

She was speaking quietly now. Stella scampered lower, so she could hear.

"She had so much promise, that girl – energy, determination, strength. A wonderful weather weaver."

Stella paused by the last opening. "She was a weather weaver?"

Velda looked up and nodded sadly. "An apprentice, like you. I think you would have liked her."

Stella ducked back out of sight and wrapped her arms round herself. *An apprentice, like me?*

She wanted to believe Velda was lying, but without her power, the sea witch *was* just a girl. Stella had seen it with her own eyes. No one else had – not even Tamar.

"It was a tragedy," said Velda. "Losing her to the sea."

She sounded genuinely upset.

Stella trotted down the last curve of the stairs, until she stood in the doorway. Velda tilted her head and considered Stella.

"You saw what she's become?"

Stella glanced through the entrance of the broch to the sea beyond. The Haken's scaled skin and needle teeth flashed into her mind and she suppressed a shudder.

"I'm willing to bet that you faced her alone?"

Stella's eyes snapped back to Velda. No way she was going to admit that – it would get Tamar in all sorts of trouble.

"It had to be you," said Velda. "Tamar can't fight her."

That wasn't right? Stella looked around the broch, remembering; reassuring herself. "Tamar *did* fight her!" she protested. "She got all her weather and came here to—"

Velda tutted, and stood up.

Stella shrank back, but Velda didn't come any closer. Instead, she moved around to the other side of the sanctuary stone. "No," she said. "Tamar relies on this." She nodded at the great slab in the centre of the broch. "This and her precious cairns. For an all-out battle? She needed you."

Tamar *wanted* her to face the sea witch alone?

Stella didn't want to believe it, but . . . Tamar *had* hurried her into learning lightning. And when the sea witch arrived, Tamar had been suddenly 'injured' – at exactly the moment she should have stepped up.

"But why?" asked Stella.

Velda stared pensively at the sanctuary stone. "Guilt," she said. "She can't get over her guilt."

Stella shifted from one foot to the other.

What was Velda getting at? Maybe she didn't want to know. Whatever it was, it would be better to find out from Tamar. She began to sidle towards the entrance, trying to make it seem casual, unhurried. The gritty mud squelched under her boots.

Velda's head snapped up. "Aren't you going to ask me what she did? Your *mentor*?"

Stella stopped dead in her tracks and clasped her hands behind her back.

"She *made* the Haken," said Velda. "The sea witch was Tamar's last apprentice."

Stella's mouth dropped open in shock. "No!"

It can't be true.

But her certainty was crumbling. What did she really know about Tamar? Was it possible? Could Tamar's training have gone so wrong that she created a sea witch? Had she trained Stella just to fight the Haken?

"Tamar trained Heather with the wrong cloud," said Velda. "And Heather refused to give him up."

There it is. You liar.

"You just want Nimbus!" blurted Stella.

Velda's eyes flashed with frustration. "That *cloud* you're so fond of, it's dangerous. You think you can control it? You can't. It'll turn on you! Or on others."

But Stella wasn't staying to listen. She turned and ran. Out of the broch. Out of reach of Velda's lies. She heard the crunch as Velda followed her outside onto the slate path, but she didn't look back.

"Tamar can't admit when she's wrong!" Velda shouted after her. "She *rushed* Heather's training, with a mismatched cloud. Created a monster..."

Don't listen. Don't listen.

"She's doing the same thing to you!"

Eight

BETRAYAL

STELLA'S thoughts pounded around her head as she ran towards the croft.

It couldn't be true. Tamar would have told her. *Would she?*

Nimbus was a perfect match for her. Tamar said so. *Tamar said so . . .*

Nimbus would never turn on me. *Would he?*

As she reached the top of the bluff, she spotted Nimbus, flying towards her at top speed – a furious ball of thundercloud.

He must have heard every word . . .

She flinched as he reached her and Nimbus stuttered to a

halt. She looked at the little cloud, suddenly wary of him. She remembered the furious arcs of crackling sparks that had seared the sea witch; sizzling and spitting. Nimbus hadn't wanted to stop, even when she told him to. What if he turned that on her? Would it do the opposite? Turn *her* into a sea witch?

Nimbus rippled white and grey and backed away from her. He looked hurt and confused.

Stella's heart pinched with guilt. What was she thinking? This was Nimbus. *Her* Nimbus – her best friend.

Velda is a liar. She's trying to push us apart.

It was the only thing she was sure of, right now.

"I'm sorry, Nimbus," she said. "Don't go. I don't know why I even listened to her."

The little cloud crept hesitantly forward. He stopped about a metre away from her and tentatively extended a small drift of mist towards her.

She reached out to touch it, but it shrank away from her hand and her heart stretched thin. "I didn't mean it," she said, her voice wobbling. "I know you wouldn't hurt me. You only ever did lightning to protect me."

Nimbus came cautiously closer.

"Please?" she said. "I'm sorry."

He settled softly around her shoulders and hot tears overflowed down Stella's cheeks. How was he still being nice to her, when she'd thought all those terrible things about him?

"Don't let me turn into a sea witch, Nimbus. Please?"

* * *

She'd talk to Tamar. That's what she'd do – tell her what Velda had said. And Tamar could tell her the *real* story. And everything would make sense again.

Stella strode purposefully down the path to the croft, Nimbus still wrapped close around her shoulders. Now that they'd made up, he didn't seem to want to let go. "Whatever happens," she whispered. "Nobody's going to come between us, okay? I promise."

She could see Tamar standing outside, doing that still-as-a-statue thing she did whenever she spoke to her clouds.

"Tamar," she said, as she came close.

Tamar's eyes snapped open. "There you are! I was worried about you. Velda's here. Didn't do us the courtesy of a blue-sky announcement this time, but she's here alright."

"She found me," stated Stella.

A flicker of shock passed across Tamar's face, swiftly replaced by rage.

"That scheming . . ." Tamar bared her teeth. "On our own doorstep! What did she want?"

"She told me about Heather," said Stella, watching Tamar closely.

Tamar jolted as though she'd been shoved. The anger drained out of her face, replaced by a hunted look. "What did she tell you?"

Stella's heart froze. She'd been hoping Tamar would deny it; say it wasn't true. But the guilt was written all over her face.

When Stella found the words, they came out clipped and certain: "The sea witch was your last apprentice."

Tamar's face crumpled. "I never . . . I didn't mean to . . ." She reached out with one hand, entreating Stella.

"It's true!" Stella took a step backwards. "You should have *told* me!"

Tamar spread her hands helplessly. "You wouldn't have agreed to train with me if you'd known."

Stella stared at Tamar in revulsion – despite all the bluster and over-confidence, all the moments of danger and the crazy plans, Stella had always trusted her. And all that time, Tamar had been risking turning *her* into a sea witch. She'd even made her fight Heather, without telling her the truth about who she was!

Tamar didn't care about Stella, any more than her last apprentice. All she ever cared about, was not being wrong.

"You *deserve* to feel guilty," said Stella between gritted teeth, then she turned and ran.

* * *

Stella burst through the door and threw herself at Grandpa, in a rush of panic and cloud.

"Hey, hey, what's wrong?" said Grandpa, flapping Nimbus out of his face and wrapping an arm round Stella.

"I might turn into a sea witch. And Tamar lied about everything. And I never want to see her again," gabbled Stella, and burst into tears.

Grandpa blew out softly and hugged her tight until the sobs subsided, then guided her to the kitchen table. "Sit down," he said. "Start at the beginning."

* * *

Stella had just finished telling him everything, when there was a knock at the door. Grandpa stood up and looked out of the window. "It's Tamar," he said.

"I don't want to see her," said Stella. "Tell her to GO AWAY!"

She stormed down the corridor with Nimbus, and slammed her bedroom door behind them.

Stella heard the front door open and the low murmur of Grandpa's voice, then Tamar's voice, high and pleading. The front door closed and the voices continued.

He'd let her in! Why would he do that?!

Stella scowled. If Tamar thought Stella was coming out, she was wrong. She could talk all she wanted. And then she could *leave*.

The low conversation continued for quite a while. How long did it take to send someone away? Stella sat down on the bed and Nimbus settled next to her.

Grandpa's heavy footsteps came down the corridor and there was a soft tap at the door. "Stella?"

"I don't want to see her!"

"I know you don't," said Grandpa, opening the door. "But hear her out before you decide that. You owe her that much."

Stella pulled her knees up to her chest and leant against the wall. Why should she listen? It would just be more lies. *Lies, lies, lies!*

Tamar and Velda. They were as bad as each other.

"Tamar didn't 'set you up' to fight the sea witch," said Grandpa. "That was never her intention."

"How do you know?" said Stella.

"I was there, remember?" said Grandpa, reasonably. "I saw her get hit by that rock."

"Whose side are you on, anyway?" said Stella.

"Yours," said Grandpa. He sat down on the end of the bed. "I might not always get on with Tamar," he said, "but I know her. She was your Gran's best friend. And your Gran was a good judge of character."

"Hmph."

"And I've heard the name Velda before . . ." he said.

Stella looked at him out of the corner of her eye.

"It was one of the only times I heard your Gran curse!" said Grandpa. "I don't know exactly what happened between them, but your Gran was *not* a fan."

Stella tried to imagine Gran cursing and a smile threatened. She hardened her face, so Grandpa wouldn't think she was coming around.

"Just hear what Tamar's got to say," said Grandpa, "then I'll send her on her way."

Stella scowled at him. He didn't deserve it – *he* hadn't done anything wrong – but she was too cross to care.

Grandpa held out a hand and Stella reluctantly shuffled off the bed. Nimbus followed.

Tamar was sitting in Gran's armchair, which immediately made Stella furious – she had no right to sit there!

Grandpa led Stella to his own chair and plumped the cushion for her. Stella sat down heavily and stared at the fireplace, refusing to look at Tamar.

"I'll get the kettle on," said Grandpa.

It was a stupid thing to say. Tamar wouldn't be staying for tea. Not if Stella could help it.

Tamar cleared her throat. "You're *not* going to become a sea witch."

Stella cast a look of betrayal at Grandpa. He'd told Tamar all her fears.

"How do *you* know?" she said.

Tamar held out a hand out towards Nimbus. He backed away from it and settled on the back of Stella's chair.

"I've never seen you this angry," said Tamar.

Stella flashed her a look of disbelief.

"But there's not even a rumble in this room," said Tamar. "Never mind the wild lightning you would have conjured at the start of all this."

Stella twisted to look at Nimbus. He was curled around the back of her chair like a guard dog, but he was utterly silent. He moved a little closer to her.

"You've mastered your fury," said Tamar. "Something Heather never did."

"Velda said you rushed her training," accused Stella. "Just like you're doing with me."

"I did," said Tamar, nodding sadly, "but not without reason. Heather struggled with wild lightning from the start. I took her in, after her family rejected her."

"*Rejected* her!" exclaimed Stella.

"They weren't weather weavers – they didn't understand," said Tamar. "When Heather's youngest sister got hurt, they felt they had to choose."

Stella folded her arms. Could Mum and Dad do that? She pictured them standing on the dock, getting further away, only this time, they weren't smiling.

Tamar looked down at her hands. "I can't judge their decision for their family, but I know it was the worst choice for Heather. Her fury became uncontainable . . ." She sighed. "I hoped that the faster I trained her, the sooner she'd be able to control it."

"But she couldn't?"

Tamar shook her head. "No. So . . . Velda suggested removing her cloud."

Nimbus tumbled off the back of the chair and landed in Stella's lap. She circled her arms around him and laced her fingers together.

"And I agreed," said Tamar, closing her eyes in pain.

"You agreed!" breathed Stella, horrified.

Tamar nodded silently. Stella looked at Grandpa. He was standing motionless with his hand on the kettle, staring at Tamar. She wondered if he realised how much it would hurt her if Nimbus was taken away.

"You *took* Heather's cloud!" repeated Stella.

"No! Velda did. Well, she tried—"

"But you agreed! When you could have stopped her—"

"I *should* have stopped her," said Tamar heavily, "but I didn't. And I will always regret it."

"You said: Velda *tried*," said Stella. "So, she didn't manage to?"

Tamar shook her head. "She didn't anticipate how hard Heather would fight to keep him. The separation was carried out at the Gathering, for 'safety'. But when the time came, Heather unleashed lightning like you've never seen."

Stella glanced at Nimbus and nodded. "We would too."

Tamar looked at her in alarm. "Don't let *anyone* hear you say that, ever!"

Stella clenched her jaw defiantly. She would – if someone tried to take Nimbus, she'd fight them with everything she had.

"Don't even *think* it, Stella!" said Tamar, fiercely. "It was catastrophic! Furious lightning, fire, cascades of ice, so many hurt . . ." Her eyes were full of horror at the memory. "Everyone was running, screaming, conjuring weather to try and stop her." Tamar's hands flew up like startled birds.

Stella pressed herself back in her chair and Nimbus swirled a threatening violet.

Tamar looked at him warily and sat back.

"So, Velda took Heather's cloud," stated Stella.

"No." Tamar bowed her head. "Heather's cloud was destroyed."

Destroyed?

Nimbus turned pale blue in shock. Stella abruptly stood up, scooping him up, and moved away from Tamar.

She'd never imagined a cloud *could* be destroyed. Just the thought of it made her knees go weak. She sat down on the far side of the kitchen table and Nimbus settled in the safe circle of her arms.

"That's why Heather gave herself to the sea," said Tamar.

How do you give yourself to the sea?

Stella pictured the ragged girl she'd seen, diving off a tall rock, plunging into the water, taking all her grief and fury with her.

"How?"

"She begged vengeance from the darkest powers of the deep. The Teran loves misery – it took her into its cold heart and made her its own."

"Turned her into a sea witch . . ."

Tamar nodded sadly. "I vowed I would never let that happen again. I would never lose another apprentice." She pushed herself up from her chair. "There is no way on earth I'm letting Velda take Nimbus from you. You can count on that."

Stella didn't answer. With or without Tamar's help, *she* wouldn't let Velda take Nimbus. Nobody would keep them apart. Even if they had to fight the whole Gathering. Nimbus let out a low growl of thunder and flickered, making Stella's arms prickle with electricity.

Grandpa stepped forward in alarm. "You've said what you came to say, Tamar. I think we'd better leave it there for now."

Tamar nodded, but paused in the doorway. "Will I see you tomorrow?"

Stella looked at Tamar and curled her lip. Tamar thought everything was forgiven?

"Hate me as much as you like," said Tamar. "But if you want to keep Nimbus, you need to enter those trials. The invitation arrived this morning."

Nine

WEATHER AND WORDS

"YOU'RE sure about this?" asked Grandpa.

"No!" exclaimed Stella. "I'm not sure about anything, right now. But I'm not losing Nimbus." She yanked her boot on.

"Do you want me to come with you?"

Stella shook her head.

Grandpa stifled a yawn. "I was up all night, thinking about this Velda business."

"So was I," said Stella.

Velda was against them, but the council had the final say – it was *them* she had to impress. If they let her enter the trials, Velda would have to lump it. And maybe Tamar, too – she hadn't decided about that.

Grandpa scratched the stubble on his chin. "I mean, how does Tamar *know* you won't turn into a sea witch?"

Stella's eyes widened. *Seriously?* She fixed him with a firm look. "I'm not turning into a sea witch, Grandpa. I promise. It doesn't just happen – you have to *want* it!"

Grandpa held her gaze, then nodded. He seemed reassured. "Can you imagine me trying to explain *that* to your parents?" He raised his eyebrows and smiled.

Stella didn't smile back.

How was she going to explain *any* of this to her parents?

Heather's parents had *rejected* her! *Rejected!* Stella hadn't been able to stop thinking about it since yesterday.

"What is it?" said Grandpa.

Stella swallowed and looked at Nimbus.

"What if Mum and Dad don't want me to have Nimbus? What if they *reject* me like Heather's parents did?"

"Come here." Grandpa pulled her to her feet and wrapped her in a hug. "Your parents would *never* reject you! Never. Not for any reason."

"But they might be scared of Nimbus . . ." Stella mumbled into his jumper.

Grandpa let go and bent forwards to look her in the eyes.

"If *I* can get used to him, anyone can. Hmm?"

Stella nodded. He was right.

"We'll get through this, together," said Grandpa. "Whatever I can do to help, you only need to ask."

It hurt her heart a little. She knew he meant it, but what could Grandpa do?

Nimbus drifted out from under the chair and Stella's resolve hardened.

She wasn't losing him.

"I just need to get into the trials," she said. "Then everything will be okay."

"That's my girl," Grandpa smiled. "And I'll be there, cheering you on."

Stella nodded cautiously. It would be brilliant to have Grandpa there. But she didn't trust that was part of Tamar's plan. Yet *another* thing she needed a straight answer about.

No more secrets. No more lies. She'd had enough.

* * *

"No. We're not doing any more lightning. Not until you answer the question!" Stella planted her feet in the sand and folded her arms. Nimbus floated closer in solidarity. If Tamar thought she was going to get away with any more half-truths, she had another thing coming.

"Of course they'll let you enter!" exclaimed Tamar. "We've got the invitation – that's half the battle – we just need the council to sign it off."

"But what happens if they don't?"

Tamar shrugged. "We'll come up with another plan."

Stella looked at Nimbus, bunched like a fist and heavy with shadows after the last lightning strike. "They can't *force* Nimbus to leave me."

"Oh, but they can."

"How?"

"I don't know how," admitted Tamar. "The Ice Weavers keep their secrets close. But Velda's perfected the process, since Heather. All the storm clouds have gone without a fight."

"Gone where?"

"To Winter's Keep," said Tamar. "The Ice Weavers are charged with holding them there, until their apprentices pass the trials."

Stella looked along the beach. *Oh.*

That wasn't as bad as she thought. Tamar had made it sound as though she'd lose Nimbus for ever.

"So, even if Nimbus did get taken away, it would just be for a bit?"

Tamar crouched down, where the last bolt of lightning had struck, and picked up her trowel. After a few moments of careful digging, she lifted a shard of fused glass out of the sand.

Like a sculpture of lightning.

Tamar pursed her lips. "Double fork again, see?" She tossed it to one side. It crumbled as it landed. "We're after a single bolt.

Clean, sharp, accurate!"

Stella shook her head, annoyed at herself for letting Tamar distract her.

"Stop changing the subject! If Nimbus got taken away, I'd get him back, right?"

Tamar winced. "That's what's meant to happen, yes," she said. "But so far, it hasn't."

Stella raised her eyebrows and let the silence stretch. She'd learnt that from Grandpa.

Tamar shifted uncomfortably, clearly considering how honest to be. "To pass the trials, apprentices first have to catch another cloud – and *not* a storm cloud. So far, I don't know of a single one who's managed it. Storm Weavers catch storm clouds. That's just how it is. It's all a huge snow job, if you ask me . . ."

"And the council are okay with that?"

"There are no Storm Weavers left to question it," said Tamar. She walked a little distance away to poke another target into the sand. "Look, the council are far from perfect – they're officious, pompous, overly cautious," she curled her lip, "but they're *not* all like Velda. They're our best hope, right now."

Intuition twitched in the back of Stella's mind.

"Did you used to be on the council?" she said. "Before Heather, you know . . ."

Tamar nodded. "This will the first time I've faced them, since then."

"Oof!" said Stella.

"Enough talking, now," said Tamar "Get that cloud sparking again."

"But it was Velda's fault!" protested Stella. "How come you got kicked out and Velda ended up in charge?"

Tamar winced and Stella snapped her mouth shut.

"She tells a convincing story," said Tamar, her voice heavy with resentment. "Velda is good with *words*. Me? I'm only good with weather."

* * *

It took the whole morning, but Tamar finally declared she was satisfied. They made their way up the steep path from the beach. Stella's head was still busy with questions.

"Will Grandpa get to watch me? In the trials?"

Tamar scratched her ear and turned away.

I knew it!

"You're planning to brain-fog him, aren't you?" said Stella.

"No, no—"

"Well, what then?" said Stella. She scampered to catch up. "What happens when we arrive? Will they stop him coming in?"

"Into the grounds? Yes, probably," admitted Tamar.

Tamar was so sneaky! She'd told Grandpa he could come and he'd just believed it.

"He'll be able to drop us off," said Tamar, "then he can stay on the boat."

"No. You have to get him in. I'm not doing this without Grandpa! Promise me!"

"But the Gathering is just for—"

"Promise!" said Stella. "You've got me into the trials. You can get him into the Gathering."

Tamar wrinkled her nose, but nodded reluctantly. "I'll see if I can pull some strings."

When they reached the clifftop, Tamar lengthened her stride and headed for the croft. Stella paused to wait for Nimbus.

Below him, the beach was a splattered mess of holes – evidence of how hard they'd been practising. Strike after lightning strike. Not as clean or neat as Tamar wanted, but most of them on target.

"Up you come!"

Nimbus put on a brief spurt of speed, then flumped down into the grass and rolled the last stretch. He looked exhausted.

They headed into the croft and Stella sat down at the kitchen table. Tamar had covered it with a tablecloth – it made the room look weirdly formal.

To hide the scorch marks, realised Stella, with a slight tug of guilt.

Tamar thumped a large book down on the table. "Homework."

Stella stared at it in dismay. "That's massive. I can't read all that!"

"It's not reading," said Tamar, "it's revision. We've covered most of it already."

Stella ran a finger over the embossed cover: *The Weather Book: Lore & Knowledge.*

"Well, apart from weather lore," said Tamar. "That may be new to you. But all you need to do is memorise it. Sharp young brain like yours? Easy."

Stella flipped the cover open and groaned. The printed text was tiny – so dense that the letters seemed to crawl like ants on the page. She flipped forward. Weather lore went on for pages and pages. She closed the book and put her head on the table.

Tamar frowned. "You look as depleted as your cloud. I'd suggest you send him out for more magic. You, meanwhile, can spend the rest of the day revising."

That was Tamar's idea of a break? To give her *homework*?

Stella stood up and slid the hefty book into her rucksack, then swung it onto her back. *It weighs a tonne.*

"You can keep that copy," said Tamar. "It's for you. But if your Grandpa's going to help you revise, tell him to keep it to himself. Sacred knowledge, that is."

Stella gave her an even look. "Don't forget about getting Grandpa in. I mean it. If they send him away when we get there, I'm leaving with him."

"Yes! Yes. You were *quite* clear," said Tamar. "Now, go on. Off with you."

* * *

"Sacred knowledge," said Grandpa, chortling. "Who's she trying to kid? It's common knowledge. More than that, it's common sense!"

Stella felt a tiny bit guilty that Grandpa wasn't treating it as sacred. But it *was* helpful, having him read it aloud. There was no way she'd get through it all on her own. She just hoped he didn't decide to share his opinions with Tamar . . .

"I bet you remember this one?" he said. "You used to sing it with your Gran. Mackerel sky, mackerel sky, never long wet, never long dry."

Stella hummed the tune.

"That's it!" said Grandpa.

"So, it's all stuff I know?" said Stella.

"I should hope so!" said Grandpa. "Your Dad knew all these, by the time he was your age. Mind you, he was a born sky-gazer. Came in handy when he was learning to sail, I'll tell you. He always had a good nose for the weather."

There was a short pause and Stella's eyes met Grandpa's – they were having the same thought.

"You think he's got a touch of magic himself?" said Grandpa.

"Dunno. Maybe," said Stella.

"I'm going to be mighty annoyed, if it turns out he knew all this and didn't tell me."

"I don't think so," said Stella. "He would have said something otherwise, when I tried to tell him and Mum about Nimbus."

Grandpa let out a puff. "You're probably right."

"Read me another one," said Stella.

Grandpa smiled. "More sacred secrets, coming up . . ."

Ten

COMPETENT
CREW

THE weather was fair for the journey up to Yell. The sky was a benevolent blue and the sea was calm; Tamar was not.

"When dew is on the grass?" she repeated, snapping her fingers impatiently.

"Rain will never come to pass," answered Stella.

Tamar gave a short nod. "A ring around the sun or moon?"

Something will happen very soon, Stella's brain supplied, unhelpfully. She leant back and rubbed her eyes. "Can we stop?

My brain is melting."

Tamar shook her head. "Knowledge is the first trial. You need to practice!"

"Give the girl a break," said Grandpa. "She's worked hard all week. Besides, while we're on the boat, she works for *me*."

Stella gave Grandpa a grateful smile. She was actually enjoying being on the boat this time. Or she would have been, if it weren't for Tamar grilling her.

"Tell me about these trials, Tamar," said Grandpa. "Are they like exams, then?"

"Exams," scoffed Tamar. "Hardly!"

Grandpa refused to be ruffled. "So? What are they? Practicals?"

"Trials!" exclaimed Tamar. "They're trials! The first is the Trial of Knowledge. That weeds out the ones who haven't put the work in."

Stella swallowed. *It doesn't matter,* she reminded herself. *I don't have to pass.*

Tamar had told her it usually took two or three tries to make it through the trials. Hardly anyone managed it first time. But that didn't stop her wanting to. How cool would that be? To enter the trials and pass them first time.

"After that is the Trial of Skill. Command, accuracy, control!" Tamar gave Stella a meaningful look.

Stella shifted uncomfortably – she hadn't told Grandpa she'd be casting lightning. "Can I go up on deck, Grandpa?"

Grandpa gave her a covert wink: *I'll keep Tamar occupied.*

Stella stood up, letting her feet find the motion of the deck. Grandpa had showed her – moving on the boat was like a dance – you had to know the rhythm. The waves came in sets, every seventh wave a big one.

Dancing with the sea! she thought, flexing her knees.

"One hand for the boat, remember?" said Grandpa.

Stella nodded. No way she wanted to fall in, lifejacket or not.

"Apprentices who pass both those trials can enter the Quest," continued Tamar. "If Stella gets that far, I'll give her a mentor gift; some useful bit of kit to take in with her. But beyond that, I can't help her. It changes every year, so there's no preparing for it. It'll challenge everything she knows about weather weaving. And finally, the Reckoning—"

Stella clambered up on the gunwale, then edged her way carefully along the side of the boat, glad to escape. Tamar had already explained the three trials to her. Hearing it again was just making her anxious – especially now they were so close.

Stella slid one hand along the roof of the cockpit, holding on tight. The waves flicked salty sea spray onto her cheeks. She sat down on the neat triangle of deck at the front and focused on Nimbus. The little cloud was scudding along ahead of the boat, skimming the waves. She took a deep breath, letting the light breeze lift her worries away.

She'd been so scared, the first time on Grandpa's boat; partly of feeling sick, and partly of what might be lurking in the shadowy depths.

"Except we know what's down there, now, don't we, Nimbus?"

At the sound of his name, Nimbus dodged left and right, showing off.

Stella smiled at him, then knelt to look over the edge. Licks of foam and sudden splashes leapt up at her, as the prow carved through the waves. A little further out, the water rushed past; deep indigo blue.

Stella stared down. Where was the sea witch now? Had she returned to midnight depth? Turned back into a monster?

Stella hoped not.

Stripped of her power, the Haken had looked almost human again. A shadow of the girl she'd once been, but no longer monstrous.

Stella leant forward and whispered. "I'm sorry for what they did to you, Heather."

The water rushed past; a tangle of hypnotic patterns.

Stella heaved a short sigh and sat up, shifting her attention to the sky. It was dotted with clouds – larger cousins of Nimbus, shaped like whales, rabbits, turtles, sheep . . .

"Are they all going to the Gathering?" she called back to Tamar, pointing at them.

"Not all of them," said Tamar. "Some are just sight-seeing or catching up with old friends. That one's definitely heading in the same direction as us, look." She pointed to a submarine-shaped cloud that had turned to head inland.

Grandpa swung the wheel to bring them into a long narrow

channel. He pulled back on the throttle and the engine settled down to a steady chug. "Whale Firth. We're nearly there, folks."

As the boat nosed along the inlet, Stella shaded her eyes and looked ahead. The channel of water they were following was long and narrow, almost like a river. It was bounded on either side by low rolling hills, carpeted in a scrub of sedge and heather.

Tamar pointed ahead. "There's a jetty down the far end."

"Right, all hands on deck, then!" said Grandpa. "Stella? You ready?"

Stella nodded eagerly and clambered to her feet, making sure to hold on with one hand. "Aye aye, Captain."

Grandpa had *said* she could crew for him, but this was the first time he'd actually asked her to do anything.

"Fenders out," he said. "Check your knots before you drop them over the side."

Stella sketched a quick salute, then flipped open the hatch in the foredeck. The locker beneath was crammed with fat, sausage-shaped rubber fenders.

For each one, Stella tied a clove hitch around the rail, checked the knot with a swift tug, and then carefully lowered the fender over the side. Four on each side, to protect the boat from banging against the mooring.

When she'd made her way all the way round, she hopped back down into the cockpit and glanced at Grandpa. He was steering the boat, a look of quiet satisfaction on his face. He was definitely impressed.

Stella smiled to herself.

"There," said Tamar, pointing. "That's where we're heading."

Stella moved across to Tamar's side of the cockpit to look. High on the hillside at the head of the firth, an old mansion stared down, its empty windows gaping like eye sockets.

"Wind House?" said Grandpa, with a note of alarm in his voice. "You're taking us to Wind House?"

"The perfect place for the Northern Gathering!" said Tamar, nodding. "We've been meeting here, on and off, for decades."

"You might want to stay on the boat, with me," said Grandpa to Stella. "Wind House is *not* a place you want to spend the night."

Tamar chuckled. "The rumours are still working, then . . ."

"Oh, what?" said Grandpa, crossly. "You're going to tell me it's *not* the most haunted house in the isles?"

A shiver crept up Stella's spine. *Stone stories,* she reminded herself. *Not the same as ghosts at all.* Even so, she wasn't keen to sleep there – especially after seeing the fright on Grandpa's face.

"They're not really ghosts, are they?" she said, partly for his benefit. "Just old stones leaking their stories."

Tamar winked. "Plus a few stories we've invented, to keep unwanted visitors away."

Grandpa grunted unhappily.

Stella kept her eyes on Wind House, trying to match it to the dreams she'd had of the Gathering. She'd imagined bright colours and lots of people, every weather you could think of, but it was nothing like that. Just a stark grey house, standing alone on the desolate slope.

The closer they got, the worse it looked.

A great crack ran the full height of the end wall. One of the chimney stacks had toppled into a pile of rubble. The windows were nothing more than crumbling holes.

"It's a ruin!" said Stella, glancing at Tamar in dismay.

Tamar smiled. "All will be revealed," she said, tapping the side of her nose. She enjoyed being mysterious. It was annoying. Especially when it was about scary stuff.

"Is that one of the guards?" said Stella, nodding at a man in a smart white uniform, approaching along the wooden jetty ahead of them.

Tamar nodded. "Yes, but don't worry. I've still got *one* friend on the council. She'll be here any minute."

Grandpa slowed the boat and ground the engine into reverse a couple of times until they were barely moving as they came alongside the jetty. He threw a coiled rope to the unsmiling guard, then turned off the engine. Silence crowded in.

Eleven

WIND HOUSE

A S soon as he'd secured the rope, the guard stepped forward
and looked suspiciously into the cockpit. His eyes widened
fractionally when he saw Tamar. "You're back!"

"By personal invitation," said Tamar, cheerfully, "from Velda."

Stella's heart jumped into her mouth. That wasn't true.

The guard didn't look convinced, either.

"Peter, isn't it?" said Tamar. "How's your little sister doing?
Has she made it to the trials yet?"

Anger flashed in the guard's eyes, then the shutters came down.
His answer was clipped. "She had a *storm* cloud. They were separated."

Stella gripped the edge of the seat, fighting the feeling of falling. *Separated.*

Tamar's mouth opened and closed, like a fish out of water. "I'm sorry," she finally managed. "I'm so sorry to hear that."

Peter turned his attention to Stella and she quickly wiped the shock off her face.

Good, friendly, no trouble – that's me.

It didn't work as well as she'd hoped.

"Who's this, then?"

"Tamar! You're here! Cutting it fine, as usual – I was starting to wonder if you'd make it."

A woman was striding towards them along the jetty – she carried herself like a queen. "Thank you, Peter. I'll take it from here."

The guard held his ground, unwilling to back down so easily. "Farah, you know I have to see their invitation." His eyes were wary, but the message was clear: *I'm not leaving until I've done my job.*

Stella sat very still and held her breath.

"This is Stella," said the woman, calmly. "She's here for the trials. You have the invitation, don't you, Tamar?"

Tamar nodded hastily and began to dig around in her bag.

The seconds ticked by and Stella's smile started to go rigid. Had Tamar lied about having an invitation?

At last, Tamar pulled a crumpled card out of the depths of her bag and held it up triumphantly. "Here we are! Knew I had it somewhere."

"Good. Everything's in order, then."

Peter still didn't look happy, but Farah stared at him expectantly until he nodded. He shot one last suspicious glance at Stella, then snapped his heels together and marched away.

Stella breathed out in relief.

Tamar put her bag down and climbed out of the boat.

"Welcome, old friend," said Farah, opening her arms wide.

"Less of the old," said Tamar, but Farah's hug muffled her protest.

Farah was tall – much taller than Tamar – and looked wonderfully unusual. She wore a long turquoise robe, embroidered with tiny golden suns, which winked and sparkled as she moved.

THAT'S what a weather weaver should look like, thought Stella. *Not all boring and tucked in, like Velda.*

Stella grinned at Grandpa, then hopped down to join them.

"You must be Stella?" said Farah. Her dark eyes shone with warmth and humour. "I've heard *wonderful* things about you."

Stella smiled at her, glowing inside.

Farah shaded her eyes and looked up at Nimbus, who was circling the top of the mast. "Yours?" she said.

Stella nodded. She beckoned to Nimbus, who swooped down to float at her side.

"What a perfect pair," said Farah. She spread her arms and bowed. "I'm honoured to tell you that I'll be your guardian, here at the Gathering."

"Thank you," said Stella, ducking her head in response. She flicked a questioning glance at Tamar. *But you're my mentor?*

Farah immediately understood. "I've put your name forward for the trials, but I haven't been able to get Tamar reinstated," she said. "Indeed, it's possible she'll be asked to leave."

Stella nodded, a flutter of nerves waking in her stomach. She glanced down at Nimbus. *No Tamar?*

She hadn't realised it until now, but she'd been banking on Tamar to help her out – not to cheat exactly, but definitely to give her last minute advice.

"You won't be alone though, whatever happens," said Farah. "I'll stand in for Tamar – speak for you, when it's needed."

"Farah will take good care of you," said Tamar. "She's a friend. You go on ahead. I'll see you up there shortly."

Stella swallowed her nerves and nodded. "Okay."

"Now," said Farah, "while Tamar and . . ." she looked questioningly at Grandpa.

"David," said Grandpa, gruffly.

"While Tamar and David unload, I'll take you up to the house."

Stella spotted a swift glance between Tamar and Farah, but nothing more was said about whether or not Grandpa should be there.

Tamar kept her word.

Grandpa towed the dinghy round to the front of the boat, and began hoisting barrels and crates up onto the jetty.

"Gently!" barked Tamar. "Don't rattle them like that!"

Farah gave Grandpa a sympathetic smile, then put a hand on Stella's shoulder and steered her away.

A narrow path snaked up the empty hillside towards the derelict house.

"It doesn't look like much from here, does it?" said Farah, her sideways glance full of laughter.

"Not really," said Stella, staring up at it with a shiver. "Looks pretty spooky."

The sky overhead was blue, but the house seemed to belong to another season. Its walls were chilly grey and deep shadows lurked amongst the fallen stones.

As they approached the house, a drift of mist rose out of the long grass, like ghosts from the grave. Stella stiffened, but Farah's warm hand on her shoulder gave her no choice – they kept walking. Stella breathed a little shallower as the world blurred around them.

"Close your eyes," said Farah.

Stella shot her a worried look.

"Trust me. It'll be worth it," said Farah, with a smile.

Stella closed her eyes and let Farah guide her forward. The mist was cool and damp on her cheeks, the peat spongy underfoot. She began to hear a murmur of voices. And she could smell . . . popcorn?

"Can I open them yet?" she said. The voices grew louder, cheerier; they were all around her. There was music, too; a bright trilling fiddle, somewhere close by.

"Now, you can open them," said Farah.

Stella opened her eyes and her mouth dropped open in amazement.

The Gathering!

Before, there had been only mossy grass and boulders. Now, the hillside was crowded with a rainbow carnival of strange structures and market stalls. The narrow alleys between them bustled with a wild and colourful mix of people – so many people!

Directly ahead of them was a living treehouse, its floors and walls sprouting new green shoots as she watched. A staircase of fat tree roots with a handrail of vines stretched up into the leafy branches. By the foot of it, a man crouched with a cloud, coaxing more vines out of the ground.

Behind him, the sun gleamed on spiralling towers of ice – a miniature frozen palace. Snow puffed out of one of the highest windows and the peak of the turret grew a little taller.

"Not so spooky now, eh?" said Farah. "Welcome to the weather market." She spread her hands with a smile.

Stella gazed around, drinking it all in. "It's, it's . . . Wow!"

"They're still getting set up at the moment," said Farah. "Wait until tomorrow – by then, it'll be in full swing."

Stella looked back down the path. She could still see Grandpa and Tamar down by the boat. Tamar was waving her arms about and pointing bossily.

"But how?" She shook her head in confusion. "How do you hide it?"

"Oh, not me," said Farah. "*They* help us stay hidden." She

nodded to a series of large humps in the grass beside the path. Each hump had a tiny door on the front and a short chimney. A thin thread of smoke rose out of one of them.

"Are those *Trowie mounds*?" whispered Stella, wide-eyed.

"They are," said Farah. "The good folk help us stay hidden. In return, we trade with them – weather magic in exchange for secrecy."

Stella clapped her hands together in delight. *Grandpa's going to be so excited!*

* * *

"WIND KNOTS! Get your wind knots here! Can I interest you in some wind knots, Miss? We have singles, doubles, and triples: everything from trade winds to full-throated gales. All tied up and ready to blow." The man waved a handful of knotted ropes at her. Stella smiled and shook her head, and he turned away to the next potential customer.

Closer to the house, the market was bustling with people; busy with trade. Every kind of weather was on display.

The next stall was almost hidden under a hedge of greenery. Yellow flowers peeped out between wiry stems of gorse. Stella didn't spot the stall holder until she popped out, right in front of her. The willowy girl put a thin whippy stick in her hand. "Wind twister," she said. "Free sample. Try it! But not near me." She laughed.

Farah turned around smartly and plucked the branch out of Stella's fingers. "Do *not* try it," she said. She gave the stallholder a withering look. "This is an *apprentice*!" she said. "Check first, next time."

"Sorry. Won't happen again." The girl backed away.

Farah shook her head in annoyance and hustled Stella away. "Honestly! It's not as though the council make rules for the fun of it! They exist for a reason."

Stella looked up at Nimbus. *He* was against the rules.

"When are the council going to decide about me and Nimbus?" she asked.

Farah glanced around furtively, then herded Stella on through the crowd. "We'll talk about that later, yes? When we're away from listening ears."

Listening ears?

The market suddenly felt less friendly. People jostled past, hurrying from one stall to the next, haggling in loud voices.

Stella's heart shrank a little. None of them knew about her and Nimbus, yet. And a lot of them wouldn't want them here. How many were on Velda's side?

Nimbus settled around her shoulders, as though to hide her.

Twelve

A SMALL TORNADO

"IS Tamar going to join us soon?" said Stella.

Farah nodded. "I'll come and fetch you when she gets here. Best if you keep a low profile, until then."

Because of Velda, Stella realised, with a chill.

That *was* the plan, of course – confront Velda, at the Gathering – but it suddenly felt a bit too real.

Farah held up an arm, indicating a pair of stone gateposts and Stella realised they'd arrived. The house loomed grey and silent, a cold contrast to the bright bustle of the market.

It was the first time she'd properly seen Wind House without its disguise. A crest was carved into the stone over the door and above it the walls ended in castellations. It wasn't huge – only two storeys high – but it still felt imposing. A shiver of nerves scampered up Stella's back. "Am I in the same room as Tamar?"

She didn't normally like sharing a room, but here, she'd be glad of it.

Farah shook her head. "You're paired with another apprentice. Gives you a chance to make friends."

Stella's heart sank. With three new schools in the last six years, she had a lot of experience at 'making friends'. It didn't always go well.

"Tamar and I were in a room together for our trials," said Farah.

Stella's eyes widened. "You've known each other *ages*, then!"

Farah's eyes twinkled. "Centuries . . ."

"Sorry," said Stella, "I didn't mean—"

Farah shook her head. "It's fine. You're right. I've known Tamar longer than anyone else here. It's not been the same since she left the council."

"Since the sea witch," said Stella, quietly.

Farah considered Stella. "You know about that, then?"

Stella nodded, but kept her mouth closed, uncertain whether they should be talking about it at all.

Farah turned the heavy iron handle and Stella followed her inside. The hallway stretched away to the back of the house, ending in two gloomy corridors leading off left and right. It smelt of old carpet and wood polish, with a faint undertone of damp.

There were four doors off the hall, all of them closed. Farah pointed at the second one on the left. "That's my office. If you need me, you can usually find me there."

Stella wasn't sure why, but she'd assumed that Tamar's 'friend on the council' probably wasn't one of the people in charge. But surely you only had an office if you were someone important?

Farah pulled the door closed with a heavy clunk and Stella hitched her bag up on her shoulder. By now, Nimbus would normally have scooted off to explore, but instead, he was staying close. She was glad.

Even without Grandpa's ghost stories, she wouldn't have liked this house. Its stone walls seemed to breathe out judgement: *unpredictable, unprepared, unwelcome.*

To their right, a narrow staircase stretched up to the second floor. "This way," said Farah, with a reassuring smile.

* * *

The upstairs corridor was cool and dark, with a door every couple of metres. *Bedrooms*, Stella guessed. There were lots of doors. Lots of apprentices, all here for the trials . . .

"When do the trials start?" she asked.

"Not straight away," Farah told her. "There's the opening ceremony tonight – that's when entries are submitted to the council."

Stella's breath caught in her throat. *So soon!*

She didn't want to think about what might happen if the

council decided *not* to let them take the trial.

"Tomorrow, you'll have the morning free – the first trial takes place just before lunch," continued Farah.

She's assuming we'll get in, thought Stella, wishing she felt that confident.

"I've paired you with an apprentice called Tassa," said Farah. "I think you'll get along. She's another of my special invitations."

Special invitations?

Farah pushed open the second to last door. "This is you," she said, with a smile. "Tassa? This is Stella, your room-mate."

The room was cramped – just enough space for two single beds and a small chest of drawers between them; nothing else. Both beds were strewn with clothes and bags and books. As Mum would say: it looked like a tornado had hit it.

Maybe it actually did . . . thought Stella. A girl was sitting cross-legged on the far bed. A wide-toothed comb was sticking out of her tight curls and the coverlet around her was covered in twigs and leaves. *Maybe she did it?*

The girl gave a small wave, making her bracelet jingle. "Hi. I'm Tas. That's you, over there," she said, pointing at the bed opposite. "Sorry. I've spread out a bit."

"I'll leave you two to get to know one another," said Farah. "Tomorrow Tassa can show you around, but for now, stay here. I'll come and fetch you when it's time."

Stella felt a tug of loss as Farah walked away down the corridor. She was nice.

Tas? She didn't know yet.

Stella gave her an apologetic smile. "Sorry you're stuck showing me around. I promise I won't trail you like a lost sheep."

"Don't worry about it," said Tas. She stood up and swept her clothes and books off Stella's bed onto the floor. "Long as you don't plan on using me as target practice like the others."

Stella dumped her bag on her bed and frowned. "Who's been using you as target practice?"

Tas nodded at the wall. "The Winter Twins – icy by name and icy by nature. They've got the room next to ours, worst luck." She sat down again and attacked a handful of curls with the comb. It was clearly what she'd been doing before Stella came in.

Stella winced in sympathy. "What did they do? Drag you through a hedge?"

"No. Dust devil," said Tas, matter-of-factly. "Bit like a tornado, but smaller – right size to hit just one person. *They* thought it was hilarious, but with hair like mine . . ."

Stella sat down on her new bed and shook her head. "You can't let them get away with it," she said. "They'll just get worse."

She knew bullies. That was how they worked.

"It's alright," said Tas. "I'm used to it."

"It's not alright!" said Stella.

Using weather against someone else? That was bad. Tamar had never said so – she hadn't had to – Stella just knew it.

"You should tell someone."

"I'm telling you, aren't I?"

"I mean someone who can do something about it," said Stella. "Someone in charge."

"Like who?"

"I don't know. Farah, maybe? Or your mentor?"

Tas shook her head. "Not right before the trials. It's not worth the trouble. *After* the trials, well, *then* they'd better watch out!" She gave a toothy grin. "Is that your cloud hiding out there?"

Stella looked behind her. Nimbus was still lurking in the corridor.

"Nimbus, you can come in," she said. "This is where we're staying."

Nimbus drifted reluctantly through the door. She smiled at him. He looked as nervous as she'd felt. It hadn't occurred to her that clouds might get shy, too. She patted the bedspread, with an encouraging smile.

Tas giggled. "What a cutey!"

Nimbus fluffed up a little and drifted over to join Stella. Tas reached out to try and stroke him, but he swerved to avoid her hand.

"Probably best if you don't," said Stella. "Not 'til he's had a chance to get to know you."

Tas snatched her hand away. "Yikes! I forgot. He's a thunder-cloud, isn't he?!"

"You know?!"

Tas nodded. "Farah gave me the heads up. Didn't tell me how you got through the assessment, though! What's your secret?"

Stella considered Tassa. Could she trust her? Nimbus drifted around and tucked himself between Stella and the wall.

"Wait! Did you *skip* the assessment?" exclaimed Tas, loudly.

Stella's heart leapt into her mouth. "Shh!"

Tas's eyes widened and she leapt up to close the door. "You did, didn't you?" she hissed, in an excited whisper. "Just snuck on through!"

Stella stared at her in alarm, unsure what to say. *Keep a low profile*, Farah had said, but she hadn't given Stella any instructions about how to do that.

To her relief, Tas broke into a massive grin. "Kudos to you, I say," she declared. "I won't tell!" She bounced back onto the bed and clapped in delight. "Check us out! Team Storm! Pow, pow, pow!" She fired imaginary lightning at the door. "Take *that*, winter!"

Stella couldn't help giggling. Maybe this was going to be fun after all. "So, why did *you* get a special invitation?" she asked. "Do you have a storm cloud too?"

"*Had* a storm cloud," said Tas. "We were separated."

Stella's heart plunged. "Oh! I'm sorry."

"No need," said Tas firmly. "I'm going to get him back. That's why I'm here."

"How?"

"By passing the trials, that's how." Tas thumped her pillows into shape and leant back. "It's taken me *two years*, but I finally found me another cloud; a nice, safe, regulation rain cloud."

Stella smiled. So, Tamar was wrong. It *was* possible.

"I didn't think anyone had managed to do that?"

"They haven't," said Tas, looking smug. "And you know why?

Because Storm Weavers catch storm clouds. It's like some cosmic rule or something. They're attracted to us."

"So, how did you catch a rain cloud?"

"Rain clouds *love* a good dancer," said Tas, winking. "And trust me, I've got all the moves." She clicked her fingers and spread her arms, striking a confident pose. "Paparuda Queen, that's me."

Stella laughed. Tas wasn't like anyone she'd ever met before, but she could already tell they were going to get on.

"Paparuda?"

"Romanian rain ritual," explained Tas. "I've been doing it since I was this big." She held a hand low to the floor. "It's really fun, and there are loads of farms round us, so calling rain's kind of a big deal."

"So, were you . . . disappointed to catch a storm cloud?"

"No!" exclaimed Tas. "Only the *best* weather weavers catch storms. That's what Bunică told me – my grandma." She touched the charm bracelet at her wrist.

"She gave you that?" said Stella, with a smile.

Tas nodded, then wagged a finger, clearly mimicking her gran. "Storm clouds are best of all – brave and true. Very lucky, if they choose you!"

Nimbus edged out from behind Stella and settled himself on her lap.

Tas looked at him with a comical expression of alarm on her face. "Wait, as roomies, we're meant to practice together . . . he won't fire lightning at *me*, will he?"

"Of course not!" laughed Stella. "Long as you don't rain on me?"

Tas grinned. "Can't promise that," she said. "My cloud's a cheeky one. I called him Drench for a reason!"

"Where is he?" said Stella.

"Out getting magic," said Tas. "Probably be ages, though. There's not much going spare round here." She shrugged. "You don't have to bring your cloud to the ceremony, though. I checked."

Stella smoothed Nimbus. She was definitely bringing *him* with her.

"So, what are you going to wear?" said Tas, looking Stella up and down.

"What do you mean?" said Stella.

"To the ceremony! It's a big deal – everyone gets dressed up."

Stella stared at Tas with a dawning sense of dread. These *were* her clothes. The clothes in her bag were no different. Tamar hadn't said anything about posh clothes!

"Don't worry," said Tas, standing up and yanking open a drawer. "You can borrow something of mine. In fact, look – this'll be perfect!" She pulled a silvery grey blouse out of the drawer. "Storm colours, so I won't be needing it 'til I pass the trials, anyway – before that, I'm orange all the way."

Stella fingered the fine fabric. The neck and cuffs were embroidered with swirling grey storm clouds. It looked too precious to lend. "Are you sure?"

"Course I'm sure," said Tas. "I told you. We're a team. Storm sisters!"

Thirteen

OPENING CEREMONY

IT felt like no time before Farah reappeared to take Stella downstairs. Tamar was waiting in Farah's office. She was wearing a dark purple skirt and polo neck, and a long grey cloak. She'd obviously made an effort to look formal, but her tufty hair and heavy boots kind of spoiled the effect.

"You ready to cause a fuss?" she said, with a smile.

"No," said Farah, shutting the office door. She glanced up at Nimbus, darting in tight triangles around the ceiling, and turned to Stella seriously. "We want no sparks, no thunder, no *fuss* of any kind," she said. "Calm control, no matter what. Can you do that?"

"No trouble!" blustered Tamar. "They're the very model of calm control, aren't you?"

Stella nodded seriously, her heart fluttering like a caged bird. The honest answer was: *No. Not usually.* But now? They'd have to be.

Nimbus, settle down!

Nimbus changed direction abruptly and ran into the ceiling light, setting it swinging slightly. Stella side-stepped to stand underneath him, like she'd meant him to do that.

Farah considered the pair of them for a moment, then nodded her approval, before turning to Tamar. "Tamar? No going rogue. Not today. Stick to the plan. Give it a while longer, then head in and find yourselves a discreet spot. I'll see you in there." She went out, closing the door behind her.

"No going rogue. The cheek of it!" muttered Tamar, pacing back and forth. "No sparks, no thunder, no fuss . . . You can tell she's on the council, can't you? If I didn't love her so much, I'd say it's gone to her head."

Stella beckoned Nimbus down and smoothed him.

Super-calm, okay? she thought. *Farah's right. We need to make a good impression.*

Barely a minute had passed before Tamar pulled up the hood of her cloak decisively. "Enough waiting. Let's head in. Get the lay of the land." Stella drew a breath to object, but Tamar was already opening the door. She had no choice but to follow.

The great hall echoed with excited conversation. It was set up like a school assembly – rows and rows of seats facing a wide stage at the far end – but that was where the similarity ended. Above the seats, the air was crowded with clouds, each of them showing off their own special tricks – a whirling kaleidoscope of weather: flurries of snow, arcing rainbows, constellations of hovering hail.

Stella glanced down at Nimbus, floating close by her side. "You stay down here, with me," she whispered.

Tamar tugged her hood higher, then made her way down the side of the hall, to a gap on the end of the third row. Stella slid in and Nimbus ducked under her chair. Tamar sat down next to her. She reached across and gave Stella's hand a little squeeze. This was it.

Tas was sitting in the front row. Her bright orange top and wild curls made her easy to spot. As though she'd felt Stella looking, she glanced back and waved cheerily. Stella gave her a swift smile, then looked away. She couldn't do cheery when her stomach was gnawing with nerves.

The lights began to dim and the jabber of voices gradually quietened. A small door opened at the side of the stage, and there stood Farah, completely transformed. Her ceremonial robes shone, almost too bright to look at.

She strode out onto the stage like a goddess of summer. As she took centre stage, she spread her arms wide, and the flickering light moved over the front row of apprentices. There was a soft chorus of 'Ooh' and 'Aah'.

Stella leant close to Tamar. "Is Farah actually glowing?" she whispered.

Tamar nodded. "She weaves with sunbeams."

"Weather weavers . . . Welcome!" Farah's voice was warm and strong. "May the sun bless you and light the path to wisdom."

A patter of clapping broke out, but was swiftly quenched by a shower of rain from overhead. Stella wiped her face and craned her head round to see what was going on.

A fat apricot oval of cloud was darting this way and that above the crowd, dropping little showers of rain. There were squeals and exclamations as it passed overhead.

Someone was going to be in trouble. Stella hoped it wasn't Tas's cloud . . .

She looked back to the front, to see if Farah was going to do something about it. There were now two people on stage. The woman who'd taken centre stage was small and wiry – much shorter than Farah. She seemed to be directing the cloud with a puckish dance, clapping her hands and tapping her toes. The long orange sleeves of her shirt gave her away – a Rain Caller.

Stella smiled. *I bet Tas is loving this.*

Satisfied that she'd created enough mayhem, the woman swept her hands inwards and her cloud joined her onstage. She stood on tiptoes and raised her arms above her head, twinkling her fingers. "May your heart always be playful and your days filled with laughter." She bowed low.

The clapping was less enthusiastic this time, but the woman didn't seem bothered. She just nudged Farah in the ribs and grinned gleefully.

Stella looked across to the door on the right. Someone else was coming through – a man, this time – a great bear of a man, a full head taller than Farah. His green tunic strained around his barrel chest and his face was weather-tanned. Only the streaks of grey in his bushy beard gave away his age.

Looks like a viking! thought Stella.

He walked silently to the centre of the stage and waited for the audience to quieten, then lifted his hands, as though about to conduct an orchestra.

A rustling curtain of leaves rushed up the wall behind him, clothing the wall in green. Flowers burst open from floor to ceiling and the hall filled with the heady smell of roses. A collective sigh of pleasure went up, and clapping broke out, though he hadn't yet finished. Vines began to spiral up the stone columns and bunches of grapes appeared, swelling from little green dots to fat red jewels.

Wow! So, that's what it's meant to look like!

The green man brought his palms together, bringing the wild growth to a gentle halt. "I gift you the strength to grow. May all your dreams be fruitful." He bowed his head with a smile.

Tears welled up unexpectedly in Stella's eyes. She wasn't sure why. She blinked rapidly. Maybe it was her imagination, but it felt like his blessing had actually landed on her.

She reached down and ruffled Nimbus.

I dream of being a weather weaver, she thought, *and never losing you.*

Perhaps the blessing would make it true.

The door opened again. Fog billowed out and spilled across the stage. The air in the room chilled and the crowd fell silent. With a sharp crackle, a pale lace of frost crept up the greenery at the back of the stage. Ice glazed the newly grown flowers. The grapes froze; some of them popped off and fell, landing with a high-pitched clink.

Velda walked out on stage, her expression as icy as the blue of her outfit.

Stella hunched down in her seat.

Velda strode to the very front of the stage, freezing fog curling around her. She looked all around the room in silence and then spread her arms.

"May ice bring you clarity and winter never find you wanting."

The applause was deafening this time. The apprentices began to drum their heels on the floor – a great rumble of noise that shook the air like thunder.

Stella glanced down the row in surprise. Were they really that impressed, or were they as scared of Velda as she was? She saw only smiling faces, bright in the frosty blue glow from the stage. Tamar nudged her shoulder and Stella started to clap resentfully. She wasn't going to drum her feet for Velda though – *stuff that.*

Velda stepped aside and a line of people began to appear through the door. The applause continued.

"The elders," muttered Tamar, out of the corner of her mouth.

Oh, that's who we're clapping for!

Stella began to drum her heels along with the others. The elders processed slowly across the stage. Two rows of chairs waited for them at the back.

If Tamar and Farah were old, this lot were *ancient*! Each of them wore robes that spoke of their weather. Two golden, like Farah – they lit up the left-hand side of the stage. There was only one other wearing orange, saw Stella with relief. And though he wore Rain Caller colours, he didn't look like he was about to rain all over the place. His back was hunched and he walked with the aid of a gnarled walking stick. There was one more green weather weaver, then four in icy blue. Twelve in all, five of them Ice Weavers, including Velda.

Nearly half the council . . . thought Stella, anxiously. *And not a single Lightning Weaver.*

"Hardly the full rainbow, is it?" muttered Tamar. "Does that look balanced to you?"

"Shh!" hissed Stella.

What if someone overheard?

At a silent signal, all of the council members sat down, except Velda. She raised her arms towards the audience. "Mentors? You may present your apprentices."

Everyone around Stella stood up. Stella scrambled to her feet, glad there was a very tall woman right in front of her. The mentors in the front row began to introduce themselves and present their apprentices. Up on stage, the wiry woman next to Farah began to fidget.

Uh oh. Is she going to rain on us again?

The woman glanced at Farah, then skipped out of her seat and pointed at the front row, her face full of mischief. "Flo, presenting Tassa. Rain Caller!"

Velda's face tightened, but she gave a stiff nod.

Farah stood and turned to face the elders. "As discussed, Tassa is a special entry. She has caught a new cloud and retrained. As stated in the Storm Laws, if she passes the trials, her storm cloud will be returned to her."

A mutter of surprise spread amongst the audience. The tall blonde apprentice in front of Stella tutted his disapproval. Stella glared at the back of his head.

The council conferred briefly, then nodded their agreement. Farah smiled in satisfaction and sat down again.

Yes! Go Tas!

Velda turned back to face the front and the introductions continued. "Freya, presenting Chanchal. Rain Caller." After each mentor had completed their introduction, they and their apprentice sat down.

Stella's heart skipped faster in her chest. Soon there would be no one left standing in front of them. Nowhere to hide.

She gasped as the second row began to take their seats. The air seemed too thin, like there wasn't enough oxygen in it. Tamar put a hand on her shoulder. "Sunshine thoughts."

Stella took a deep breath and looked down at Nimbus.

No thunder, no matter what, she thought. *Best behaviour. We can do this.*

Fourteen

A SPLIT VOTE

"HELGA," said the mentor in front of Stella, "presenting Flynn – Wind Whistler."

She and Flynn sat down and there was nowhere left to hide. Tamar pushed back her hood and Velda's eyes widened in shock.

"Tamar, presenting Stella – Lightning Weaver."

A murmur of shock ran through the crowd.

"No!" said Velda. "Storm clouds are forbidden to novices. This entry is void." The elders leant their grey heads together and talked amongst themselves.

Farah stood up, her robes flaring gold. "I second Stella's entry in the trials," she declared. "Stella is not a novice. She's a fully trained apprentice."

"Fully trained," scoffed Velda. "Tamar can't be trusted train to anyone. That's why she's no longer a mentor!"

Tamar stiffened and an electric whiff of ozone rose from her cloak. Stella gave her an urgent nudge. *Stop it!*

Behind Velda the elderly Rain Caller banged his stick on the stage. "Give the girl a chance, I say!" He smiled impishly. "It's been a long while since we saw anything lively."

Stella's heart danced with gratitude. Not everyone was on Velda's side . . .

"It's too dangerous!" declared Velda, turning to face the elders. "The council have a responsibility: to serve and *protect*."

The Ice Weavers on the end of the row all nodded their agreement. Obviously, *they* were going to agree, but Stella was worried to see two green elders nodding too.

Velda swept her arm dramatically towards the wall on Stella's left and everyone turned to look. Stella looked too.

The long crack in the wall had been gilded silver, so it still looked like a bolt of lightning.

From when they tried to separate Heather from her cloud, Stella realised.

The damage had been hidden behind whirling clouds before, but now they'd settled, it was clearly visible. An accusation, written in stone – commemorating the violence of the apprentice who turned sea witch.

"*That* is what happens!" intoned Velda.

The apprentices close to Stella shrank back, their eyes bright with fear; all except Flynn, the Wind Whistler. He glowered at Stella with undisguised hostility.

"When an apprentice is *not* properly trained," said Velda, striding along the front of the stage. "*That* is what happens. It's why novices are assessed *before* they are trained. The Storm Laws exist to protect us all!" She spread her arms wide and then turned back to face the council. "Are you willing to risk the lives of everyone here? Or have you forgotten?"

The Verdure Weavers who had been nodding along with her stiffened and one of them stood up – a gaunt old woman wearing a cloak embroidered with ivy.

"We forget nothing," she said, coldly. "Perhaps *you* have forgotten that these decisions are not yours alone. Besides, it's too late for assessment – she's already been trained."

Stella glanced at Tamar in delight, but her jaw was still set. The argument wasn't won. Not yet.

Farah stepped forward and nodded respectfully. "May I point something out?"

The gaunt woman inclined her head.

"With all this fury, all this uncertainty, with accusations flying, I have not heard even a whisper of thunder. That, to me, suggests *perfect* control."

The green weather weaver turned and pinned Stella with a sharp gaze.

Wow, she's not someone to mess with.

"Where is your cloud?" said the woman.

"Er, here," said Stella, pointing at her knees.

"Have him show himself."

Stella looked down. "Nimbus, can you come up here a minute?"

And do your very best innocent look – like you do when we're with Grandpa.

Nimbus fluffed himself up a bit and then slowly rose until he floated at Stella's shoulder. He hung there, pale and round, looking like he'd never fired lightning in his life.

The old woman turned her gaze on him and looked at him for a long minute.

"Thank you," she said to Stella. "You and your cloud are excused. This will need further discussion."

A look of spiteful triumph flitted across Velda's face, but Farah nodded in satisfaction, then Tamar was leading the way of the hall. Stella kept her eyes on Tamar's back, ignoring the stares and whispers that followed them.

Tamar strode to Farah's office and closed the door behind them. She blew out her cheeks. "Glad that's over."

"Did I do alright?" said Stella.

Tamar's eyebrows shot up. She took both Stella's hands in hers. "You were *magnificent*. Both of you." She looked up, to include Nimbus. "Remarkable. You made that . . . *schemer* look like a raving fool."

Stella grinned at Nimbus. *Magnificent!*

Tamar shrugged. "Now, we just have to hope the council see sense."

"I think that green lady was impressed," Stella pointed out.

"Ilana? Hmph, let's hope you're right," grunted Tamar.

Before long, a cacophony of voices filled the hallway, but after a time, it fell quiet again. Stella wound her fingers together and leant closer to Nimbus.

The ceremony was over. Nobody had come to get them. Did that mean the council had decided against including them?

She sat up straighter as the door handle turned. Farah's robes lit the room with a warm glow. "Stella," she said, smiling. "It's time."

Farah looked relaxed. Surely that was a good sign? Stella stood up, shadowed closely by Nimbus.

Tamar stood up too, but Farah shook her head. "Just Stella." Tamar growled in annoyance, but Farah held up a hand, quelling any disagreement.

* * *

The hall looked different when they went back inside – bigger. The rows of chairs had been rapidly cleared away and the frozen greenery had gone, leaving the walls looking stark and bare. Stella approached the stage with Farah, their footsteps echoing in the empty space.

The council's chairs weren't in a line anymore – they were arranged in a tight arc at the back of the stage. Velda stood before them – she'd obviously been talking until the moment they came in. She watched them approach with a stiff smile.

The lady in green beckoned and Stella climbed the stairs at the side of the stage.

Stay close, Nimbus. And unless I tell you, stay calm!

Farah moved aside to leave them standing alone in front of the council. Stella looked at Nimbus, then at her feet. She didn't like all these people staring at her.

"Stella."

Stella looked up. It wasn't Ilana that had spoken, it was one of the Ice Weavers – a woman with a pinched mouth and an elaborate gown dripping with crystals.

"You were trained before being assessed, correct?"

Stella nodded, raising a mutter of disapproval from the council.

Ilana cleared her throat. "Nevertheless, she *has* been fully trained."

Stella allowed herself a tiny smile – Ilana *was* on their side.

Ilana sighed. "You have divided the council," she said, getting to her feet. "We have a split vote."

Stella looked at the uneven rainbow of robed elders and wondered who else had voted in her favour.

"Velda would like to see you assessed, without delay."

Stella tried not to react, but a flicker of expression escaped. Ilana's sharp eyes caught it. "You don't want to be assessed?"

Stella swallowed. "There's no point," she said. "You all know Nimbus is a thundercloud."

"But is he a *danger*?" said Ilana. "That is the question."

"No! He's not. I promise!"

Velda stepped forward, her face a picture of reasonable concern. "Given the nature of your cloud," she said, "and the irregularity of your training, many of us feel that assessment would be the safest course of action – for you, too, Stella."

"You just want to take Nimbus," said Stella. "I don't know why. We haven't done anything wrong!"

"Nobody is suggesting you have," said Velda. "But a storm cloud is a grave responsibility. One that, perhaps, you're not ready for?"

Stella glanced down at Nimbus and saw with dismay that he was gradually shading darker. *Not now, Nimbus! Please! Happy thoughts.*

But it was hard to hold onto hope, with Velda standing right there, threatening to take him away.

"We're ready!" said Stella. "Please. Just give us a chance!"

Velda's expression didn't change. This wasn't a conversation, Stella realised. It was a performance – for the council's benefit, not hers.

"That brings us to the second option," said Ilana. "Many of us feel that, having completed your training, it's only fair you should have the chance to prove yourselves."

Stella straightened her back and Nimbus bobbed a little higher.

"However, we have one condition."

Stella nodded eagerly, but Ilana's face remained worryingly solemn.

"Usually, the trials are simply a test – to determine whether you are ready to receive deeper knowledge. But given that you've not been assessed, they will test more than that, for you."

Stella bit her lip.

"You will take the trials."

Stella grinned and Nimbus bobbed a little higher.

"*But* if you fail—"

Stella's breath froze in her chest.

"You will submit to the standard Storm Laws," interrupted Velda.

Ilana's nostrils flared and she gave a small sigh. Velda was clearly testing her patience. Stella stared at the stern row of faces behind them. "What does that mean?"

"It means," said Velda, with a predatory smile, "you agree to be separated from Nimbus – *without* any fireworks."

Stella shook her head. "But why?" she appealed to Ilana. "Can't we just promise no fireworks and stay together?"

Velda looked down her nose at Stella. "Understand that you have broken the law," she said imperiously. "And you are being granted a reprieve. I suggest you take it."

"Pass the trials," said Ilana, "and there will *be* no further discussion." She cast a sharp glance at Velda.

Stella looked down at Nimbus. He trembled slightly and she ran a hand lightly over him to calm him.

We can still prove Velda wrong. We can do it.

Nimbus subtly shifted from white to faintest yellow. No one

else would have noticed, but it was enough for Stella. Nimbus agreed.

"Thank you," she said to Ilana. "We'll do our best."

Behind Velda, there was a murmur of approval from the council. Velda smiled thinly, as though this was what she'd intended all along.

Ilana simply nodded.

* * *

"So?" said Tas, as Stella pushed open the door.

"I'm in," said Stella.

Tas whooped and leapt to her feet, grabbing Stella by the hands and dancing her in a circle. "Both of us in the trials! It's going to be epic!"

Stella didn't really feel like dancing. She gently detached herself from Tas and sat down on her bed. Nimbus settled next to her.

"There's a catch," she said.

"There's always a catch," said Tas. "Go on?"

"We have to pass first time, or they'll take Nimbus. And I'm pretty sure Velda's not going to make it easy . . ."

"Not up to her though, is it?" said Tas.

A sharp rattle of rain at the window made them both jump.

Tas drew the curtains. "Drench! You're back. You took your time!" She unlatched the window and her cloud flew in. He bumped Tas playfully as he passed, leaving a damp patch on her shoulder. Nimbus bounced up off the bed and Drench stopped abruptly.

"Drench, Nimbus. Nimbus, Drench," said Tas.

The two clouds circled each other once, then settled side by side. Tas smiled at them. "See? Best friends already. Now, stop worrying. You did it. You're in. And together? We're going to ace these trials."

Stella nodded, searching for the little glow of certainty she'd felt back in the hall, but all she could remember was Velda's thin smile.

Like she'd got them right where she wanted them.

Fifteen

PRACTICE MAKES PERFECT

BREAKFAST was porridge, which suited Stella just fine. Tas poked mistrustfully at the gloopy mixture. "Is it meant to be grey? It's not like this at home."

"Trust me. It's good," said Stella. "Have some honey."

As they carried their bowls back to their room, Nimbus and Drench rushed ahead, raising a squeal down the corridor.

"Sorry," called Stella.

The apprentice took one look at her and disappeared back

into her room.

Stella rolled her eyes. "We're not about to start zapping people in the corridor!"

"Yeah, but you *might*," said Tas with a wink. "You could start with the Winter Twins. Make everyone's lives a bit easier."

"Tas!"

Tas smiled. "Just saying . . ."

"Are the Winter Twins actual twins?" asked Stella.

Tas shook her head. "That's just what I call them. They're Ice Weavers – Bianca and Neve – this year's favourites."

"Why? Have they got special skills, or something?"

Tas dropped her voice as they approached their room. "No, nothing amazing." she said. "But they're Velda's apprentices. Be a surprise if they *weren't* the favourites."

Great, thought Stella. *Velda's apprentices. In the room next to ours.*

* * *

Tas was quiet as they ate breakfast – she seemed subdued.

"You worrying about the trial?" said Stella.

Tas shook her head. "No. It's just . . ." She let out a short huff. "Do you feel different, when Nimbus isn't with you?"

"How do you mean?" asked Stella.

"Like a pull, inside?"

Stella scraped her bowl and nodded. "Stretched – like elastic."

"That's it!" exclaimed Tas. "I thought it might just be me."

"Why do you ask?"

"It's gone," replied Tas. "The feeling's gone."

Stella looked up at Drench, but Tas shook her head. "Ever since they took my storm cloud, I've had that feeling the whole time," she explained. "The *whole* time."

"Eesh!"

"But today . . . it's gone," said Tas.

"That's good?"

"But don't you see?" said Tas. "Arca must be *here*, at the Gathering!"

Stella smiled. "Makes sense. Velda's got to be ready to give him back, doesn't she?"

Tas nodded, her eyes bright. "Now all I've got to do is *find* him!"

Stella frowned, suddenly worried for her new friend. "Wouldn't it be better to wait until *after* the trials?"

"Would you wait, if it was Nimbus?" retorted Tas.

Stella looked up at her cloud. *No. I wouldn't.*

But that still didn't make it a good idea.

"Arca's close," said Tas, "I can feel it." She moved to the window and pointed to the courtyard and the outbuildings beyond. "That's all out of bounds to apprentices, so I reckon that's the best place to look."

"No, Tas! You'll get in massive trouble."

There was a soft tap at the door and they both froze, as though Stella had summoned trouble.

"Can I come in?" came Farah's voice.

"Yes," called Tas, with a smile.

The door swung open. "Ah, good. You're both up."

"We were just about to start revising," said Stella, glancing at Tas.

"Stella was," said Tas. "I'm helping Flo . . . at the market."

Was that true? Tas wouldn't meet her eyes.

"Ah," said Farah. "Well, make sure you're back on time."

Tas nodded.

"I'll show you to the study room, then," said Farah, smiling at Stella. "Bit comfier than revising here. Oh, you won't need that," she said, as Stella reached for *The Weather Book*. "There's a whole library downstairs."

* * *

The study room was on the ground floor, along one of the gloomy corridors, but when Farah opened the door, it was surprisingly bright. A wide bay window spilled sunlight across empty rows of desks. The room was silent, but for the tock of a pendulum clock.

Stella walked to the window. It looked out onto a long sloping field, full of tumbled stacks of overgrown granite boulders – a narrow strip of wilderness, contained by tall stone walls. *Not much of a garden.*

Farah lifted a copy of *The Weather Book* from the shelves and set it on the desk nearest the window. "That's the practice field," she said. "You may see some apprentices out there, but you should have peace in here."

Nimbus pressed himself against the glass, eager to be outside, but Stella gave him a stern look. He grudgingly moved away from the window.

"If he needs some fresh air, you can let him outside," said Farah, indicating a door in the far corner. Nimbus perked up, but Stella shook her head. She didn't want to let him out of her sight; not with Velda prowling around.

"I'll take you out later, Nimbus. Promise." Nimbus settled sulkily on the desk and Stella glanced at the clock. "How long have we got?"

"Until the trial? Three hours," said Farah. "It's at eleven o'clock."

Three hours?! That wasn't long enough!

Farah gave her a searching look. "Knowing Tamar, I'd guess you didn't start your training with theory?"

Stella shook her head and bit her lip.

"But you've done some revision?"

"Mostly weather lore . . ."

Farah nodded. "Good."

"I've barely started weather knowledge, though," admitted Stella. She opened the book and riffled through the remaining pages. There were far too many.

"Weather is in the heart, not in the head." Farah smiled. "You have everything you need, right here." She pointed at Stella's chest. "You just need to listen."

Stella put a hand over her heart, beating rapidly inside her ribcage. *The trials. The trials. The trials.*

"Breathe . . ." said Farah.

I don't have time for relaxing! I should be revising.

The clock ticked. Farah waited.

Stella took a deep breath – the room smelt of beeswax and dust, leather and paper.

"Now, close your eyes, and notice the weather," said Farah.

Stella closed her eyes and took another breath. The sun glowed pink through her eyelids. She could feel it too, warm on her cheeks. Her heart began to slow.

"What do you feel?" said Farah.

A sweet feeling rose inside Stella, swelling with each breath. It reminded her a little of the sanctuary stone's song of courage, but gentler, somehow.

"Um . . . warmth and happiness? Hope, maybe?"

Farah laughed. "See? You *do* know. You've just named the key ingredients for summer sun."

Stella opened one eye a crack and squinted. Farah's gown glowed gold – it was like staring into the sun.

"Sorry, let me tone it down a bit," said Farah, dimming its light.

Stella blinked until the bright after-image faded.

"Remind yourself of the weather lore," said Farah, patting the book. "Beyond that, trust yourself! Tamar has taught you well."

* * *

Stella had been revising for almost two hours before Nimbus

began to get restless. She rubbed her eyes. "You're right. I need a break, too."

She opened the door and Nimbus plunged through it. Outside, a short flight of steps with a stone balustrade led down onto a flat stretch of grass. Stella perched on the top step.

She could hear the clock inside; the minutes dripping away.

Just a quick break, she told herself, *so Nimbus can let off steam.*

But where had he gone?

Stella's heart quickened. She'd only looked away for a second! She shaded her eyes and squinted. There he was; way up high.

Come down!

The little cloud sank swiftly towards her.

You scared me. Stay close, will you?

Nimbus wrapped himself around her.

A wooden door in the far wall opened with a creak. Stella shrank back behind the balustrade. Two girls dressed all in pale blue appeared, trailed closely by two clouds.

The Winter Twins?

Stella sat very still and watched. One girl moved to the middle of the lawn and the other to the edge of the slope. They were passing a gust of wind back and forth with flicks of their fingers, like a game of invisible catch. Their clouds rode the circling wind like a fairground ride.

Behind them, a third cloud began to bulge through the gate. It was large, so getting through took a long time.

Silly thing. Should have gone over the top.

A tall boy in a long green coat appeared behind it. He walked a little way down the hill, away from the girls, and slumped down on a low stone bench, his hair hanging over his face.

The big cloud began to roll slowly along the end of the house towards Stella, sending streamers of green scrambling up the stone; clothing the wall with honeysuckle. Sprays of flowers flourished like trumpets amongst the lush foliage.

Stella watched in admiration and envy. *Imagine being able to grow stuff that easily!*

Nimbus was still wrapped around her. It wasn't clear if he was feeling shy, or protective, but either way, she was glad of it.

A flash of rainbow caught her eye. The girls had moved onto rain now, sending a glittering spray of water high into the air. The fountain of rain arced up from one cloud and the other one caught it as it fell. No wonder Tas had called them the twins – they were definitely a team – and seriously well-practised.

A look passed between the girls and their clouds began to relay across the grass. It was clear what they were up to. Each sparkling arc brought them a little closer to the stone bench.

The boy didn't notice, until it was too late.

"Hey! Don't rain on me!" He jumped to his feet, shaking water out of his hair and wiping his face angrily.

"Why? What are you going do, Magnus?" said the taller of the two girls, moving closer to him, hands on hips. "Go crying to Mummy?"

Her cloud let out another jet of water, splattering the wall next to him. Magnus jumped out of the way, beckoning impatiently to his cloud. It turned ponderously and began to slide back towards him. The sprouting grass seemed to grasp at it, slowing it down.

Stella thought about what the twins had done to Tas and a knot of annoyance hardened in her chest.

The second girl joined her team-mate and they linked hands. Their clouds circled each other, then laced themselves together, growing heavy and dark. In a few moments, there was just one huge cloud, looming over Magnus's head.

"You're not afraid of a little rain, are you? I would have thought you'd be *used* to being *wet*!"

It was obvious what they were going to do.

Nimbus!

She barely had to think it. He was already shooting across the grass. The cloud cover sprang up around Magnus a split second before the deluge started.

Stella smiled to herself. *Ha! That spoiled their plan.*

She stood up and walked down the stone steps.

The downpour faltered and gradually petered out. A brief scowl of frustration passed between the two girls and they turned to see Stella approaching across the lawn.

Nimbus, keep an eye on their clouds.

Sure enough, before she was even halfway across, the big cloud split into two. The clouds curved away from Magnus and began to circle Stella. Nimbus swiftly furled up his cloud cover and darted back to her.

"What do we have here?" said the taller of the two girls. "The new girl."

"Sweet," said the other girl. "Magnus has got himself a little friend."

"I'm not his friend," said Stella. "I don't even know him. I just don't like bullies."

"Bullies?" said the tall girl. "We weren't bullying him – we were *helping* him. He needs the practice! How's he going to make it through the trials, if he can't even call his own cloud cover?"

The girls burst into unkind laughter and Magnus hunched his shoulders and looked at his feet. His cloud had finally reached him. It wrapped itself around his legs in apology, but he flapped it away.

The taller girl cupped her mouth with one hand. "*We* don't think he's ready," she said in a loud stage whisper. She glanced back at Magnus, who was trying to disentangle himself from the thicket of meadow flowers that had sprung up around his knees. "He should count himself lucky he's got *us* to help him practice."

"Maybe someone should help *you* practice?" said Stella.

Above her, Nimbus darkened to purple and let out a low rumble.

The girls' eyes widened and they moved closer together, suddenly less sure of themselves. "You can't do that. It's not allowed."

"Oh?" said Stella. "I thought this is where we come to *practice*?" Nimbus flickered and deep growl of thunder trembled through the air. The girls' faces paled.

An unkind delight rose up in Stella. *See how you like it!*

The girls backed rapidly towards the wooden door, staring at Stella with a mixture of fury and fright.

"You can't do that!"

"It's dangerous!"

"We'll tell."

"See what happens then, Sparky!"

Stella's delight dissolved in a rush of worry.

"Sparky and Damp Patch!" crowed the shorter of the two girls. "A perfect pair. Wait 'til your mum hears about this, Magnus!"

They darted through the door before Stella could come up with a good answer. It closed behind them, with a resounding thump, and the sound of their cackling moved away.

Stella let out a shaky breath.

Why was it so hard to stay out of trouble?

Sixteen

A DANGEROUS GAME

STELLA turned towards Magnus. His back was pressed to the wall, his face pale and his eyes fixed firmly on Nimbus. Nimbus let out another low growl of thunder and Magnus visibly trembled.

"Sorry!" Stella took a deep breath and filled her mind with happy thoughts.

Puffins. Shortbread. Grandpa's bad jokes.

Nimbus was soon back to his normal self – small, fluffy, friendly-looking.

Magnus gaped at her. "How did you do that?"

"Do what?"

"He was all . . ." Magnus pulled a furious face and mimed lightning with his fingers. "And now he's . . ." he spread his palms and looked at Nimbus.

Stella frowned. "I just . . . asked him to stop."

Did Magnus think thunderclouds went round thundering all the time?

"You've never met a thundercloud before, have you?" she asked.

Magnus shook his head. "Of course not. They're dangerous!"

Stella breathed in through her nose to stop the anger rising again. Why did everyone keep saying that? It wasn't true!

"Nimbus *isn't* dangerous!" she said firmly. "He only does lightning if I ask him."

Magnus gave her a doubtful look. "That could be dangerous."

"I expect your cloud *could* be dangerous," said Stella.

Magnus let out a nervous laugh. "Only if you've got hayfever."

Stella's cheeks heated up and she scowled. "He might! He could – I don't know – wrap somebody in thorns? Strangle them with vines, or something?"

Magnus stared at her in horror.

"I'm not saying he would!" said Stella. "That's the point! Even your cloud *could* be dangerous, but he's not. Because you'd never do that. Just like I'd never fire lightning at someone."

Magnus pushed his fringe out of his eyes and watched Nimbus scooting back and forth at the edge of the lawn. He seemed to be trying to entice Magnus's cloud into a game of chase.

"What's he doing?" he said.

"Trying to get your cloud to play," said Stella. "Unless you think that's too *dangerous*?"

Magnus's cheeks flushed slightly and he nodded at his cloud. "Go on then, Briar!"

The big cloud surged forwards across the grass. Nimbus turned a swift loop-the-loop of joy and scooted away down the slope.

"Thanks," said Magnus.

"What for?"

"For seeing off Bianca and Neve."

Stella gave a slight shrug. "S'alright. I couldn't just stand there and watch."

Magnus's face was full of questions, but he didn't say anything more – just turned to watch the two clouds. They made a comedic pair. Briar was lumbering down the slope in long slow hops. Tufty clumps of sea pinks bloomed wherever he touched down. Nimbus zigzagged around him, raining on them.

Maybe he'll pick up a few tips, thought Stella. *That'd be good.*

"So, how come they let you stay?" said Magnus. "Storm clouds are banned."

"You can't ban storms!" snapped Stella. "That's just stupid."

Magnus flinched slightly.

"Sorry," said Stella. "It's not your fault. But it is stupid."

"It's to keep everyone safe," said Magnus, cautiously.

"It's not keeping *me* safe, is it?" said Stella. "I love my cloud."

Magnus looked down at the two clouds and his expression

140

softened. He loved Briar too – it was obvious.

"Taking people's clouds isn't right," she persisted. "I mean, if they're *actually* dangerous, maybe. But not if they haven't done anything wrong!"

Magnus thought about it and a small hope kindled in Stella's chest. If she could convince one person, maybe she could convince everyone?

"The Storm Laws aren't right," she said, daringly. "You don't ban cars because of one car crash. You don't ban running because one person fell over . . ."

"It's a good point," said Magnus. "I mean, the Storm Laws are meant to protect everyone, but they're not protecting *you*, are they?"

He glanced up at the house.

Were there people listening up there?

Stella folded her arms, suddenly less confident. Maybe she and Nimbus should have stayed inside. Stayed out of trouble. She gnawed on her lip. "Do you think they'll tell Velda?"

"Mum? Yes. Probably. They're massive tell-tales."

Stella blinked at him. *What?*

Magnus quailed. "Oh, root rot! You didn't know, did you?"

The realisation tumbled through her like a rockfall. "You're *Velda's* son?"

Magnus nodded, his face full of apprehension.

Velda's son!

Stella wished she could reverse time; swallow the whole

conversation back into her mouth. Why hadn't anyone warned her?

Stella turned away. *Time to go, Nimbus.*

Nimbus didn't respond immediately – he was too excited by this new game.

"Now, Nimbus!"

Nimbus reluctantly floated up out of the maze of rocks, shading to sulky grey and deliberately taking his time about it.

Magnus shifted uncomfortably. "If the twins get you in trouble, I'll back you up, yeah?"

Stella nodded stiffly. That might help.

"And you've got a point, about the Storm Laws," he continued. "I'd never really thought about it like that. If you want to talk more, another time . . ."

Stella looked at him and bit her lip. He was Velda's son. *Velda's* son! Velda, who wanted to take Nimbus. No matter how nice he was being, they couldn't be friends.

"I'll see you around," she said noncommittally, and ducked out of the wooden door.

* * *

Stella opened the front door a crack. No sign of The Winter Twins – the hallway was empty. She scampered across and tapped on Farah's office door.

"Come in."

Stella slipped quickly inside with Nimbus and closed the door. "I need to see Tamar."

"Is everything alright?" said Farah, standing up from her desk. She held out a hand towards the small leather sofa. "Sit down. Tell me."

Nimbus circled the ceiling, before tucking himself into the corner. Stella sat down.

"I think I'm in trouble."

Farah's face grew serious. "What happened?"

"Neve and Bianca were picking on Magnus," said Stella. "So, Nimbus and I stopped them. And now they're going to tell Velda."

"Stopped them, *how*?" said Farah, her eyes sharp with worry.

"Nimbus thundered at them. Scared them away."

All the consequences were crowding into her head now, a great tangled heap of worries, but the biggest one pushed its way to the top.

What if Velda stops us taking the trials?

"You thundered at them?" said Farah, giving Nimbus a stern look.

Nimbus slid down the wall and hid behind Stella.

Stella nodded. "Someone had to do something! They're bullies."

Farah closed her eyes, summoning patience. When she opened them, her face was serious. "Please tell me you didn't use lightning?"

"No! We would never—"

There was a sharp rap at the door.

"Enter."

The door swung open and Velda appeared. Her eyes settled on Stella and Nimbus. "There you are. Follow me."

Farah nodded heavily and Stella's throat tightened in fear. *Please? We can't have blown it already!*

She followed Farah and Velda into the hall, with Nimbus trailing close behind.

Neve and Bianca were hanging over the upstairs balcony, smiling spitefully. Tassa was scampering down the stairs, an anxious frown on her face. Her eyes widened as she saw the grim procession. Stella shook her head.

Don't get involved.

Velda led them to a door just beyond the great hall. "Wait here," she said, and went inside, closing the door behind her.

Farah wrung her hands in frustration. "I thought I'd made myself absolutely clear?" she said. "You need to be the very model of control."

"It wasn't for no reason," protested Stella. "I was standing up for—"

"It doesn't *matter* what you were standing up for!" whispered Farah. "You *can't* be fighting with people, Stella. Not here." Her fingers beat an anxious rhythm on her knuckles. "While you are here, you do *not* have the luxury of losing your temper. Is that understood?"

Stella scowled. She never liked being told off, but it was worse when it didn't feel fair. She avoided Farah's eyes.

"Is that *understood*?" repeated Farah in a low voice.

"Understood," mumbled Stella.

"We can't give Velda any reason to take you out of the trials."

It should be Neve and Bianca in trouble! Not me and Nimbus. Stella clenched her fists and Nimbus let out a low grumble.

"Not a peep out of you!" warned Farah. "Not if you want to stay with Stella."

Nimbus immediately faded to white and made himself a bit smaller.

The door opened, flooding the corridor with cool light. Velda motioned for them to come inside. Beyond her, the lady in green, Ilana, was sitting in a tall wing-back armchair.

Stella went in with Farah, glancing back to check Nimbus was following.

"I think it's best if her cloud waits outside?" said Velda.

Stella saw Nimbus start in confusion as the door closed, shutting him outside.

Wait there, Nimbus. Be good.

Stella took in the room at a glance – this must be where the elders spent time, when they weren't busy with council stuff. Three narrow windows overlooked the courtyard; between them were display cases, filled with arcane instruments and curios.

Ilana cleared her throat and Stella's attention snapped back to her.

"I understand that you had some sort of altercation—" she began.

"Stella used weather against my apprentices!" said Velda, impatiently. "She forfeits the trials."

An icy stream of fear coursed through Stella.

"I am aware of the rules, thank you, Velda," said Ilana. "But it's customary to hear both sides before making a decision."

Velda clamped her mouth shut angrily and Ilana turned her attention to Stella. "Well?"

"I didn't!" protested Stella. "*They're* the ones using weather on people! They set a dust devil on Tassa! And they half-drowned Magnus."

"Did you see this dust devil?"

"Well, no . . . But Tas's hair was full of . . . I saw them do it to Magnus. He'll tell you."

Ilana shook her head. "They claim they were training with Magnus, when you attacked them."

"I did not!" exclaimed Stella. "I didn't *do* anything. All Nimbus did was rumble a bit and they ran away."

"You thundered at them?" Ilana's tone was sharp.

Stella opened and closed her mouth. She looked at Farah for help, but her face was stern. Farah drew herself up tall. "Stella, did you fire lightning at them?"

"No! Of course not! I'd never—"

"Did you rain on them?"

"No."

"Set a wind on them?"

"No!"

"Freeze them?"

"No!"

Farah nodded, thoughtfully. "So, your cloud just . . . thundered a little?" She raised her eyebrows slightly and looked at Ilana.

Stella nodded. "Yes."

"You threatened them!" said Velda, triumphantly.

Stella opened her mouth to answer, but Ilana heaved a deep sigh and pushed herself to her feet. "There is no rule against that," she declared. "Though I *strongly* suggest, Stella, that from now on, you stay *well* away from Bianca and Neve. Consider this your final warning."

Stella nodded. "I will. I'm sorry."

The hint of a smile passed over Farah's face. Velda looked like she might explode.

Ilana nodded once, and extended an arm towards the door. "Stella, you may go. You have about half an hour until the first trial. Use it wisely."

* * *

Stella bounded up the stairs and sprinted past the Winter Twins. Tas was waiting anxiously in their room. Stella closed the door after Nimbus, shutting the sound of Bianca and Neve's animated conversation out in the corridor.

Let them wonder . . .

"You're back! How much drama was that?" said Tas. "The twins told everyone you're getting kicked out?"

Stella sat down on her bed and patted the coverlet for Nimbus to join her. She didn't even want to imagine the amount of gossip going round.

"Not today," she said.

"So? What happened?"

"Nimbus thundered at them."

"Ha!" Tas clapped her hands in glee. "That'll teach them for picking on a Storm Weaver."

"They weren't picking on me. They were picking on Magnus."

"Magnus?" said Tas, frowning in confusion. "What are you sticking up for him for? You know who he is, right?"

"I do now."

"And Velda *still* came down on you about it?"

Stella nodded. "She's really got it in for me."

Tas let out a puff. "You and me, both."

Seventeen

WEATHER LORE

THE hallway buzzed with nervous chatter. There were about thirty apprentices waiting outside the great hall. Stella and Tas had arrived early, but hung back when they spotted the Winter Twins, already standing by the big double doors. 'Stay away from Neve and Bianca,' Ilana had said – easier said than done.

Magnus had taken up a spot not far from Stella, slouching against the wood panelled wall. She wasn't sure if she was meant to steer clear of him too, so she was currently pretending he wasn't there.

"Bianca's got *two* clouds," said Tas, wrinkling her nose and peering along the hallway. "Did she have two this morning, when you and she—"

"No."

Stella twisted her fingers into a knot. The trial was all she could think about, right now. *I bet Velda's going to give me the hardest questions.*

"So, where's the other one appeared from?" Tas craned her neck to look. "I'm sure she never had two before . . ."

"It was probably gathering magic," snapped Stella. "Stop staring at them!"

Tas widened her eyes and zipped her mouth shut.

What did she expect? She needed to concentrate now. Nimbus nudged her hip and she stroked him absently.

Did she know enough? How many questions did you have to get right? All of them? Would they find out straight away, if they'd passed or not?

Red sky at night, sailor's delight. Red sky in the morning, sailor's warning.

Revising the rhymes this morning, that one had leapt out at her. Dad used to say it. Trouble was, now it was all she could hear – an earworm – going round and round on repeat. She just hoped it wouldn't make the other rhymes fall out of her head.

"Red sky at night?" said Magnus, from behind her.

"Sailor's delight," answered Stella automatically, then frowned. "How did you . . ."

"You've been repeating it under your breath, Sparky," said

Magnus, with a smile. "You know it's 'shepherd's delight', right?"

Stella stared at him, horrified. The one rhyme she was sure of, and it was wrong?

Magnus shrugged. "Shepherds, sailors, I shouldn't think it matters. Main thing is the weather."

"Leave her alone," said Tas, stepping between them. "She doesn't need *you* making her nervous."

The big double doors opened and Stella's heart leapt into her throat. It was time.

* * *

"Which clouds warn of high winds?"

Velda's nail tapped against the wooden lectern as she waited for the answer. It was distracting.

"Cirrus?" said Stella.

"Final answer?" said Velda, and Stella nodded.

"And the rhyme?" prompted Velda.

"Mare's tails and mackerel scales make tall ships carry low sails."

Velda's mouth tightened. She marked the page with a sharp tick. So far, Stella hadn't got a single question wrong.

"Fair weather clouds?" said Velda.

"Um . . ."

She'd learnt it. She knew it – somewhere in her brain. It was one of the ones she'd revised at home, with Grandpa. But he'd just called them fair-weather clouds. What was their real name?

Nimbus floated a little higher beside her. He was being so good – doing his best impression of a little sheep.

That's it!

"Woolly fleeces bestow the heavenly way, no rain will come today. Cumulus!" She grinned at Nimbus and glanced down at the apprentices in the front row of seats. Tas gave her a double thumbs-up. A little way along the row, Magnus nodded encouragement.

"Good," said Velda. "You seem to have at least a passing knowledge of Weather Lore."

A passing knowledge?

Stella bristled – she'd got every single question right! She glanced at Farah, who gently tilted her head towards Velda: *stay focused.*

"Let's see how you do with Weather Knowledge."

Stella took a deep breath. She'd seen how it went with the apprentices who'd gone before her. One weather question for each season. Four more questions and she'd have passed this trial. *Just four. I can do this.*

"Rain," said Velda. "Orange is the colour, but what is the feeling?"

Stella glanced at Nimbus and smiled. "Playfulness," she said, confidently.

She ought to know that one by now! How many times had Nimbus rained on her out of the blue? It was his favourite trick when he was in a cheeky mood.

"How would you conjure a breeze?" said Velda.

"With joy," said Stella.

"A gale?"

Stella hesitated. She wasn't expecting another wind question.

"Er . . . joy, with a thrill of excitement."

"A hurricane?"

Another wind question? This wasn't right.

And she'd only ever used one of Tamar's bottled hurricanes. She'd never tried to create one.

Why would you? Only a sea witch would actually want to . . .

"I've never conjured a hurricane," she said.

"How might you *try*?" said Velda, her voice cool. Stella glanced across at the council. The old man in orange gave her a nod – maybe it *was* just a normal trial question?

She closed her eyes and tried to remember what it felt like to wield a hurricane.

Power, raw power. Wide as the sky. Thrilling and wild.

"More thrill than joy. Hardly any joy. A raw excitement that wants to rip things apart," said Stella. She opened her eyes to see Velda smiling and her heart dropped like a stone. Whatever trap Velda had laid, she'd just walked right into it.

Velda turned to address the council. "It's clear that Tamar's lessons have ranged a little wider than the approved training."

"Tamar didn't train me in that," protested Stella.

Velda whipped round and gripped both sides of the lectern. "You simply *know* how to call a hurricane?" she said. "That's what you're telling us?"

"Um, yes?" said Stella.

"So, it's part of your character?" said Velda, raising her eyebrows. Stella shook her head.

A susurration of whispering rose from the waiting apprentices. Now *everyone* was going to hate her.

"Natural tendency to violence," said Velda, writing something on the sheet, before glancing at the council.

"No, no!" blurted Stella. "I told you, I've never—"

"Moving on," said Velda. "Verdure. Can you tell us what one adds to rain to grow a rose?"

"A sense of belonging."

"And?"

And what? That's it – a sense of belonging.

"A rose, specifically," said Velda impatiently. "What else does a rose need?"

"Er, sunshine and . . . compost?"

A titter of laughter ran round the hall. "Compost!" someone repeated.

Stella's cheeks burned. You did need compost! Earth would probably do, but compost would be better. She scowled in embarrassment at the apprentices in the front row.

Magnus was mouthing something at her, but she couldn't make it out.

"A sense of belonging, friendship, and hope," said Velda, counting them off on her fingers. "Perhaps you're lacking in those?"

Stella drew a breath to answer back, but Nimbus suddenly

bobbed up between her and Velda. He was right. No point in rising to it. And if he could stay calm, she could, too.

Thanks, Nimbus.

The little cloud glimmered gold and moved back to her side.

Velda drew a cross on the sheet in front of her, a look of smug satisfaction on her face. She nodded to herself, then looked up at Stella. "Winter weather."

Stella shivered – the temperature had suddenly dropped in the hall.

"Ice," said Velda, her blue eyes glittering.

She knew this one. "Clarity and purpose."

"Exactly," said Velda, inclining her head, as though Stella had given her a compliment. "How about snow?"

How many questions was she going to have to answer? It wasn't fair.

Just keep calm, and get them all right.

"What kind of snow?" she checked.

"Light snow. Small flakes," said Velda.

"Fear," said Stella.

"Your fear, or someone else's?"

Stella wrinkled her nose in confusion, then realised – it was another trick question. You had to *feel* weather to be able to make it.

"My own."

"What are you afraid of, Stella?"

You, thought Stella.

But she wasn't about to say that. Was this even part of the trial?

"What are *you* are afraid of, Stella?" repeated Velda, quietly.

Deep water, heights, wild lightning, failing, losing Nimbus . . . but most of all, YOU.

Beside her, Nimbus dropped a small flurry of snow.

Velda watched the last flakes settle on the stage with satisfaction. She knew.

"We've surely covered all the seasons now," said Farah, stepping out of the shadows at the edge of the stage. "Are you satisfied that we've heard enough?"

Several of the council members nodded, but Velda wasn't going to be hurried. She scribbled something on the bottom of Stella's question paper and circled it, with a flourish.

Stella shifted awkwardly on the spot, trying to ignore the growing murmur from the front row.

Was it finished? Could she go?

The busy scratching of Velda's pen was loud in the anxious silence. After a moment, she looked up and seemed surprised that Stella was still there. "That'll be all," she said.

Stella breathed out in relief and scampered down the steps before Velda could change her mind. She didn't make eye contact with the other apprentices as she made her way back to her seat. Their laughter was still echoing in her ears.

Eighteen

ROSES AND THORNS

As the apprentices swarmed out of the hall, Stella found herself walking within an empty circle – people were avoiding her. This morning, there had only been rumours, but Velda's questions in the trial had made them true – Stella was dangerous.

Tas caught up with her and punched her playfully on the shoulder.

"Check you out, Sparky! Mad, bad, and dangerous to know!"

"I'm not," said Stella.

"Well, don't tell this lot!" said Tas. She snarled at the nearest apprentices and they cowered away.

"Seriously, Tas – don't. You'll only make it worse."

"Oh, come on, it's fun!" Tas hurled an imaginary hurricane at the apprentices in front of them and the crowd scattered, making a clear path to the doors. "Ooh! The power! If you decide to turn sea witch, I'll be your sidekick, yeah?"

"That's not funny."

Tas pulled a monstrous face and began to lumber towards the back of the hall, arms outstretched, moaning like a zombie. If they'd been on their own, it would have been hilarious, but here it was attracting a lot of unwanted attention.

Stella glanced back at the stage, to see Velda watching with narrowed eyes. She ducked her head and hurried towards the door. Tas quickly caught up and took her arm.

A cluster of Ice Weavers barged past them in the hall and Nimbus swelled slightly, a small but determined bodyguard.

Neve glanced at the little cloud, then caught Stella's eye. "Compost!" she said, and the whole group burst into giggles. Stella's cheeks burned.

"Ignore them," said Tas. "They've got tiny brains. Like goldfish. They'll have forgotten in two seconds."

A rich smell of food was wafting in through the open front door. The garden had been turned into a make-shift canteen; a long line of wooden tables laden with food. As all the apprentices poured out of the house, the sky filled with jostling clouds. Nimbus stayed close to Stella, seeing off anyone who looked like they were getting too close.

Tas was right, though. By the time they were all outside, the Ice Weavers had lost interest in her. The conversation turned to Bianca and her brand-new cloud. She was parading it up and down, like a prize poodle, making it float left and right, up and down, while the rest of her group cooed in admiration.

Stella couldn't imagine Nimbus putting up with that. "Have you ever seen a cloud that well behaved?"

Tas looked at Bianca's cloud critically. "Practically robotic," she said. "Makes sense. Clouds choose people like them – no wonder it's got no personality."

Bianca's head snapped round. She glared at Tas and a whisper of anticipation passed around the winter group. "Did you have something to say, Tassaaaa?" she asked, loudly.

Tas flinched. "No."

"You're certain?" demanded Bianca.

Tas shook her head. "Nothing. Nothing at all."

"I didn't think so!" said Bianca, turning away with an air of dismissal.

Tas hung her head and Drench deflated. Stella squeezed her arm. How much bullying had Tas endured before, that she'd back down this easily? It hurt Stella's heart to see her and Drench so subdued.

Tas looked up, with shame in her eyes. "I'll go find us a quiet spot, yeah?" She looked towards the far end of the garden.

Stella nodded. "Go for it. I'll grab us some food and come and find you."

Tas moved away and Drench followed, drizzling despondently.

A queue had already formed, with the Winter Twins and three other pale-haired girls at the front. Stella joined the far end of it. It was a lot like getting lunch at school; everybody in pairs or groups – everybody except her.

Stella patted her leg and Nimbus stopped investigating the nearest table and floated back to her. She picked up two plates from the stack and eyed the food. Was there anything Tas didn't eat? She hadn't thought to ask.

"Hello, Sparky," said a voice behind her.

Stella whipped round. It was Magnus. Again.

She gave him an awkward smile. *Your mum wants to take my cloud. Why are you even talking to me?*

"Hi," she said. She turned away and held out the two plates for a serving of vegetables, hoping that would end the conversation.

Magnus didn't take the hint. "Are you going to do lightning for the skills trial?"

The serving spoon fell, with a sudden clatter.

Thanks Magnus, just shout it out, why don't you? Stella gave the woman serving a tense smile. She was dressed in blue and white – an Ice Weaver. She didn't smile back.

Stella waited until they were further along the queue, before confronting him. "Can we *not* talk about it *here*?" she said.

Magnus was unrepentant. "After you sent Neve and Bianca running? Trust me. It's all anyone's been talking about."

Oh, no.

Stella glanced at the Winter Twins. They'd spread out blankets in the middle of the lawn, taking up more space than they needed to. A large group was gradually forming around them. The cool crowd.

"Luckily, you're not the hottest topic anymore," said Magnus. "You seen Bianca's new cloud?"

"Hard to miss," said Stella.

"It's almost unheard of – catching a cloud at the Gathering," said Magnus. "Everyone's treating it like a sign from the skies or something. As if her head wasn't big enough already!"

"She was bad enough with one cloud," agreed Stella, earning a chortle from Magnus.

Bianca was still standing in the middle of her group, revelling in the attention.

"— and it found me, in my hour of need!" she concluded dramatically. She looked directly at Stella and raised her eyebrows in a silent challenge.

Stella looked away. She didn't need another confrontation with Bianca. Especially not here, in front of everyone.

On the far side of the lawn, a willow fence suddenly sprouted out of the ground and began to twine itself into an intricate dome around a small group. Verdure Weavers – they must be.

"Is that your group, over there?" she asked Magnus.

He grimaced and shook his head. "They hate my guts. They think since my mum's in charge of the trials, I'll get an automatic pass."

"And you won't?" challenged Stella.

Magnus snorted. "No! Mum would be happier if I'd never even *caught* a cloud. If anyone gets an automatic pass, it'll be Bianca. She's got *potential*, apparently."

Oof! She didn't really know what to say to that.

Magnus shrugged. "I'll give it a go, though. I'm pretty sure I'll get through the first two trials. The Quest, who knows?"

He sounded genuinely nervous and Stella felt a sudden wave of sympathy for him.

"It's not like you need a free pass, anyway," she said, glancing down at his cloud. "That honeysuckle you grew this morning was brilliant. I reckon you'll do fine."

"Thanks." Magnus flushed and looked away.

Briar turned golden with pride and let out a delicate patter of rain. A climbing rose scrambled quickly up the nearest table leg.

"Briar!" hissed Magnus.

The rose continued to climb, throwing out sprays of blooms like fireworks.

"Stop it!" Magnus rubbed a hand over his face in embarrassment. "Sorry. I'm really sorry. He does this when he likes people. It's so embarrassing."

Stella stifled a giggle. The rose was taller than their heads now, though the top was beginning to droop – it wasn't strong enough to support its own weight.

"Briar, enough already!" said Magnus. He roughly plucked a small spray of roses and held it out stiffly in Stella's direction.

"There. You happy now?"

His cloud stopped raining.

Stella shuffled the plates so she could take the flowers. Briar fluffed up smugly.

Unkind laughter broke out on the picnic blankets behind them.

"Stella! Over here!" Tas's voice cut across the lawn.

Stella turned to see Tas waving her arms in the very far corner.

"I've got to go," she said.

"Yeah. Course," mumbled Magnus, looked at his feet.

"Hey!" said Stella.

Magnus looked up at her sheepishly.

"I like your cloud," she said, then turned and marched smartly over to Tas, ignoring the whispers and giggles from the group in the middle of the lawn.

"Thought you might need rescuing?" said Tas, as Stella sat down.

"Bit late," said Stella. She passed Tas a plate of food.

"So?" said Tas. "What was that all about?"

"Nothing, really," said Stella. "I don't think he's got many friends, is all."

"Well, duh!" exclaimed Tas. "This is Velda's son we're talking about! I expect you need signed permission to even to talk to him."

Stella shrugged. She looked back to where Magnus was edging his way forward in the food queue, putting some distance between himself and the rose.

She let out a puff. *Why could nothing just be simple?*

Nineteen

GRANDPA'S
GOOD NEWS

WHEN the nearest apprentices had finished their food and departed for the house, Tas leant in close. "So . . . do you want to hear about my adventure this morning?" she said.

"You didn't!" said Stella. "You snuck out the back?"

"Course I did," said Tas, looking pleased with herself.

"And?" said Stella. "Did you find Arca?"

Tas's smile faded. "No. I only got to look in one door, then I had to hide. It was a storage shed – stacks of magic yarn and a bunch of old looms. No clouds."

"Are you sure no one saw you?"

Tas nodded confidently.

"How did you get past the guards?"

"Secret route," said Tas, winking. "I'll show you later, if you want?"

Stella shook her head. "I'm on my final warning, remember?"

"Suit yourself."

Tas looked across at the Ice Weavers and frowned. Bianca was still showing off her new cloud – using it to grow a widening boundary of crystalline flowers around their group.

"Stella!"

Farah was standing by the front door, waving. Stella scrambled to her feet, her heart in her mouth. Had she failed the trial? Were they going to take Nimbus?

"Good luck," said Tas.

Stella picked her way carefully across the crowded lawn. There was a low two-tone whistle as she approached the Ice Weavers. She glanced over.

Bianca was waving goodbye.

Stella set her jaw and took an amount of satisfaction in crunching straight across the delicate ice flowers that encircled the winter group.

Farah shepherded Stella and Nimbus quickly through the front door.

"Did we pass?" said Stella, as soon as they were inside.

"We'll know later this afternoon," said Farah.

"I hate waiting!" exclaimed Stella.

Farah gave a slight shrug and smiled sympathetically. There wasn't any point in arguing, realised Stella. The council could take all day, if they wanted.

Farah led them through the house, and out of a back door that led to the courtyard. She waved aside two guards who stepped forward as the door opened.

What was so secret that it needed guards? Perhaps Tas was right about Arca being back here? Or maybe, this was where they brought you to have your cloud taken . . .

"Where are we going?" said Stella, stopping abruptly.

"To see Tamar," said Farah, in surprise. "You wanted to see her. Your Grandpa's been asking after you, too."

"Oh!" Stella's heart lightened. *Grandpa!* Nimbus turned a tight loop of delight beside her. She followed Farah across the courtyard with a spring in her step.

Farah glanced curiously at the spray of rosebuds tucked into Stella's button hole. "I noticed you speaking to Magnus earlier," she said. She nodded at the flowers. "Are you two friends now?"

"Sort of," replied Stella.

"Hm!"

The note of surprise nettled Stella. "I told you! We stuck up for him."

Farah raised her eyebrows, thoughtfully. "I wonder what Velda will make of that."

Rebellion prickled in Stella's veins. "She can make what she likes of it!"

Farah didn't reply, but her expression counselled caution.

A heavy wooden door in the back wall led to a quiet path behind the house. Here, Farah's pace slowed. She drew a breath, then closed her mouth and carried on walking, clearly weighing up whether to tell Stella something. Stella matched Farah's pace and held her tongue. Farah didn't seem like the sort of person you could pester.

"Has Tamar told you how the Storm Laws came about?" asked Farah, at last.

Stella stuck her hands deep in her pockets and shrugged. "She doesn't like talking about it. It makes her cross."

Farah nodded. "So, you don't know about Velda's husband?" she said.

Stella shook her head.

"*He* was a Lightning Weaver."

Stella's mouth fell open in surprise. *Velda and a Lightning Weaver!*

"Tamar mentored him, way back when," said Farah. "He was brilliant. Truly gifted. In due course, he became a mentor himself."

"Wait, you said 'was' – he *was* a Lightning Weaver," said Stella.

Farah nodded. "He was killed – by wild lightning." Farah shook her head sadly. "An accident with one of his apprentices . . . He always did take pride in training the wildest ones."

Realisation crackled through Stella's brain, lighting new

connections. "Magnus lost his dad to lightning?"

Farah's face clouded. "Magnus was very young at the time, only a toddler. But yes, Magnus lost his father, and Velda lost her husband. That's when she began campaigning for the Storm Laws—"

"And we thundered right in front of him," exclaimed Stella, smacking a hand against her forehead and staring at Nimbus. *No wonder he was terrified!*

"Well, he doesn't seem too traumatised," pointed out Farah, with a smile. "He's still speaking to you. I just thought you should know."

Stella heaved a sigh. "Thanks."

* * *

Tamar's stall was a large grey canvas tent, set a little way apart from the Wind Whistlers. Its sides billowed and flapped each time a gust escaped from the neighbouring stalls. Tamar and Grandpa were sitting on a pair of crates just outside.

"I'll leave you here," said Farah. "You can make your own way back."

As Stella approached, Grandpa jumped to his feet. "Stella! How did it go?"

"I don't know," said Stella. "They haven't posted the results yet."

"But they let you enter?"

Stella nodded. "Yes."

Grandpa punched the air. "I knew it! They'd be fools, not to. I'm glad they recognise star quality when they see it."

Tamar gave a slight smile and disappeared into the tent.

"How many people in the trials?" asked Grandpa.

Stella shrugged anxiously. "Loads."

"Hmph. Not *one* of them as good as you, I'll bet," said Grandpa, pulling her into a bear hug. Nimbus swooped down to join in, making Grandpa huff and blow. "Stop it, cloud! Let me have a minute with my girl." He didn't flap Nimbus away though, so the little cloud settled around them, a soft golden haze.

"Now, do you want the good news, or the good news?" said Grandpa, letting her go.

"Both," said Stella, with a smile.

"I've been making friends," said Grandpa.

"Really?! With who?" She immediately regretted how rude that sounded, but Grandpa didn't even notice.

"The good folk!" His face was a picture of excitement.

"You've seen them?" said Stella, looking around wide-eyed. She knew they were here – Farah had said so – but she hadn't spotted any.

"Oh, you won't see them now," said Grandpa. "They don't come out by day. But I got chatting to them last night, when I was lugging all Tamar's stuff up here."

"You *got chatting* to them . . ." repeated Stella. It sounded both unlikely and unwise. Most of the stories she knew about Trows involved people getting stolen away.

Grandpa nodded blithely. "Turns out one of them knew your Great Gran – just think of that! When they found out the family connection, they invited me back to theirs and it turns out they're short a mason. So . . . guess who's going to be working with them?"

"You?" said Stella, in disbelief.

Grandpa nodded. "We're building the course for the Quest!"

"The Quest?" Tamar popped her head out of the tent flap, her eyes bright with interest. "You'll be able to give her a few tips then? A bit of insider information?" She tapped the side of her nose.

Grandpa shifted uncomfortably. "Well, no . . . they swore me to secrecy."

"Even to your own granddaughter?" persisted Tamar.

"You don't break a promise to the good folk," said Grandpa, crossing himself.

"Typical." Tamar rolled her eyes in disgust, and disappeared inside again.

For a split second, Stella wished that Grandpa wasn't so superstitious – she could do with some help. But then she thought better of it. She wanted to pass because she was good enough – not because she'd done something sneaky. And if Grandpa went back on his word, he wouldn't be Grandpa.

She patted his arm. "It's alright. I don't want to cheat. Especially if it would get you in trouble."

Grandpa gave her a grateful smile.

"So, what's the other good news?" asked Stella.

"Are you sure you want to know?" said Grandpa. "It's meant

to be a surprise. I only mentioned it because Tamar said you were having a tough time."

Stella nodded. "Go on?"

"Your parents are on their way!" said Grandpa, spreading his hands wide.

"Here? No!"

There were so many reasons that was a bad idea, Stella didn't know where to start.

Grandpa's smile faded. "I thought you'd be excited?"

"This place is meant to be *secret*!"

"Well, sure, but I couldn't bring you up here without letting them know."

"Aren't they meant to be working?"

They can't come here. They'll get in the way. They'll stop me taking the trials. They'll think it's dangerous.

"They had a break and wanted to surprise you. They were going to meet us at home, but now we're up here, so they're coming here."

Stella shook her head in dismay. "You've got to stop them!"

Grandpa shook his head. "I can't, now. They're on their way. But it'll be fine. You'll see. They'll be amazed – delighted and amazed by all this."

But the doubt remained, cold as a sea witch's kiss.

What if they're not?

Twenty

A BIRD'S EYE VIEW

As she walked back, Stella's head whirled with thoughts of Mum and Dad. What would they do when they got here?

Stella pictured Mum trying to overpower the guards and a panicked giggle escaped like a hiccup. The nearest stallholder looked curiously at her. Stella ducked her head and jogged up the front steps.

Two apprentices were coming across the lawn carrying bags. One of them was crying. Were they leaving?

The trial results!

Stella burst through the front door, but found the hallway

blocked by a milling crowd; glimpsing Tas down the far end, she pushed her way through.

Tas let out a whoop when she spotted her and stabbed a finger at the results board. "Stella (Lightning Weaver) – Trial 1 – Pass!"

Elation rushed through Stella. "We're through?"

"Yep! Both of us," confirmed Tas. "Storm weavers for the win!"

"Storm weavers for the bin," contradicted Neve.

"Oh, zip it, Neve," said Stella, with a stab of annoyance.

Bianca joined Neve. She looked up the list deliberately – their names were right at the top, both of them 'Merit', rather than 'Pass'.

"Oh, they've made a mistake, look," said Bianca. She pulled a pen from her pocket and scribbled Stella's name off the list. "There, that's better!"

Having her name crossed out didn't make it true, but it felt like it. Stella snatched for the pen, but Tas grabbed her arm.

"What are you going to do?" said Bianca. "Thunder? Go on. I dare you."

Nimbus darkened to furious purple and Tas's eyes widened. "Don't, Stella!"

Stella gritted her teeth. *Calm, Nimbus!*

Tas looked from her to Nimbus and back again. "Lightning Weaver, coming through!" she yelled and the crowd of apprentices pressed themselves out of the way in alarm. This time, Stella didn't even mind.

She bounded through the gap, up the stairs and along the corridor to their room, followed closely by Nimbus.

"Why can't they leave us alone?" she burst out, as Tas closed the door. Nimbus let out a rumble that rattled the glass in the window. He'd done well to hold it in.

Tas put on her rucksack, climbed onto her bed, then unlatched the window and threw it open.

"What are you doing?"

"Taking you outside," declared Tas. "You need some air."

"Are we allowed on the roof?" said Stella.

"In emergencies, yes," said Tas. "And this is an emergency."

"Nimbus isn't going to—"

"Even if the twins come in?" interrupted Tas. "They've followed me in here before! They're not going to leave you alone – not now they've seen you're rattled."

Stella looked at Nimbus, swirling purple and gunmetal grey. Honestly? She wasn't sure *what* he'd do if the twins came barging in here.

She leant out. A steeply pitched roof extended out at the back of the house, making the building a sort of T-shape. *The great hall.* On either side of their window, the main wall rose up like the battlements of a castle. Behind it, was a flat lead gulley – a hidden pathway.

"You've been out here before?"

Tas nodded. "It's my escape route. Budge over." She climbed onto the drawers and stepped out through the window. "See? Perfectly safe."

Stella clambered up after her and Nimbus followed, still

grumbling. Luckily, he seemed to have understood about staying hidden. He tucked himself down into the gulley and flew all the way to the far end of the house.

"You want to know how I got to the courtyard?" said Tas, with a smile. She pointed at a narrow iron ladder a little further along.

Stella peeked over the wall. It wasn't as tall as the broch, but it was still pretty high. It made her head spin. A guard appeared down below and Stella ducked back. "We shouldn't be out here," she whispered.

Tas pulled the window closed. "No, but we are," she stated. "It's the safest place to be until you calm down. Follow me."

Stella shuffled along behind Tas. Staying low, they crept all the way along the back of the house and round the corner, onto a flat roof.

Nimbus was there, waiting for them. Tas sat down, her back to the wall, and Stella joined her. Nimbus settled next to her in a disgruntled heap.

He didn't like holding everything in. Neither did she. Stella heaved a sigh and leant back against the sun-warmed stone.

"Bit better?" asked Tilda

Stella nodded.

"You get the best view from up here too, look," said Tas, pointing.

Off to the left, the colourful stalls of the market stretched away down the hillside. From up here, it looked magical. Puffs of snow and ice burst up like fireworks from a group of blue and white stalls. There was a sudden burst of laughter as a vine reached for the sky above one of the green huts.

Stella heaved a deep sigh. "Thanks, Tas."

Tas shrugged. "I'm not having you blowing your chances for those two."

"They totally deserve to be thundered at."

"They do. But it's not worth it."

"It's not like it would hurt them. Just shut them up a bit."

Tas shook her head. "Trouble is, most people hear thunder and they think *that*." She leant over and pointed at the great hall.

"But thunder is just—" Stella looked back and the protest curdled in her throat. Halfway along the great hall, a massive, jagged repair ran all the way down the side of the building. The wall around it was scorched black.

Lightning strike. The Haken. Her scalp tingled cold. The battle must have been brutal, desperate; nothing held back.

Tas sucked her cheeks in and made a fierce expression. "A danger to the weaving community! An avoidable threat!" she intoned. It was a pretty good impression of Velda.

"We're not a danger to anyone," protested Stella.

"Not even the twins?" said Tas.

"No," said Stella, seriously.

"Hey, I'm kidding. Course you're not. You'll show 'em. Prove we're not all like that." Tas nodded towards the great hall.

Stella pressed her lips together. *Neither was Heather,* she thought. But she didn't quite dare say it out loud.

And she couldn't be sure. Would Heather have turned sea witch if Velda hadn't tried to take her cloud? Probably not. Would she have done something else bad? Maybe.

It was impossible to know. It made her head hurt just thinking about it.

Stella heaved a sigh.

"What?" said Tas.

Stella shook her head. It was too tricky to explain.

"Tell me about your storm cloud," she said, changing the subject.

"Arca?" said Tas. "He's a snow cloud. Blizzard class – freeze you solid as soon as he looks at you. You should have seen us in snow ball fights! No one stood a chance." She grinned. "I taught him a bunch of cool tricks, too – flash freeze, ice roses." A shadow of sadness flitted across her face. "Drench is great," she said, "but Arca? We just got each other. You know?"

Stella looked at Nimbus, brooding beside her, and sighed heavily. She did know.

"Let it go," said Tas. "Seriously. Don't let them get inside your head. We're going to pass these trials and walk away as Storm Weavers. I'm not having it any other way. Deal?"

"Deal," agreed Stella.

"Here," said Tas, fishing in her pocket. "This is for you."

Stella opened her hand and Tas dropped something small and sparkly into her palm. A tiny lightning bolt; one of the charms from her weather bracelet.

"Thank you!"

"Whenever they're getting to you, just hold that, and remember why you're here." Tas looked meaningfully at Nimbus.

Stella nodded. "I will." She turned the charm between her fingers and looked out across the patchwork rainbow of the market. The sky stretched wide above them and Tas's shoulder was warm next to hers.

Beyond the market, the silver channel of water shone in the evening sun. She couldn't quite see Grandpa's boat from here – the jetty was hidden by a roll in the hill. The firth was empty of boats, for now . . .

"It's not just the twins winding me up," she admitted. "I just found out my parents are coming."

"Is that not a good thing?" asked Tas, tentatively.

"They're not weather weavers!" exclaimed Stella. "They don't know about me being a Lightning Weaver. They haven't even met Nimbus . . ."

"Wow! How d'you think they're gonna take it?"

"I don't know," said Stella, heavily. "How did your parents take it, when *you* caught a storm cloud?"

Tas glanced up at the sky. "I mean, they're both weather weavers, so it's a bit different. Everyone assumed I'd find a rain cloud, like them. So, surprised, I guess? And sad – they knew Arca would get taken away."

Stella heaved a sigh. *Mum and Dad. Here.*

"Your parents love you, right?" said Tas.

Stella nodded.

"So, they'll be happy for you?"

Stella shrugged. She couldn't imagine Mum being happy about any of this.

Mum and Dad would never *reject* her – she knew that. But what if they asked her to stop weather weaving? Give up Nimbus?

Nimbus rolled against her leg, making her jump. He was icy cold; spinning with frost.

Hey, stop it! Whatever they say, I'm not giving you up. She scooped him towards her.

Tas eyed the sparkling cloud. "Bianca was putting on a proper show at lunch. Did you see that ring of frost roses?"

"Hard to miss," said Stella, remembering the crunch of them underfoot.

"Arca used to grow ones just like that," said Tas, looking suddenly vulnerable.

Stella nodded sympathetically.

"Only, I've never seen another cloud make them," said Tas. A dark suspicion crossed her face. "Clouds can't be brain-fogged, can they?"

"I don't see how?" said Stella.

"But what if they made him forget me somehow?" persisted Tas.

Stella stroked Nimbus protectively. Nobody could ever make him forget her, could they? Nimbus moved a little closer to her.

Tas chewed on the end of a curl. "It's just, Bianca's cloud seems kind of . . . blank."

"No." Stella shook her head firmly. "No way."

There was no way Bianca's new cloud could be Arca. "Look, think about it!" she said. "Velda's *got* to give him back to you, or she'll have the whole council after her. Besides, Arca would never choose Bianca, would he?"

Tas sighed. "No. Never. You're right – the waiting is just doing my head in, especially knowing he's so close." She drummed her fingers in frustration. "He's here, somewhere. I just wish I knew where."

Tas closed her eyes and turned her head, as though trying to pinpoint a faraway sound. Stella watched her silently, but after a minute she opened her eyes and shook her head. "No good," she said.

"Hey, you'll get him back soon." Stella nudged Tas's shoulder and smiled. "I can't wait to meet him."

Tas's eyes lit up. She rooted in her rucksack, then paused. "Can you keep a secret?"

"You know I can."

Tas lifted a small blue jar out of the bag. She cupped it in her hands and stared at it for a moment, before passing it to Stella.

Stella took it carefully. It felt cool in her hands. The jar shone and sparkled, pulsing with little flashes of white and blue. She peered closer – it was filled with tiny crystals, tumbling and turning, like a miniature blizzard.

"Beautiful," said Stella, reverently. "What are they?"

"Seeds of winter," confided Tas, her eyes fixed on the jar. "Arca made them."

Stella watched the tiny storm for a moment longer, before handing it back.

Tas took the jar and held it to her chest. "It's how they knew he was blizzard class. I wasn't meant to keep any. But they're all I've got left of him, so I hid them."

Stella eyed the jar curiously. "Why aren't you meant to have them?"

"Too powerful for a novice, they said." Tas snorted. "Arca used to make them all the time. These, and frost roses." She smiled sadly. "They were kind of his party trick . . ."

"Some party trick!" said Stella.

"Says you, lightning girl!" said Tas, with a grin. She tucked the jar back into its hiding place, then pulled a packet of corn puffs out of the bag. "Pufuleti," she said. "We should be celebrating, remember?"

Stella grinned. It hadn't really begun to sink in until now. The first trial was done.

And we passed, Nimbus!

She ruffled the little cloud, leaving trails of cheerful gold in his surface.

Together, they could take on anything. Even Velda.

Twenty-One

GREEN FINGERS

AS Stella and Tas climbed back through the bedroom window, they could hear the Winter Twins talking loudly in the room next door.

"Probably wondering where we are," whispered Tas, covering her mouth in silent mirth. "Let's keep them guessing – we can hide in the practice field."

It was a good plan – there were enough hills and hummocks, bushes and boulders, that even if the twins came outside, Stella was pretty confident they could stay out of sight. But when they got there, Tas didn't follow her down the slope.

"You not coming?" asked Stella.

Tas looked at a gate in the far wall, raised her eyebrows and shrugged.

"What?" said Stella.

"It leads through to the courtyard . . ."

Stella shook her head firmly.

"Just a quick look?" said Tas.

"Wait until after—"

"I can't!"

"What are you going to do," asked Stella, "if you find Arca?"

"I'm not going to let him out, or anything. I just have to *see* him; make sure he's okay."

Stella sighed. She didn't trust that was true. But she knew there'd be no talking Tas out of it. She began to trudge towards the gate.

"No!" said Tas. "You stay here. I don't want to get you in trouble. You've still *got* Nimbus."

"But I don't want *you* to get in trouble, either!"

"I won't," said Tas. "I've got a million excuses. Anyway, the council aren't worried about me. Drench is no threat to anyone." She glanced up at Nimbus and quickly backtracked. "I mean, not that you are . . . I didn't mean—"

"I know what you meant," said Stella. "Just promise you won't get caught?"

Tas saluted. "Promise. I'll meet you at supper, yeah?"

* * *

Stella found an ideal hiding spot near the bottom of the field; a huge stack of granite boulders, facing the sea. About halfway up, a massive slab formed a natural shelf, wide enough to sit on. Hidden from the house, and far enough away that if the twins came out to practice, they probably wouldn't spot her.

She leant back against the stone and let the wind lift away a little of the worry in her heart. Nimbus settled next to her and she combed her fingers through him.

"We're going to have to be so careful," she said. "No thunder at all. Everyone's just waiting for it; waiting for us to prove Velda right."

She sighed. Normally, she was good at facing problems head-on, but you couldn't do that against gossip and rumours. They were like fog – creeping, silent – sneaking up behind you when you weren't looking. *Freezing fog. Velda's speciality.*

"Here you are! Cor, you're not easy to find."

Stella startled and looked up to see Magnus, perched on the rocks high above her.

"That was kind of the point," said Stella, dryly.

"You not practising for the next trial?" he asked.

Stella shook her head.

Special skills – lightning. Just the thought of it made the back of her neck crackle with tension.

"I don't think we'd better practice lightning," she said. "Not here. We'll save it for the skills trial."

Magnus climbed quickly down the rocks. For someone so

tall, he was surprisingly nimble. "Well done on knowledge this morning," he said, stepping down onto her ledge. "You aced it."

"Apart from the compost," said Stella, wincing at the memory.

"Ha! Yeah, but still – you answered everything else right – even the obscure stuff about hurricanes."

Stella sighed. "Trouble is, now everyone thinks I'm a hurricane-wielding sea witch."

"Oh," said Magnus. "You're not?"

"No!"

"Shame." He gave her a sly smile. "Might liven things up a bit."

"You don't want to let your mum hear you say that."

"I'm done caring what she thinks."

Stella glanced at him in surprise. His eyes were full of hurt. Magnus caught her looking and rearranged his face into a studied look of boredom. "She wants me to drop out of the trials."

"What?! But why? You did brilliantly. You got every question right!"

Magnus looked down. "She's convinced Briar isn't an 'appropriate' cloud for me. I'm a 'huge disappointment', apparently." He plucked a tuft of moss off the rock and rolled it between his fingers. Briar quickly slid forward to grow some more.

"A disappointment?" repeated Stella, quietly. *Ouch!*

"She also said I'm not to speak to you." He snuck a sideways glance at Stella. "So, I told her to get stuffed."

Stella stared at him in surprise and then began to laugh.

"What? It's not funny," said Magnus.

"It kind of is . . ." said Stella. "She's in charge of the whole Gathering, and everybody's scared of her, and you just told her to 'get stuffed'!"

"Well, I think what I actually said is: I'm going to choose my cloud and choose my friends, and there's nothing you can do about it."

"Huh!" Stella nodded in approval.

Magnus the rebel – who would have thought it?

Magnus grinned briefly and looked away. "That's not the worst of it."

"Tell me."

"Briar grew a skunk cabbage."

Stella guffawed. "Sounds stinky?"

Magnus nodded. "Right in the middle of her office carpet."

"Remind me not to annoy you . . ."

"Oh, you'll know about it," said Magnus, waving his hand under his nose.

"Well, I'm glad you stuck up for yourself," said Stella. "Good for you. You and Briar are perfect together. You'll do brilliantly."

"Hope so." Magnus's face grew serious. "Don't know about the Quest though," he said. "Bianca and Neve were right about that. Briar and I aren't much use in a fight. If the council start chucking sleet and hail at us . . ." He shrugged.

Stella looked doubtfully at Briar. She couldn't imagine the gentle giant battling anything, much. "Fighting isn't really *you*, is it?" she said.

"No," agreed Magnus. "We'll probably get hammered." He

ran a hand through Briar, who was busily painting a patchwork of lichen across the bare rock. "I was thinking, though, we might stand a chance . . . if we could learn cloud cover?"

Stella looked at Nimbus, looping in and out of the maze of rocks below them.

What do you reckon, Nimbus?

He immediately swooped towards them and settled on the rock next to Briar. Stella smiled – that was a pretty clear answer.

"Nimbus and I will teach you cloud cover . . ." she said.

Magnus smiled.

". . . if *you'll* show us verdure?"

"Deal," said Magnus, quickly. "We'll make a grower of you in no time. It's easy."

Easy for you, maybe.

She slid down the front of the boulder to the ground. "Just so you know, the only thing we've grown so far is one measly beansprout."

"Was that with or without compost?" teased Magnus.

Stella scowled at him.

"Hey, I'm joking," said Magnus, scrambling down the boulder to join her. "A beansprout is good!"

"You wouldn't say that if you'd seen it."

* * *

Teaching cloud cover was harder than Stella had anticipated.

Briar was slow-moving and easily distracted. And he was determined to make gaps for every insect that flew past, so his cloud cover came out looking more like a colander – full of holes.

"I'm sorry," said Magnus. "I told you we're useless at it."

Stella looked critically at the wobbling cloud cover and frowned. "Perhaps we're going about it the wrong way?" she said. "Did you see that willow dome the others made at lunch? Maybe you could do something like that, instead?"

"What, like a shield?"

"Yes! A living one."

"Hmm . . ." Magnus rifled through his pockets. His coat had lots of pockets, all of them stuffed with little wraps and packets of seeds.

"Something strong," said Stella. "Think hail-proof."

"Flexible, strong-rooted too, in case of gales," added Magnus. For the first time since they'd started, there was a spark of excitement in his eyes. "*Phyllostachys Glauca*!"

"Bless you!" said Stella.

Magnus rolled his eyes. "It's a type of bamboo."

* * *

It wasn't cloud cover, but it worked. Nimbus had even thrown sleet and hail at it. Nothing got through the dense thicket of stems. Best of all, Briar could grow it in seconds.

But now, Magnus was pouring seeds from one hand to the

other and looking at her expectantly. "It's easy," he said. "You use a sense of belonging to root you to the ground, and let the seeds do the rest."

Stella hunched her shoulders. "What about if you don't belong?" she mumbled.

"What do you mean?" exclaimed Magnus. "You've got a cloud, don't you? Of course you belong."

"I don't *feel* like I do," admitted Stella.

"Alright, who do you think *does*?"

"Everyone else," said Stella.

"What about Bianca? Do you think she belongs here more than you?"

"Probably . . ."

"No, I'm being serious," said Magnus. "Do you think she's got a better cloud than you?"

"No! Nimbus is the best," said Stella. "No offence, Briar."

"Is Bianca stronger than you?" said Magnus.

"I doubt it."

"Kinder than you?"

"No."

"Braver than you?"

Stella shook her head.

"So, what makes you think Bianca belongs here, any more than you do?" said Magnus, spreading his hands.

"She's got loads of friends."

Magnus raised his eyebrows and snorted. "That's entirely

debatable. But a useful insight." He crouched down and sprinkled a few seeds on the ground. "For *you*, belonging means having friends," he said.

"Well? It's true, isn't it?" said Stella. "People make you feel like you belong. Or like you don't . . ."

"And who makes you feel like you belong?" said Magnus.

Grandpa? But maybe because he doesn't belong here, either.

"Tas," she realised.

Magnus smiled. "Right, Tassa's going to be your magic spark for verdure."

Well, that's as clear as mud.

Stella scrunched her nose up. "How, exactly?"

"Think of all the best times you've had with Tassa," said Magnus, "and then get Nimbus to rain all over these."

Stella heaved a sigh, but Magnus nodded at her, so she closed her eyes and remembered:

Dancing in the bedroom.

Tas's impressions of Velda.

Sharing a blanket for lunch.

Sitting side by side on the roof, with the whole world in front of them.

She heard a light pattering as Nimbus began to rain, then a short laugh from Magnus. She opened her eyes and gaped in amazement.

"Nimbus! You did it!"

Twenty-Two

THE COLD
SHOULDER

"SEE?" said Magnus. "Told you, didn't I?"

The ground in front of them was now a verdant riot of green. It was still visibly growing, branches splitting into twigs, sprouting into leaves, tiny flowers bursting open. It made a soft rustling sound, busy with life. Nimbus darted back and forth, adding a drizzle here and a splash there.

"You should be a mentor," said Stella.

"One day, maybe . . ."

"Seriously! I never thought I'd get this . . . But you just explained it, in a way I could understand!"

Magnus shrugged bashfully.

As she watched, a lone bee buzzed in and began to investigate the purple heather.

My heather! That I grew! From bare earth!

"Stella!"

She stood up to see Tas jogging down the field towards them, followed by Drench. Nimbus swooped up the hill to greet them.

"Are you alright?" said Tas, breathlessly.

"Yes. I've been practising!" said Stella. "Look!"

Tas glanced at the heather. She didn't look impressed. "Supper's served. I've been waiting up at the house for ages."

"Sorry," said Stella. "I *meant* to come and find you, but Magnus offered to show me verdure." She gave him a brief smile of gratitude.

Tas's expression cooled. "Fine. Well, don't let me stop you." She turned and started back up the slope again.

"No, wait, I'm coming!" called Stella. She turned back to Magnus. "I've gotta go."

He nodded.

"Thanks," she said.

Magnus gave a modest shrug.

"Friends?" She stuck out a hand.

Magnus shook it with a smile. "Friends," he agreed.

On the way back, Nimbus and Drench circled overhead, trying to out-do one another with sudden bursts of rain.

Tas sidestepped quickly, well-practised at dodging Drench's downpours. "So, what was all that about?" she asked. "I thought you were trying to steer clear of Magnus, given the fact that his mum is *evil*?"

Stella shook her head. "He's not *like* his mum."

"If you say so," said Tas. "But watch yourself. And if he starts bad-mouthing me, don't listen!"

"Actually, he was nice about you," said Stella. "Turns out I need friends to grow stuff. He called you my 'magic spark'."

Tas stopped and looked at Stella in surprise. "*Magnus* said that?"

Stella nodded.

Tas grinned. "Huh! He can't be all bad, then. Magic spark?" She twirled on the spot. "I like it!"

Stella hooked her arm through Tas's. "So? Where are we going?"

Tas grinned. "Upstairs," she said. "We need to plan for tomorrow – the skills trial is a big spectacle. Everyone turns up to watch."

"Wait, everyone?" Stella's confidence shrank like a frost-bitten bud.

Tas nodded cheerfully. "Let's grab food first, or were you planning to skip supper?" Stella's stomach grumbled and Tas laughed. "I'll take that as a no."

Tas kicked the bedroom door, but it didn't open.

"Can you?" she said. "Hands full." She held up the plates.

Stella's hand stuck to the metal door knob. "Ow! Cold!" she said, letting go and rubbing her palm.

Tas leant forward and squinted at the frosty palm print on the door knob. "I've got a bad feeling about this . . ."

Stella pulled her sleeve down to cover her hand and tried again. The door seemed to be stuck. She gave it a shove with her shoulder and it opened with a sharp crack. As it swung open, Stella gasped.

The entire room was iced white.

Tas pushed past her, put the plates down, and turned on the spot. "I don't believe it. Our *beds* and everything!" She flipped the coverlet back, throwing a shower of snow into the air. Nimbus and Drench nosed in through the door and began to explore the frozen room.

Stella picked up *The Weather Book* and cracked it open. The pages were warped, the edges rimed with frost.

Tas gave a growl of frustration. "We can't let them get away with this."

"It's not like we saw them do it," pointed out Stella. "It'd just be our word against theirs."

"I'm not talking about *telling* on them," said Tas. "Nobody would do anything about it anyway. No. We'll think of a way to get our own back."

Stella dusted the snow off her bed and sat down. "Leave it, Tas. They've already got me in trouble once today. I don't want to start a war."

"Start a war?" said Tas. "*Start* a war!" She spread her hands, taking in the icy room. "In case you hadn't noticed, it's already started!"

Drench settled on the curtain rail, making the icicles on the curtains jingle.

Tas glanced towards him and her face paled. "Arca . . ." she breathed. She leant towards the window.

Stella quickly got up and joined her. She squinted through the frosted glass.

"No. Look." Tas pointed and Stella focused closer. The ice on the window formed a spiral of perfect petals.

"It's *my* frost rose," said Tas. "Bianca's got Arca!" Her eyes filled with tears and she looked at Stella in horror. "*That's* why I couldn't find him!"

Tas spun towards the door, but Stella caught her by the arm.

"Stop! Think! We can't just go busting in there."

"This is proof!" cried Tas, pointing at the window. "She's taken him! She's got my cloud!"

Stella looked anxiously at the frost flower. It might be proof to Tas, but was she right? And would anyone else believe it?

With the door standing open, it was already beginning to thaw.

"We have to get Farah," she said. "Show her, before it disappears."

They didn't even knock – just burst into Farah's office, both of them talking at once.

"She's got my cloud!"

"They iced our room!"

"You can't let her keep Arca!"

Farah held her hands up. "Girls! Stop! One at a time."

Stella looked at Tas and nodded. It was her story to tell.

"Bianca's got my storm cloud!" she blurted, her eyes wild. "I suspected it at lunch, but now, I'm sure."

Farah's brow furrowed and she stood up. "That's a serious accusation."

They didn't have time for a lecture.

"Come and see," said Stella, tugging at her sleeve. "Quickly! Before it melts."

The three of them hurried upstairs, Tassa leading the way.

"It was there!" said Tas, helplessly. "Stella saw it."

Stella nodded. But the frost had melted to small droplets. One of them ran down the window like a teardrop.

Farah heaved a sigh. "Tassa, I can't accuse Bianca without proof."

"But you can't let her take the trials!" exclaimed Tas. "If they complete the Reckoning together, they'll be bound. I'll never get Arca back. Ever!"

"I won't let that happen," Farah assured her. "But you can't tell anyone about this. Not now. Not when you're this close. Especially not without proof."

Tas clenched her fists, trembling with frustration.

"Pass the trials and you *will* get your cloud back. I promise," said Farah. "But please, don't do anything rash. We've worked too hard for this!"

Tas nodded stiffly, but there was a spark of defiance in her eyes.

Stella rubbed her arm – they'd get Arca back. She didn't know how yet, but they would.

Farah ran a fingertip along the icy bed frame and rubbed her fingers together. "There are spare rooms now, following the first trial," she said. "Gather your things. I'm moving you to the far end. The more distance between you and those winter girls, the better."

* * *

The new room was bigger than their old one – it even had a wardrobe. Nimbus and Drench had taken up residence on top. Farah had thawed out their belongings, but now the whole room smelt vaguely steamy, like a bathroom.

Tas lay on her new bed, facing the wall. Farah had made her promise not to confront Bianca and she was still stewing about it.

Stella gave her a gentle shake. "You'll get him back, Tas."

"You don't know that."

"Come on, we're so nearly there. Storm sisters, remember?"

Tas looked over her shoulder and gave Stella a sad smile. All the spark seemed to have gone out of her.

Stella sat down by Tas's feet.

"When you pass the trials, Velda *has* to give your cloud back. She said so, in front of everybody – she can't back out of that. That's what you've got to hold onto. Passing the trials!"

"But it was a message!" exclaimed Tas, thumping the mattress in frustration. "A message to me, from Arca. He needs my help!"

Stella didn't want to contradict her flat out, but the more she thought about it, the more it didn't make any sense. Tas was *so* desperate to see her storm cloud. What if she was seeing him where he wasn't?

"Why would Arca choose Bianca?" she said.

"He didn't. That's the whole point. She's forcing him to do what she wants."

Stella looked up at Nimbus and frowned briefly. She couldn't imagine anyone *forcing* him to do anything. "How could she?" she said, reasonably. "Nobody tells a storm cloud what to do."

Tassa sat up abruptly. "How do the council make *any* of the storm clouds do what they want?" she said. "You ever thought about that? You think the storm clouds *want* to leave?"

Stella shrank from the fury in Tas's voice. She hadn't thought about it; not in any detail. Mostly she'd been trying *not* to think about it.

"I just figured if their weather weavers agreed, then—"

"Would *you* agree? I didn't! I mean, we went along with it –

with all the guards and assessors there, you kind of have to – but Arca and I had this whole plan. He was going to escape – fly back to me. We were going to hide."

Stella's eyes widened. She'd considered exactly that plan herself – tell Nimbus to pretend to go along with the separation, then escape later.

"But Arca never came back?"

Tas shook her head. "Which means they stopped him."

A chill skittered up Stella's spine and she glanced at Nimbus.

"What did you mean about being bound?" she said. "You said if Bianca gets through the trials, she and Arca would be bound, at the Reckoning?"

Tas laughed in disbelief. "You're taking the trials, and you don't even know what they're *for*!"

To keep Nimbus.

Stella looked at the floor, suddenly feeling stupid. Beyond that, she had no idea. She'd just rushed ahead; tried her best. What else was she supposed to do?

Nimbus tumbled down off the wardrobe and poured himself into her lap.

"Sorry. I'm sorry," said Tas. "That was mean."

Stella shook her head wordlessly and ran her fingers lightly over her cloud.

"The trials prove the bond between weaver and cloud," said Tas, gritting her teeth, "and the Reckoning makes it official. If Bianca passes with Arca, there's no getting him back. In the eyes of the council, he'll become *her* cloud. Forever."

Stella swallowed hard and smoothed Nimbus. "Farah won't let her keep him," she said. "If Bianca *has* taken Arca, she'll get him back for you."

"Yeah, because trusting the council worked out *so* well for me before," said Tas.

Twenty-Three

FOUR SEASONS
IN ONE DAY

THE following morning, Stella kept Tas distracted with stories about their training mishaps, but by lunchtime, Nimbus was getting antsy.

"I'm going to take him outside," she said. "You coming?"

"No. I can't face seeing Bianca. Not now." Tas gently shook the seeds of winter, making them twinkle. She'd been clutching the jar all morning.

Stella paused in concern. "Are you going to be alright at the trial?"

Tas shrugged. "I'll have to be, won't I? How else am I going to get him back?"

* * *

When Stella got back to the room, Tas wasn't there. She looked around with a pang of alarm, before noticing Drench on top of the wardrobe. Tas couldn't have gone far.

Sure enough, she reappeared about five minutes later, looking cheerier than she had all morning. "Where have you been?" said Stella.

Tas smiled secretively. "Had to sort something."

Stella's heart sank. "You've been to see Bianca, haven't you?"

"No!" Tas closed the door and breezed past Stella.

"I got you lunch," said Stella, nodding at the plate she'd brought up.

"Thanks."

"So? Where were you then?"

"Went to hunt for my weather bracelet," said Tas, around a mouthful of sandwich.

"You've lost it?"

Tas held up her bare wrist and nodded. "I just hope I didn't drop it when I was sneaking around out the back . . ." She sighed. "I just went to check our old room, but it wasn't there. You don't think the Winter Twins could have nicked it?"

Stella shrugged. *Maybe?* Or it might just be lost. She scanned the mess on the floor. "I can help you look, if you want?"

"Later," said Tas, lifting her orange rucksack off the floor and dumping it on Stella's bed. "Now, it's time to get dolled up – get you looking the part."

She pulled out a long silver dress and held it up in front of Stella. "Super glam, but perhaps too sea witch? What do you think?"

"It's not very me," said Stella dubiously. "Anyway, this trial is in a field, isn't it?"

"Well, sure, but you're not planning to perform in your jeans and raincoat, are you?"

"What's wrong with my jeans and raincoat?"

* * *

A ring of standing stones crowned the hill, surrounding a small arena of gritty sand – a stark bald patch amidst the lush green. Stella and Tas joined the queue of apprentices waiting to take their places.

All around the circle, people jostled for the best view. A handful had brought stools or crates to stand on. So many faces, eager with anticipation.

Bianca was already in the circle. Stella couldn't actually see her, but she could see the distinctive pair of clouds, floating above one of the tall stones. One of them seemed agitated, bobbing up and down, the other was perfectly still.

Was one of them really Tas's cloud? If so, which one?

Stella glanced at Tas, but thankfully, she wasn't focused on the pair of clouds. She was staring out at the water, her eyes clear and her chin high.

Probably rehearsing her performance in her head.

Until Tas had described it to her, Stella hadn't realised the skills trial was meant to be an actual *performance* – she'd figured that was just Tas talk.

But no. Tas had hers all planned out – a show and a dance and everything.

Stella hadn't practised anything like that. Mainly her goal had been staying on target.

She looked along the queue. All the others were dressed like they were going to a posh party – dresses, suits. She looked down at her own clothes and sighed. Too late now.

"What are you huffing about?" said Tas, coming out of her daze.

Stella tugged the front of her yellow raincoat and tilted her head at the other apprentices. "You were right."

"Don't stress. It's perfect. You do you."

Stella gave her a grateful smile. "Good luck, Tas."

"Us Storm Weavers? We make our *own* luck," replied Tas.

* * *

The council were seated on a small raised stage, giving them the best view of the arena. Stella spotted Farah and Ilana amongst them. If Tamar was here, she was staying out of sight, which was probably a good thing.

Velda stood in the centre of the circle, directing apprentices to their places. Stella's heart lurched when she saw where Velda was pointing for her.

Between Bianca and Neve. Of course.

The girls smiled coldly at her as she took up her spot.

Neve leant forward to look past Stella at Bianca. "Surprised she's still here!" she said. "Thought we'd given her the *cold shoulder.*" Both girls broke into giggles.

Stella's head filled with a high-pitched hum of hatred, but she didn't react; not even slightly. She just checked Nimbus, joined her hands behind her back, and turned to face the centre.

Fifteen stones, fifteen apprentices – only half had made it through the first trial. How many would make it through this one?

Stella swallowed, her nerves coming back full-force.

Lightning! In front of all these people, all pushing to get closer.

Standing between Bianca and Neve in their pristine outfits, she suddenly felt grateful for her jeans and raincoat. They made her feel like herself – the familiar armour of home. If they were good enough for facing a sea witch, they were good enough for the trials. Anyway, she wouldn't have been able to concentrate if she'd borrowed one of those long flappy dresses.

She quickly located Tas, who gave her a thumbs up. Stella gave her a swift smile and bounced on her toes.

We've got this, Nimbus. He bobbed in agreement.

Magnus was across the far side. He wasn't looking in Stella's direction. Not really surprising, with his mum standing right there.

A chill found its way between Stella's socks and the bottom of her trousers. She looked down to see mist creeping between the stones and pooling in the centre of the circle. Nobody had noticed yet – the babble of conversation from the crowd was still loud. The low cloud formed a sparkling whirlpool around Velda's feet.

Velda turned slowly on the spot. Satisfied that each of the apprentices was where they should be, she flung her arms up in the air. The freezing fog fountained up in a sparkling geyser.

"Ooh!" rose from the crowd, then they fell silent.

"Welcome, one and all," said Velda, her voice sharp in the cool air. "As part of their trials, our apprentices must show their mastery of weather conjuring. Each has a cloud aligned to their talent."

Velda looked in her direction and Stella tensed.

"Today, they will present their unique skills. We give you . . . four seasons in one day!"

Clapping and cheering erupted. Velda let the clamour continue for a few moments, before sweeping her arms wide to send the icy fog tumbling out over the crowd. There were squawks and exclamations as it found its way inside coats and collars, rapidly shushed by others who had seen this before – the show was about to start.

"We open, with Tassa, Rain Caller."

Tas grinned at Stella, then stepped away from her stone and

mimed putting up an umbrella. There was a sudden rustle as people zipped coats closed and pulled on hats. Umbrellas popped up like mushrooms.

Stella smiled – Tas was good at this. A real performer. She was playing to the crowd – making them part of the act.

Tas looked up at the clear sky, then spread her hands and gave an exaggerated shrug and shook her head: no rain today – sorry. There was a murmur of disappointment and two of the umbrellas closed and disappeared.

Tas wagged a finger in the air – scolding them for doubting her – and Drench swooped in and drenched them.

Squeals and laughter broke out.

Then, Tas began to dance – a wild rhythmic dance, with high flung arms and finger clicks, that sent Drench darting and tumbling over the gathered crowd. A downpour here, a sneaky drizzle there. One or two lucky souls smiled smugly when they were left dry, but Drench dashed back, leaving them spluttering.

When she was satisfied that almost no one was dry, Tas rose on tiptoes and swept one arm in an arc above her head. Drench followed, leaving a fine mizzle of rain above the circle of stones. It caught the morning sun and shone – a perfect rainbow.

Tas bowed low to the audience, then took a moment to soak up the delighted applause, before strutting back to her stone.

Stella clapped enthusiastically along with the crowd. Only yesterday, Tas had been ready to confront Bianca – throw it all away. But now look at her! She had the whole Gathering cheering her on. Stella's heart swelled with pride. Tas was made for this trial – she'd done brilliantly.

Not all the performances went as well as hers. One of the Rain Callers unleashed a solid deluge that raised howls of protest from the crowd. The grass became a muddy quagmire as people scrambled to escape the over-enthusiastic downpour.

The following girl couldn't convince her cloud to rain at all. It seemed to have stage-fright – just kept darting back to the edge of the circle, to hide behind the stone. Probably it had gone fine when they'd practised, but that was *a lot* different than doing it in front of masses of people.

Stella really felt for them. Especially when Velda wouldn't let them leave. The girl clearly just wanted to disappear, but instead she had to stay there, trying to comfort her anxious cloud, as the performance carried on without them.

The Sun Weavers were next up, which was a welcome relief for the people who'd got properly soaked – they steamed gently in the baking heat. Stella turned her face to the sky and closed her eyes, enjoying the kiss of sunlight on her cheeks; letting the glow fill her with hope.

Autumn was largely represented by Verdure Weavers, though there were a couple of Wind Whistlers too – they seemed to be divided by season according to their favoured winds.

Magnus was amazing. When Stella had practised with him, she'd grown heather. Magnus had said that would be easy, because it grew naturally here in Shetland.

But now? He wasn't going for easy.

Briar floated in the centre of the circle, blushing like a peach at all the attention. At a nod from Magnus, he began to monsoon – a solid wall of steaming tropical rain, falling straight as stair-rods. In minutes, a lush tropical garden burst out of the barren patch of ground – shiny spears of green leaves and sprawling vines adorned with flamboyant flowers. A small palm tree arched upwards, its leaves unfolding like feathers. It looked magical, and entirely out of place on a Shetland hillside.

Only thing missing is parrots, thought Stella, with glee.

Two of the other Verdure Weavers did well too, but Magnus was definitely the best of the group. Stella was pretty sure he'd make it into the third trial, whether his mum liked it or not.

The first performer for winter was Flynn, the Wind Whistler who'd sneered at Stella at the opening ceremony. Stella hoped he did badly.

As he walked forward into the circle, a grey behemoth of cloud loomed over the crest of the hill. A whisper of concern rippled around the crowd and umbrellas began to appear again. The air grew heavy with the grey scent of storm.

Smells like thunder, thought Stella, glancing at Nimbus. He'd shaded to a dark graphite grey that matched the sky above. *No joining in! Save it for our turn. Okay?*

Flynn was a *Wind* Whistler, so what was he up to?

He stretched his mouth wide in a strange frog-like expression and let out a sharp trill. The wind shrieked an answer, streaking up the hill from the water. The icy wind whisked over the gathered crowd, whipping hats off heads and turning umbrellas inside out.

Flynn turned slowly, making certain he'd got everyone's attention, then pursed his lips and blasted out a series of deafening whistles. Above him, the storm cloud divided into sharp-edged triangles. He was wielding the wind like a sword!

Nimbus dropped to hug the ground. *Good idea. Stay there.*

She was glad when Flynn's routine came to an end.

It was almost her turn – just Neve to go, then she and Nimbus would be up.

"I'm looking forward to seeing you fail," whispered Bianca, from behind her.

Twenty-Four

FLASH FREEZE

STELLA turned and scowled at Bianca. "We're not *going* to fail."

Bianca smiled. "Not what I heard."

Stella gritted her teeth. *She's trying to rattle you. Just ignore it.*

She glanced down. How Nimbus was resisting thundering at Bianca, she had no idea, but she was grateful.

"Good luck catching another cloud," said Neve. "You're going to need one."

Stella whirled to face her, but it was too late to answer back. Neve was already stepping forward. Velda greeted her with a smile.

Stella glared at the pair of them, until Velda glanced in her direction. She flicked her gaze down to Nimbus.

I'm not letting Velda take you, Nimbus. No matter what.

In the centre of the circle, Neve's dress sparkled like diamonds as she twirled on the spot. Snow began to dance like petals through the air.

Stella's turn came too fast. In no time, Neve was flouncing back towards her, a smug smile on her face. Stella ignored Neve and focused on Velda, waiting for her cue.

Velda nodded.

"Say goodbye to your cloud," said Bianca quietly, so that only Stella would hear.

It was like a knife between her ribs, but Stella couldn't react. Not now. Lightning needed calm. Calm fury. Not even a hint of jittery or distracted.

She set her jaw and walked forward, Nimbus at her side.

She was dimly aware of Tas to her left, and Magnus, standing still as a tree to her right, but she blocked out both of them, focusing only on Nimbus.

You need to stay in control, okay? Perfect aim. Single bolt.

"Lightning!" announced Velda, loudly. "You may wish to stand a bit further back for this one."

An expectant hush fell over the crowd. Nobody moved.

"Very well," said Velda. "Let's hope she's been practising her aim." She leant closer to Stella. "If you hit *anyone*, with so much as a *spark*," she said softly, "you can consider that a *fail*." Velda stepped away, leaving Stella standing alone.

At a nod from Stella, Nimbus took his position in the centre and rose a little higher.

Stella scanned the circle of apprentices and the curious faces behind them with unease. They were too close. They'd never done lightning with so many people close by. What if they hurt someone?

Just do it like we practised on the beach.

"Um . . ." She cleared her throat. "Nimbus needs something to aim for?"

Velda rolled her eyes and stepped back into the circle. "She needs someone to aim for . . ." she proclaimed loudly. "Would anyone like to volunteer? Perhaps you, sir? Or you, madam? No?" There was a ripple of nervous laughter.

"Not someone," said Stella. "Some*thing*."

Velda sighed dramatically, as though Stella was being intensely demanding. "Very well. You can aim for *this*," she said. She pointed at the small palm tree Magnus had grown.

Stella's heart sank. She looked across at Magnus. He gave a resigned shrug.

The small patch of tropical garden was looking a bit frostbitten after Neve's performance, but it was still beautiful.

Oh, Magnus. I'm sorry.

Velda stepped back again and Stella zeroed in on Nimbus. He was still all pale and fluffy, but it was time for that to change.

Right now, I'm thinking of people who steal clouds, Stella told Nimbus.

She let the silent fury build inside her – words unspoken, outrage, pain.

Nimbus darkened to grey.

The sea witch with her slaves. Velda with her scheming. Neve and Bianca, too.

Nimbus let out a deafening clap of thunder. It ricocheted around the stones and rumbled away across the hillside.

Why do they have all the power?

Enough! Nimbus, you're my family. We're not letting anyone steal you.

Nimbus paled slightly.

"No!" exclaimed Stella, raising a mutter from the onlookers.

They've promised to take you away.

Are we going to let that happen?

Stella closed her eyes and felt the fury build inside her, like a white-hot fire.

It's not just wrong. It's CRUEL!

There was a sudden wasp's nest buzz, and the sharp smell of electricity prickled through the air. Stella opened her eyes. Nimbus was flickering white and blue.

She kept the memories coming, one on top of another:

'Dangerous!'

The strobing flashes resolved into crackling sparks.

'Outlawed!'

Fine tendrils of lightning began to climb out of the furious thundercloud, threading their way higher, searching for the clouds above.

'Say goodbye to your cloud!'

The overcast sky flashed and boomed with sympathetic rage, lending them power.

Stella waited as long as she dared, then pointed.

"Fire!"

Lightning crashed down, blinding bright.

Hot sand spattered Stella and she skipped back, hands up to protect her face.

Too close!

The thunder rolled away across the sky, crashing and booming, out into the distance, leaving a shocked silence behind.

Stella took a breath, dropped her hands, and looked around anxiously. Pale faces stared back at her. Smoke from the singed palm leaves drifted over the frozen crowd, but no one was screaming; no one was hurt.

Phew.

Nimbus faded to a murky purple and waited, just like they'd practised.

Stella stepped forward and crouched by the base of the tree, dusted the sand away carefully, then wrapped her sleeve around her hand and pulled.

The lightning glass came free in one piece. A fragile shard of fused sand. One clean bolt. She held it high so it caught the light.

A huge cheer rose around her, followed by a thunderous wave of applause.

Nimbus drifted over to her and settled around her shoulders, exhausted.

We did it, Nimbus.

Her fury cooled into a trembling thrill of success.

Velda stepped forward and shooed Stella back to her place. She raised an arm and the crowd simmered down. "A lively display of fury and destruction there. Did anyone think to bring a fire extinguisher?"

Laughter broke out and the elation slipped away, leaving a wobbly tiredness in its wake. Stella sagged back against the cool stone. She looked across at Magnus, but he was staring at his feet. He looked crushed.

"Happily, our next apprentice is well equipped to put out any fire," said Velda, raising another laugh from the crowd. "Taking the trials with *two* winter clouds, one old familiar and one newly captured."

Captured? The word jarred.

You don't capture clouds, they choose you, thought Stella, glowering at Bianca.

"A cool-headed contrast to the last performance," continued Velda. "Bianca! Would you mind?" She pointed at the smouldering garden, inviting Bianca to put things right.

Unlike her teammate, Bianca was wearing pale blue trousers and a white shirt. They looked unnaturally bright and neat against the ragtag backdrop of the watching crowd. She walked confidently into the circle and quieted her audience with a raised hand.

Like a mini version of Velda.

The two clouds followed her into the circle. One of them gliding smoothly, under perfect control. The other erratic, bouncing higher and lower, sparkling with frost.

Tas caught Stella's eye from across the circle. She was miming something with wide-eyed excitement, but Stella couldn't tell what she was trying to say.

Bianca stood right in the centre, with her clouds directly over her head. She raised a hand and made a swift dusting motion at the palm tree. Sleet streaked out of the agitated cloud, dousing the smouldering leaves. There was a soft hiss and a column of smoke rose out of the ruined garden. Uncertain clapping started, but rapidly petered out as Bianca raised both arms above her head and posed like a gymnast.

Bianca muttered something to her second cloud. It swelled, towering up in a great white concertina above her, then squished suddenly flat, as though someone had stepped on it. Stella started in surprise, then began to laugh.

It had a dumped a snowdrift. Right on Bianca's head!

Instant snowman! Something had definitely gone wrong. Stella put her hand over her mouth and glanced at Nimbus in delight. He'd shaded to a mirthful orange – he was enjoying this as much as she was.

Bianca stepped out of the snowdrift and shook the snow off herself; angry as a cat. She threw a sharp glance at Velda, who gave an impassive nod: continue.

Bianca raised a threatening finger at her cloud. "Get down here!" She pointed fiercely at the ground, but the cloud didn't come any closer.

She glanced at her mentor again, but Velda just watched, her mouth a thin line of disapproval.

Stella couldn't hear what Bianca hissed after that, but it was obvious she was giving her cloud a serious talking to. The cloud didn't like it at all. He abruptly dropped a silver torrent of rain.

Bianca was a picture of silent fury, her fists clenched at her sides, her mouth open to shout. The cloud gave a shudder and detached itself from the rain with a sharp *crack*. And then Stella realised – it wasn't rain, it was ice.

Bianca was *frozen solid*!

A perfect ice sculpture, solid and glistening.

There was a heartbeat of silence, before all hell broke loose.

Twenty-Five

SEEDS OF WINTER

THE cloud sped away down the hill, intent on escape. *Tas was right! It wasn't Bianca's cloud!*

Stella watched it go, but a shout brought her back to the chaos unfolding in the stone circle. Bianca started to topple, like a falling statue. Velda leapt forward and caught her.

Would she have shattered otherwise? The thought made Stella's stomach turn.

Velda lowered her rigid apprentice carefully to the ground. Farah came rushing forward, her gown blazing gold, heat rippling off her in waves. Ilana followed, sweeping her hand in a wide circle. A willow screen sprouted with a hurried rustle, hiding them from sight. Bianca's original cloud darted anxiously to and fro, overhead.

Could Farah thaw out a whole person? Stella hoped so. Bianca might be horrible, but she wouldn't wish her dead.

Stella looked around for Tas, but she wasn't by her stone any more. *Where are you, Tas?* The fugitive cloud had disappeared in the direction of the house. *Maybe she followed it?*

Ilana appeared from behind the willow. Her voice cut across the loud chatter. "All apprentices back to the hall! Now!"

Tamar appeared furtively at Stella's side. "Come," she said, putting an arm round Stella's shoulder. "Let's get you out of here."

They pushed their way through the press of onlookers, many of them still craning to see into the circle.

"Best not to be here, now," said Tamar, quietly. "Don't want people thinking *you* had anything to do with that. You didn't, did you?"

Stella gaped at her. "No! Of course not! Do you really think I'd—"

"No! It was only a thought!" blustered Tamar. "But if I wondered, you can bet other people did, too. It's no secret that Bianca's a difficult character – I wouldn't have blamed you."

Stella pulled away in horror. "How can you say that?!"

Nimbus let out a low rumble and the crowd around them backed away.

"Great," said Tamar. "So much for a quiet exit. Always with the drama—"

"Tamar, it's not just a drama! Bianca might die!"

"Unlikely!" snorted Tamar.

Stella couldn't take any more of Tamar right now. She took advantage of the sudden gap in the crowd and ran.

"Nobody's going to die," Tamar shouted after her. "Farah's right there!"

A couple of people gave Stella startled looks as she ran past, but none of them tried to stop her. She sprinted round the garden wall and bounded up the steps through the front gate. Magnus was there. He looked as shaken as she felt.

"That was awful!" she said.

"Yeah."

The Ice Weavers appeared through the gate, all of them clustered around Neve, competing to comfort her. They fell quiet as they passed Stella. She didn't make eye contact with them, but she could feel them glaring. They disappeared through the front door and Stella let out a breath. "They all think I did it," she said.

Magnus shot her an anxious look from under his fringe. "You didn't, did you?"

"Seriously? You too?!" exclaimed Stella. Nimbus shaded to an indignant purple and moved closer to her.

Magnus held his hands up nervously and took a step back.

Velda chose that moment to appear through the gate, along with two guards. She took in the scene in an instant. "Magnus? Inside, now!" she snapped.

Magnus bolted for the door without a backward glance and Stella's heart plummeted.

"Stella, you will wait in the great hall with the other apprentices," said Velda. "Choose a spot far away from my son."

"I wasn't—"

Velda held up a hand and pointed silently to the front door. Stella hung her head and made her way up the path.

* * *

It was a long anxious wait in the great hall. No chairs had been set out – everyone was just clustered in small groups. The air frothed with gossip.

Tas came in a while after everyone else. She didn't spot Stella – just made her way over to the far corner and slid down to sit on the floor. She looked utterly dejected. Stella hurried over to join her. As she sat down, Tas gave a sad smile and shuffled a bit closer.

"At least it got away," she said.

"What do you mean?"

"Bianca's cloud. It escaped."

"You think she'd trapped it, somehow?"

Tas nodded. "Did it look like it was happy to you?"

"No." Stella shook her head. "And I did think it was weird when Velda talked about *capturing* it."

"Wasn't Arca, though," said Tas, her eyes brimming. "He would have come back to me, otherwise."

"But that's a good thing!" insisted Stella. "Means you'll definitely get him back after the trials."

"You think?" said Tassa. She looked around the hall, as though committing it to memory.

"I don't just think, I know!" exclaimed Stella. "You stormed that trial! You're a proper performer – rained all over everybody *and* made them laugh about it!"

Tassa wiped her eyes and smiled. "You reckon they enjoyed it?"

"They loved it! In fact—"

A loud banging interrupted her. Everyone turned towards the double doors. Velda and four other council members had entered the hall, their faces serious.

Velda stepped forward and a hush fell over the hall. "You all saw what happened to Bianca," she said. There was a shuffling of feet and a few people nodded.

"I'm sure you'll all be *relieved* to know that Bianca is going to make a full recovery," said Velda. "And, in the interests of fairness, she *will* be taking part in the third and final trial."

Stella groaned. *Fair? How is that fair?*

Tassa gave a soft snort. "Surprise . . ."

"We have determined that the flash freeze was in no way her fault. Someone *tampered* with Bianca's cloud."

Except it's not her cloud. Otherwise, why would it want to escape?

It was all Stella could do, not to blurt it out in front of everyone. But Farah's advice rang loud in her head. *You can't tell anyone – not without proof.*

"We have completed the search of your rooms," announced Velda, nodding at the two uniformed guards behind her.

A discontented mutter of conversation swept around the room. Stella scowled – the guards had been going through their stuff? Looking for what?

Velda held up a large orange rucksack and Stella's heart sank.

It was Tas's.

"We have found the person responsible for Bianca's misadventure," announced Velda. "It was *Stella*."

Stella scrambled to her feet, her heart racing. A circle was rapidly opening around her and Tassa, as the other apprentices backed away.

"It wasn't me!"

Nimbus lifted from her shoulders and turned a thunderous purple. It was so tempting to let him spark up, but she mustn't. It would only prove them right.

Stella's throat knotted as she stared at Tas's bag.

Tas was her only friend. But she couldn't take the blame for this! She'd lose Nimbus. She shook her head, trapped.

The two guards stepped forward from behind Velda, clearly intending to march her out of the hall. The sight of them filled Stella with panic. "It wasn't me!" she shouted. Nimbus echoed her with a low growl.

The room went suddenly silent.

"Then perhaps you'd like to explain how this came to be on your bed?" said Velda, shaking the bag at Stella. She opened the top and pulled out a blue bottle.

"*Seeds of winter!*" she said, triumphantly.

Tas got to her feet; her eyes steely with determination. She gave Stella's hand a quick squeeze.

Velda stared around the hall. "Would anybody like to tell me what happens when seeds of winter are given to an ice cloud?"

There was a lot of whispering.

"Anybody?" said Velda staring around the apprentices. Nobody answered. "Flash freeze!" she said. "The idea that an apprentice would *maliciously* feed these to Bianca's cloud before the trial . . ."

Everyone was staring at Stella again, hard enough to make her skin prickle.

Tas let go of Stella's hand, stretched expansively, and yawned. "I hope none of you are buying this rubbish. You really believe Stella did this?"

In a flash, all eyes turned to her and Stella wilted in relief.

Velda drew herself up tall. "We've *all* seen what Stella is—"

"Get real!" interrupted Tas. "This is the girl who sleeps with the rule-book under her pillow! I should know. I have to listen to her snoring . . ."

There was a ripple of laughter, quickly stifled.

"It was me. I fed the seeds to Bianca's cloud."

"This was a direct attack on another apprentice," said Velda, still looking at Stella. "An automatic expulsion from the trials."

"Oh, but don't you want to know *why* I did it?" said Tassa, spreading her hands wide and looking around. "Maybe you're not

225

asking, because you already know?" She was performing for the crowd, now.

The guards began to push their way forward, but people weren't moving out of the way – they were too riveted by the unfolding drama.

Tas tilted her head and raised her eyebrows as though expecting an answer. When none came, she shrugged. "I did it because Bianca is a bully and a liar. Just. Like. YOU!" She pointed a finger at Velda and smiled brightly.

There was a collective gasp and Stella looked at Tas in awe.

"You want to *join* your friend?" boomed Velda. "So be it. *Both* of you are expelled from the trials."

"Stella had nothing to do with it. It's my bag," announced Tassa. "I left it on her bed this morning."

The guards were getting close now. Tas skipped sideways and began to weave between groups of apprentices.

"If you search," she called, "I mean *actually* search, properly, the bag's got my name sewn into the pocket." She dodged behind the long curtains at the side of the hall, popped out further along and scampered up the steps onto the stage. "Probably not the best place to hide stuff," she said in a comedic whisper. "But I wasn't planning on getting caught . . ."

Stella saw a few faces bright with admiration – Tas and Stella weren't the only ones Bianca and Neve had been picking on. There were more than a handful of people who'd be glad to see Bianca get her comeuppance, even if it *had* massively backfired.

Tas ran to the centre of the stage, taking Velda's usual spot, and looked out at the crowd. "FYI people, seeds of winter *don't* cause a flash freeze," she announced. "Not unless your cloud hates you. All they do is power it up to do what it WANTS!"

"Bring her here!" barked Velda.

The guards blundered up onto the stage, but Tas jumped lightly off the front before they could reach her, leaving them battling a determined rainstorm. Drench was living up to his name.

One of the council elders took the bag from Velda, undid the flap on the pocket, and squinted inside it. She nodded and raised her eyebrows at Velda.

Velda's face contorted in rage. "Tassa! Out!" she shrieked. "Fetch your things and get out of Wind House!"

One of the guards stepped forward to take Stella's arm, but Velda shook her head, her eyes burning with frustration. "Not her."

For now, Stella was in the clear.

Tas skipped in and out of knots of apprentices, making fools of the guards. Stella watched, perfectly split between love and despair.

"Thought for the day," shouted Tas over the hubbub. "How did Bianca catch a cloud that hates her?" She held up her hands and stared around, challenging anyone to give a good answer.

She lingered too long and the guards caught her by the elbows. They hurried Tas to the door, her feet barely touching the floor. "Think on it, people!" she called over her shoulder. Velda grabbed her roughly by the collar and marched her out of sight.

Twenty-Six

A WEB OF LIES

STELLA had been hoping to give Tas a hug before she left, but the corridor upstairs was quiet. She padded along it with a sinking feeling. The door to their room was ajar. She pushed it, and it swung open with a low creak.

Tas's bed was neatly made. There was nothing on the floor. Stella's copy of *The Weather Book* sat alone on the chest of drawers.

The room looked so bare without Tas's mess; without Tas.

Stella beckoned Nimbus inside, then pushed the door closed and sat down on her bed. Something crinkled. She pulled back the blanket and found a hastily scribbled note.

Give them a show, Sparky. And hold tight to that cloud of yours. I bet your parents will love him. Stay stormy! T x

A tear landed on the paper, making the ink blur. Stella wiped her face on her sleeve, then carefully blotted the note dry. She slid it under her pillow and curled up on the bed. How could things get any worse?

Her best friend was gone.

The Quest was *tomorrow*.

And Mum and Dad were due to turn up at any moment.

She could just picture Mum's face if she found out about lightning weaving. Maximum worried. And that would be followed by a hard: "No."

Not even Dad will be able to talk her round, thought Stella miserably. *He might even agree with her.*

What would she do, if Mum and Dad tried to drag her away?

Nimbus settled on the blanket next to her. He'd turned twilight blue. It matched her mood exactly. "It'll be alright," she said, trying to reassure him. But she didn't believe it. Nimbus could tell – he nestled in closer.

Right now, she felt anything but 'sparky'.

"Drippy, more like?" she said, with a sad hiccup of laughter.

If only Tas was here. She made everything feel possible.

Nimbus lifted off the bed, but he didn't settle on the wardrobe this time. Instead, he bumped softly against the window.

Stella sat up. "What?"

Nimbus bounced off the glass again.

Stella frowned briefly, before realising what he meant. "The roof . . ."

Stay stormy.

"You're right. Tas wouldn't be in here moping, would she?" Stella bit her lip and looked at Nimbus. "And it *is* easier to think out there."

Nimbus bobbed and Stella stood up.

She unlatched the window. The evening air smelt green and full of promise. Above the rooftops, the simmer dim glowed – a peachy golden twilight.

Stella clambered out into the lead gulley. It felt good to be doing *something*, even if she wasn't yet sure what. She pulled the window closed and began to edge her way along towards the flat roof. At least their new room was nearer the end – not as far to go.

She'd got halfway there before she realised Nimbus wasn't with her. He was floating out above the courtyard.

"Nimbus!" she hissed. "Come back!"

Nimbus didn't move.

What if somebody spots him?

She glanced down and gasped. In the centre of the courtyard was a cloud – not moving; not doing anything; just sitting there on the ground, like someone had dropped it.

The escaped cloud.

Stella glanced at the iron ladder Tas had pointed out. Some sort of very basic fire escape, she guessed. It looked solid, but not easy to get onto.

Tas did it, she reminded herself.

Stella eased herself up until she was straddling the wall. She wriggled round until she had both feet firmly on the first rung of the ladder and looked down.

Mistake! Stella's fingers locked around the cold metal.

She closed her eyes and tried to quell the churning in her stomach, then began to climb down, as steadily as she could, by touch alone. One rung, slide, another rung, slide – hurried by the thought that someone else might find the cloud first.

At last, her toe met solid ground. She opened her eyes to see Nimbus swooping down to join her.

The other cloud still hadn't moved.

Stella moved slowly, so as not to startle him, but the gravel crunched. The cloud jolted and lifted a little way off the ground.

"Shh, shh," soothed Stella. "It's only me . . . and Nimbus. He's nice, too."

She held up her hands and edged forward, Nimbus at her side.

The cloud lunged towards them and loosed a spatter of sleet. Stella flinched back and motioned for Nimbus to stay back, too.

No way she wanted to get turned into a human ice pop. Especially when nobody knew where she was.

But now, it was a stand-off. She didn't dare get too close. Going to fetch Farah didn't feel wise either. By the time she dragged her back here, the cloud might be gone.

After a minute, Nimbus grew tired of waiting and began to drift slowly forward. The cloud didn't react, so Stella risked moving a couple of steps nearer.

"We just want to make sure you're okay," she said softly. "That's all."

The cloud didn't look okay – not at all. Its surface boiled with shimmering fractals of ice and every movement was jerky and erratic.

Seeds of winter. But that doesn't change who you are, does it?

"It seemed like Bianca was being pretty mean to you," she said softly. "Is that what made you cross?"

The cloud darkened and contracted into a tight ball.

Stella nodded. "Nimbus gets annoyed with *me* sometimes, too. Though he mostly just rains on me."

Nimbus turned apricot orange and drifted back towards her.

I didn't mean now!

There was a loud bang as a door on the other side of the courtyard flew open, and Stella's heart quickened. *I'm not meant to be here.* She sprang back towards the great hall, ducking into the shadow of a stone buttress.

Final warning, said Ilana, in her head.

Stella made sure Nimbus was out of sight, then peeked round the edge.

It was Velda.

As she approached, fat flakes of snow began to fall out of the little cloud – a steady tumbling flurry of white that settled soft as feathers on the ground.

"There you are . . ." said Velda. "I thought we might have lost you, this time."

Stella's eyes widened. *This time.* The cloud had tried to escape before?

Velda reached into her coat and pulled a fine mesh of silver out of an inside pocket. A shiver crept up Stella's spine. She'd seen one of those before, during the sea witch battle – a cloud-catching net. Tamar had one.

But Tamar would never use it on a weather weaving cloud. She was sure of that.

Velda's hand shot forwards and the net swept wide in a shimmering arc. It stuck to the cloud like cobwebs to a fly. The little cloud pressed himself to the ground, but Velda hauled him towards her, the net tightening as she pulled. "Did you think I'd just let you go? You've got a job to do."

He's terrified, poor thing!

"As for freezing Bianca," said Velda. "You should know that I'm very, *very* displeased."

The cloud made one last desperate dive for the ground, bulging against the net, but Velda yanked him back. "You're making it worse for yourself. There *is* no escape."

Horror flooded through Stella, making her legs tremble. What was Velda going to do to him?

Velda gathered the loose ends of the net in her hand and strode towards the outbuildings, towing the little cloud behind her.

In the centre of the courtyard, surrounded by a perfect circle of snow, something glittered on the ground.

A small silver charm bracelet.

* * *

"Don't you see? This is the proof! Tas was right!" yelled Stella.

Farah's face was blank with shock, but Tamar was already on her feet.

She'd been sitting on the sofa deep in conversation with Farah when Stella burst in, but she recognised an emergency.

Stella held up the bracelet and shook it, the tiny weather charms glinting and jingling. "It was Arca. He came back to look for Tas. He promised he would. And he recognised *this*! She lost it in the courtyard."

Tamar stabbed a finger at Stella. "I told you! I told you, didn't I? I knew Velda was up to no good!"

"*Yes*, you were *right* . . ." said Stella, impatiently. "But, hurry! We've got to help him."

Farah stood up and reached for her robes. "I'll assemble the elders."

"No, we've got to go, now!" said Stella, urgently. "Velda netted him. She's going to do something horrible to him." She opened the door.

"Perfect," said Tamar grimly. "We'll catch her in the act!"

Stella made a beeline for the back door and sprinted across the courtyard. She glanced back. Tamar was only a pace behind. Farah appeared at the back door with Ilana and one of the Ice Weavers.

Stella rushed over to the building Velda had entered, and burst inside. "There she is!" she blurted. "Stop her!"

"Stop me?" said Velda, raising her eyebrows. "Stop me doing what?"

"Coercing clouds," said Tamar, stepping through the door, her tone grim. "Trapping them, threatening them, stealing their free will."

Farah and the two council elders followed her inside, their faces stern.

"Ah, Tamar," said Velda. "Still so bitter."

Stella frowned. Why wasn't she worried? Were they too late?

"Where's Arca?" she demanded. "The cloud you trapped! What have you done with him?"

"Arca?" Velda smiled. "Oh, you mean Bianca's cloud? I think there must be some confusion."

"Where is he? I want to see him," insisted Stella.

Velda gave a curious frown. "Why? He's right here." She drew a hand towards her and the little cloud nosed slowly into sight from a dark corner.

Velda looked at the little cloud fondly. "Come here," she said, stretching a hand out. The cloud made his way to her side. She ruffled her fingers through him affectionately.

"Arca, we're here to rescue you," said Stella, beckoning urgently.

Nimbus flew round behind the little cloud, trying to herd him towards the door, but Arca just hung there, completely passive.

"You don't need rescuing, do you?" said Velda.

Stella's mouth dropped open. "You're controlling him!"

"Well, of course! Control is important, as you well know. *Especially* with over-powered clouds." She levelled her gaze at Nimbus, who wisely darted back to Stella's side.

Velda turned to the council elders and bowed her head respectfully. "I thought it best to keep Bianca's cloud company until he recovers," she explained. "Seeds of winter take a while to wear off. And as we saw today, the effects can be . . . appalling." She nodded at the little cloud and pointed to the corner. "Back you go." Arca drifted back into the shadows.

Stella gaped. What had Velda done to him?

Velda shook her head and gave Stella a sympathetic smile. "What *has* Tassa been filling your head with, I wonder?" She looked at Tamar and her eyes took on an icy glint. "I *suggest* you leave now, unless you've anything else to add?"

Tamar shook her head stiffly, her lips tight with frustration. The council elders glared at her; their faces stiff with disapproval. Tamar turned towards Farah, but Farah refused to meet her eyes.

As Stella followed Tamar outside, she could already hear Velda weaving her web of lies. "Unwise to let Tamar stay . . . still holds a grudge . . . an embarrassment, really . . ."

Then the door closed on the conversation, shutting Tamar and Stella outside.

Twenty-Seven

ALL GROWN UP?

"I WASN'T making it up," said Stella. "I promise!"

Tamar patted her shoulder. "I know you weren't. And you did the right thing, coming to find us. There's definitely something wrong with that cloud. Keeping it company? Pah!" She shook her head in disgust.

"Do you know how she's controlling it?"

Tamar shook her head. "If I knew that, I'd set it free in a heartbeat."

Stella looked back at the closed door. "Are you sure Farah is on our side?"

Tamar sighed. "She is. I'd trust her with my life. But she can't just go flinging accusations around. To bring it to the council, she needs cold hard proof. This will already cause her no end of trouble."

She looked at Stella and pursed her lips.

"What?"

Tamar sighed. "We have another problem."

Another problem? Stella couldn't take any more problems, right now.

"Your parents are here."

Stella froze. Her brain just stopped.

"They're down at the jetty with your grandpa. They were more than a bit agitated to find you weren't *with* him. So, I need you to come down and reassure them that you're fine." Tamar blew her cheeks out, as though parents were the most inconvenient thing in the world.

Stella stared at Tamar. She'd missed Mum and Dad so much when they first left; counted the days until they'd come back. But everything was different now. Complicated. And she wasn't fine. Not even close.

"Have you told them about weather weaving?" she said.

"Your grandpa filled them in on what he knows," said Tamar, raising an eyebrow. "Didn't seem any point in denying it. We need them onside."

Stella nodded. "And how did they take it?"

Tamar shrugged. "Your dad knows all the stories, from when

he was small. He's his mother's son. Your mum, well . . . she's going to need to hear it from you."

* * *

Stella's stomach fluttered with nerves as they headed down to the jetty. She wound her fingers into knots. What would she say to them? How would they react? What if they wanted to take her away from here, away from Nimbus?

But when she caught sight of Dad down the other end of the jetty, all the worries flew out of her head. She took off at a sprint, hammering along the wooden planks.

"Oof!" Dad laughed, as she launched herself into his arms. "It's good to see you too!" He ruffled her hair. "How have you been, little star?"

Stella smiled up at him. "Amazing."

Mum climbed down out of their boat and joined in with the hug, sandwiching Stella in the middle. Her fears and doubts melted away – Mum and Dad! They were here. And they still loved her. And everything was going to be okay.

Dad tensed slightly. "What the . . ."

Mum turned, and Stella looked round to see Nimbus approaching cautiously along the jetty, Tamar hurrying to catch up.

Stella swallowed. "Mum, Dad?" she said. "This is Nimbus. My cloud."

* * *

The cockpit of Mum and Dad's boat was bigger than the one on *Curlew*. It had long cushioned benches all the way round. There was even space for a wooden table in the middle. Even so, it felt crowded.

Tamar and Grandpa had taken the curved seats at the back. Mum sat next to Stella, clutching her hand, and Dad was performing a very slow game of chase, following Nimbus wherever he tried to land.

"Dad, can you just let him be?" said Stella.

"I want to see if . . . is he literally like a normal cloud?" said Dad, reaching out again to try and touch Nimbus.

The little cloud lifted off the bench and floated up out of reach. He was being very patient, but Stella wasn't sure how long he'd be able to keep that up. Mum's suspicious glare wasn't helping, either.

"He's a bit like a normal cloud," said Stella. "Except he's mine. He chose me."

Mum gripped her hand a bit harder.

"Ow, Mum!" Stella pulled her hand away. "We've been learning weather magic together. And everything's fine. We're all fine. Aren't we, Grandpa?"

"Mm hm," nodded Grandpa. "Been getting on like a house on fire."

Stella caught his eye and shook her head very slightly.

Do NOT tell them about the lightning!

Grandpa gave a slight smile. He understood.

Mum was still staring at Nimbus like he might explode at any moment. Nimbus was starting to look a bit agitated. Stella stood up and crossed over to the opposite bench where Nimbus hovered. She raised her eyebrows at Dad, who took the hint and sat down by Mum.

Nimbus considered the new setup for a moment, then settled on the seat and snuggled up next to her. Mum's eyes widened.

"You don't need to worry," said Stella. "We've just got one more trial tomorrow, and then we're going home to Grandpa's."

"Trial?" said Mum.

"The Quest," nodded Tamar. "It's a proper challenge, but Stella and Nimbus are going to storm through it."

Mum's face paled. "Storm?"

Oh, no. "She just means we'll do really well," hedged Stella.

Mum didn't look at all reassured. She glanced at Grandpa, then narrowed her eyes at Tamar. Her worry coalesced into a look of determination that Stella knew all too well.

"Well, I think now we're here, we should have a good look around," said Mum firmly. "Find out a bit more about this 'Quest'. *Then* we can talk about whether Stella should be taking part."

Stella stood up abruptly. "No!"

Mum pulled her chin in, unused to having her dictates challenged. Dad put a hand on Mum's shoulder and gave Stella a warning look: *this is not how we resolve things.*

But Mum was going to spoil everything!

Stella set her jaw. "You can't just go away and *leave* me here, then come back and boss me about! You're not even meant to *be* here!"

Mum's mouth fell open. "Boss you about?"

"You don't get to decide!" said Stella. "I'm doing it. I've worked really hard for it. You can't just stop me!"

She turned and clambered quickly down the side of the boat, closely followed by Nimbus. Mum jumped to her feet. "Stella, come back here!"

"No!" said Stella. "Grown-up and independent! That's what you said when you left! And that's what I'm being!"

She stomped away down the jetty, shutting her ears to Mum's exclamations and the low warmth of Dad's voice, as he tried to calm her down.

* * *

Tamar caught her up as she got to the market. "Well, that went well . . ."

"What did you *want* me to do? Take her on a guided tour! Introduce her to Velda?"

"There's always brain-fog?" said Tamar, glancing back down the hill.

"No! I *want* them to know," blurted Stella, suddenly realising it was true. "I don't want to keep secrets from them. I just want them to stop treating me like I'm five years old!"

"Grown-up and independent?" said Tamar, with a smile.

"Yes!"

Was that so unreasonable?

Tamar twitched her eyebrows. "Well, you certainly showed them independent. Grown-up? Meh."

Stella huffed. Tamar couldn't talk! It didn't take much to make her lose her temper.

"I'll say sorry tomorrow," she said. "After the Quest."

* * *

It took about an hour for the guilt to kick in. Stella tried to hold onto feeling cross, but she couldn't. She just felt bad. They'd come all the way back to see her, only for her to yell at them. It wasn't their fault. None of this was.

It felt weird walking down through the market without Tamar or Farah, but she couldn't find Farah, and Tamar was bound to say something that would worry Mum.

No. She needed to do this on her own.

Music was drifting from the Trowie mounds – bright trills of fiddle and the jolly wheeze of an accordion. Stella hurried past, keeping her hood up and her head down. Grandpa might be friendly with the Trows, but that didn't change the stories. And most of them were warnings.

Mum jumped to her feet as she approached the boat. "Stella!"

Stella climbed up wordlessly and Mum pulled her into a hug.

"I'm sorry I shouted at you," mumbled Stella, tears starting in her eyes.

Mum squeezed her tighter. "I'm sorry, too," she said. "I should have listened, before wading in and taking over."

Stella gave a wet sniff. Mum fished a tissue out of her sleeve and handed it to her. "It's clean. I haven't used it."

"Thanks." Stella blew her nose.

Mum sat down and patted the cushion next to her. "Grandpa tells us you've been working your socks off, practising for this thing?"

Stella nodded and sat down. "We've been training every day."

"Do you think you might . . . show us?" said Mum, glancing at Dad. "I'm still not sure I understand exactly *what* you've been doing."

Dad was staring intently at Nimbus again. At least he wasn't chasing him round the cockpit this time.

What could she show them? Not lightning.

Grandpa appeared up the steps from the cabin, carrying two steaming mugs of tea. He set them down on the table and Stella raised her eyebrows at Nimbus, with a secret smile.

Stella pointed firmly at one of the mugs and Nimbus glistened briefly.

Mum looked expectantly at Stella, still waiting for the trick.

Stella picked up the mug and turned it over. The frozen block of tea fell out onto the table with a clunk. Mum and Dad gaped at it.

Stella bit her lip and Grandpa let out a low chortle of laughter.

Dad picked up the solid block of tea. He sniffed it and opened his mouth as though to taste it.

"Don't lick it!" squeaked Stella. "Your tongue will stick!"

Dad put the block of ice gingerly back in the mug. "Well, I'll be . . ." he breathed in amazement. Mum shook her head, her face covered in questions.

"We can do other stuff, too," said Stella. "But probably not on the boat?"

"Definitely not on the boat," said Grandpa. "Save it for tomorrow."

"That's not all I've been learning . . . Grandpa's been teaching me sailing stuff," said Stella, giving Dad a shy smile. "I'm his crew, now."

"Very handy she is, too," said Grandpa. "Got some salt in her veins."

A swift glance of surprise passed between Mum and Dad – probably remembering Stella's fear of deep water, then Dad beamed. "That's wonderful!"

"And I don't get nightmares about sea witches anymore," said Stella, gaining in confidence. "Hardly any." Grandpa patted her shoulder.

Mum smiled at her wistfully. "My little girl! I want to hear *everything* that's happened."

"That could take a while," grunted Grandpa, looking at his watch. "And I'm fairly sure this one's got an early start tomorrow."

Stella nodded.

There would be plenty of evenings to explain everything that had happened. A bit at a time. After they were home.

For now, it was enough that they were here.

Twenty-Eight

CALM BEFORE
THE STORM

THE following morning, Wind House was eerily quiet. It wasn't just Tassa who'd left, though she was the only one expelled. Less than half the remaining apprentices had passed the second trial. Those who didn't had packed their bags and left the house.

Now, there were only six apprentices in the great hall, including Stella. The Winter Twins, Flynn and Magnus had all made it through. There was also a girl, Chanchal – one of the Rain Callers.

She wasn't as good as Tas.

All of them were eyeing each other nervously, as they waited for their mentors to arrive. Stella couldn't take her eyes off Bianca and her two clouds.

If you didn't know Arca didn't belong with her, you'd never guess it. He was trailing her so closely, it looked like she had him on a leash.

Bianca saw her staring and made a face, so Stella looked away. Magnus gave her a cautious smile and she smiled back.

Magnus sidled over, looking nervous. "I'm sorry about yesterday. I didn't really think you did it."

"S'alright," said Stella.

"You get any sleep?" he asked.

"Not much."

"Me neither."

Stella looked at the other four apprentices. "How many people get through the Quest?" she asked. "Is it only half, like the other trials, or is there, like, one winner?"

Magnus shook his head. "Could be all of us?" he said. "Could be none of us. It's timed, so it's whoever makes it through alive before the time's up."

Stella stared at him. "People die?"

Magnus gave her a startled look and shook his head. "Not literally! No."

Stella let out a breath in relief.

"It *is* dangerous, though," said Magnus, "so we have to pair up in teams. I was thinking, maybe, if you wanted—"

The double doors opened and Velda strode in, followed by four other mentors. Stella gave Magnus a quick nod of agreement, then moved away to greet Farah.

Farah swept over and put a warm hand on her shoulder. "You're ready for this, Stella." Her tone was certain, her smile encouraging.

Stella took a deep breath and nodded. When Farah said it like that, she could almost believe it. "Let's hope so."

"I know so," said Farah. She put an arm round Stella and led her out of the great hall. Stella glanced back.

"Bianca's back. Did you see?" she whispered. "She's in there with Tas's cloud! We can't let her—"

Farah tutted and shook her head. "Let *me* worry about that," she said. "*Your* only focus is the Quest. Have you got someone to pair with?"

Stella nodded. "Magnus."

Farah's eyebrows shot up, but she didn't argue.

* * *

The path leading to the Quest course was signposted by colourful fluttering flags. Tamar was waiting for them by the first flag. She looked agitated, pacing back and forth, and her hair was poking out at all angles.

As Farah and Stella approached, she patted her hair down and smoothed her cardigan, but her mouth was tight with unspoken words.

"What's wrong?" said Stella.

"This is as close as I get," said Tamar. "After last night . . . They've banned me from attending the Quest."

Stella's face fell.

"But you've got Farah!" said Tamar, hurriedly. "She's your mentor now. Officially."

"What? Forever?" said Stella, staring at Tamar in dismay.

"No! Just for today. You don't get rid of me that easily . . ."

Stella nodded. "Okay. Good."

"But it means I can't gift you anything for the Quest." She curled her lip in frustration. "I had it all planned out but . . . that's a mentor's privilege." She looked at Farah.

Farah nodded and reached into the deep pocket of her robe. She pulled out a golden scarf and held it out to Stella. It glimmered and glowed, painting starbursts of light on her skin.

"For you," she said. "To aid you in your Quest." She smiled.

"Thank you!" Stella took the scarf. It was warm to the touch, but it dimmed as she took it from Farah.

"Find your joy," said Farah. "It's woven from the brightest summer sun. May it light the darkest places and ward off winter's bite."

Tamar took the weather bag off her shoulder and handed it to Stella. Stella slipped her head through the long strap and slung it over her shoulder.

Farah frowned. "We can't afford to bend any rules today, Tamar,"

"I'm not!" said Tamar. "It's hers. I'm just returning it to her. I gifted it to her ages ago. And I'm not sending her into the Quest without a weather bag."

Farah fixed Stella with a serious stare. "Tell me truthfully, have you used this bag before?"

Stella nodded. "Almost every day."

Farah pursed her lips and nodded. "Very well, then. That should be allowable."

Tamar hesitated for a moment, then stepped forward and took Stella's hands.

They stood there for an awkward moment, then Tamar met her eyes. "I know I've not always been the best teacher . . ." she began.

Stella shook her head. "You have!" she said.

"Shh, let me say my piece," said Tamar. "What I mean to say is, you and Nimbus belong together. You're the most naturally gifted pair I've ever had the pleasure of teaching." She gave them both a tense smile. "Trust each other, and trust yourselves. It's been an honour to bring you this far."

A ship's bell began to ring in the distance, each cold clang sending a little shiver of nerves through Stella's chest.

"Use your weather wisely," said Tamar, letting go of her hands. "And look after your partner. May the wind be at your back."

* * *

Stella looked up at the small cloud that had been assigned to her and Magnus. An 'observer' cloud, so the council could watch them. All the teams had one. She wasn't sure she liked it, but then she looked at the entrance to the course and changed her mind. The wide cave gaped like a mouth in the hillside, waiting hungrily for them. Maybe it *would* be good to have someone watching.

Velda's hand rested on a large glass sand timer, on an ornate wooden stand. Stella stared at the fine sand in the bottom of it. How long would that take to run through? An hour? Two?

There was no point in guessing. As fast as they could – that was how long the Quest would take.

"—using your weather skills only. You are not permitted to hinder each other, nor bring harm on each other. Take care of your partners. Prove your worth and your weather. Good luck."

Velda rolled up the paper she'd been reading from and smiled at the Winter Twins.

I bet she's told them about the whole course, thought Stella, with a stab of resentment.

Velda's smile faded as it panned across Stella and Magnus.

Nobody had objected to them pairing up. Well, nobody but Flynn, who got stuck with Chanchal. Stella wasn't sure who Flynn would have preferred to be partnered with – her, or Magnus? But he'd kicked up a bit of a stink about being paired with a Rain Caller.

She couldn't really imagine Flynn being happily paired with *anyone.* There was a toothy competitiveness about him. *Does not play well with others*, thought Stella, remembering one of her old school reports.

But that wasn't true of her anymore.

She looked up at Magnus and gave him a nod of encouragement.

The bell rang once more. With great ceremony, Velda turned the large glass timer over and set it down. The sand began to run through in a fine stream and as one, the apprentices ran towards the cave.

* * *

The cave funnelled back into a wide tunnel, lit by sputtering lanterns. The air smelt of peat and damp stone. Nobody spoke. The only sound was the steady drip of water and the gritty crunch of their feet on the path.

The tunnel got gradually narrower and darker, until they were walking single file. That's when the rain started.

The first Stella knew of it was a curse from up ahead, then the water was gushing at her from all directions, choking in its intensity. "Nimbus! Cloud cover!"

The bubble of cloud popped into place around her, ringing like a drum as it absorbed the pounding rain all around. Stella reached through it and pulled Magnus inside.

He coughed and snorted. "Went right up my nose."

"This is what they call rain?" said Stella, looking up at the trembling cloud cover.

"Deluge, more like," said Magnus.

"Time to try out your cloud cover, I reckon?"

Magnus wiped the water out of his eyes and looked up nervously. "Briar? Can you give Nimbus a hand?"

The cloud cover turned milky white as Briar joined in, strengthening the thin shield around them, and Magnus visibly relaxed.

"See? Not so hard," said Stella. "Let's keep moving. Nimbus? Lead the way."

The bubble of cloud bulged and elongated into a shimmering tunnel and Stella jogged forwards into it, leaving Magnus standing gaping behind her.

She glanced back and smiled at his surprise. "It's called a sky tunnel," she said. "Next level cloud cover. Just get Briar to copy Nimbus."

* * *

As the sound of the rain died away, a crackling sound filled the tunnel.

"Arctic blast!" said Magnus. "It's a classic Quest challenge – deluge followed by ice. We need to get dry. Quick! Or we'll freeze."

Stella pulled Farah's scarf out of her bag and Magnus's eyes widened. "A sunbeam scarf!" he said in awe.

Stella hung it between her two hands like she'd seen Farah do, and closed her eyes.

Joy, she thought.

Mostly she felt damp. And increasingly cold. Her teeth began to chatter. Where was joy, when you needed it?

Magnus cleared his throat softly and Stella opened her eyes.

"Can I?" he asked, holding out his hands.

Stella hesitated, but then handed him the scarf, her hands trembling with cold.

Magnus took the scarf and held it up with a look of reverence. A child-like delight crept onto his face. "I've always wanted to try one of these!"

The scarf began to glow, softly at first, then brighter and brighter, until Stella had to cover her eyes against the glare. Magnus kept it up until they were both bone dry, then let the scarf dim to a sunset glow. It was enough to keep them warm as they hurried on.

Stella strode out, straining her ears for sounds up ahead, but all she could hear was the steady drip of ice melting in the tunnel behind them. They'd lost the other teams. Had they missed a turning?

She glanced back and spotted the small observer cloud, trailing along behind Magnus. It stopped when she did, but didn't give any clue about where they were meant to go next.

"Hey," said Magnus, catching up to her. "This is yours." He held the scarf out.

Stella smiled briefly. "Hold onto it, for now," she said. "We might need it again."

Twenty-Nine

THUNDERWOOD

THE air was thick with moisture, each breath heavy in her lungs. It coated her cheeks like mist and beaded on her eyelashes. She didn't like it.

With each step forward, the dripping walls of the tunnel seemed to press closer. Stella tried hard not to imagine what it would feel like to be squashed by them.

Something rustled up ahead and she started, straining her ears to pinpoint the noise. *A rat?* Weather, she could deal with, but she hadn't banked on anything living down here.

The rustling continued. And it seemed to be coming from more than one direction. Echoes crawled along the curved stone walls. Not one creature. Lots of them . . .

Maybe it's the Trows? Stella suppressed a shudder. She did *not* want to meet them down here, in the dim twilight of the tunnels. She tugged Magnus's sleeve. "Can you hear that?"

Magnus nodded. "Sounds like verdure," he said, his toothy grin glimmering in the shadows. "My place."

The way ahead was blocked by a row of vertical bars. *Vines!* Stella realised, as Magnus easily pushed them aside. The tunnel opened into a huge cavern, swarming with plants. A shaft of sunlight shone from high overhead, illuminating the jungle below.

"I think you'd better lead for this bit," said Stella.

Magnus nodded. "Stay close," he said.

Stella trailed close behind as Magnus pushed his way forward through the dense undergrowth. The cave was alive with the sound of leaves unfurling and the constant drip of water. Huge leaves arched overhead, their fat stalks bristling with thorns. "Don't touch those," said Magnus, needlessly.

Stella snorted. "I'm not stupid."

Magnus ambled forward looking closely at one plant after another. Every now and then, he paused, to pluck a few leaves, or shake a seed head. Everything he gathered went into his pockets.

Probably he had a plan, but after a few metres moving at an excruciatingly slow pace, Stella couldn't take it anymore.

"Magnus, this isn't a field trip!"

"But these might be useful!"

"We're being timed! And the others are already ahead . . ."

She pictured the sand, slipping fast and silent through the hourglass; Velda tapping it impatiently. And Magnus wanted to meander along like they were blackberry picking?

Magnus shook his head firmly. "We can't hurry – not in here."

"But we've *got* to—"

"Look out!" Magnus yanked Stella out of the way as a plant erupted out of the earth behind them. Stella shoved it back as it reached for her face. "Argh!"

She scowled in embarrassment. *Scared of a garden shrub.*

Its red stem was still growing, splitting; like a raw network of veins. Green leaves and sprays of pale flowers erupted like silent fireworks. Magnus moved away.

As she turned to follow him, her hand began to burn. A sharp prickle at first, then a searing pain that leapt up her arm like fire. Stella yowled and Nimbus darted towards her.

"Ach! Did it get you?" said Magnus.

Nimbus wrapped himself around her shoulders, uncertain how to help. Stella cradled her hand and whimpered. There were blisters. Actual blisters! It didn't just feel like it was burning, it actually *was*.

Briar circled them, throwing up a screen of bamboo to hold back the encroaching foliage and Magnus quickly grew a small succulent plant. He plucked one of its juicy leaves and split it half, revealing a spongy gel-filled core. "Here, give me your hand."

Stella held it out, trembling with the effort of not shouting in pain. Magnus smeared the cool goo over her hand. The relief was immediate.

Stella blew softly on it, suddenly deeply grateful that Magnus knew what to do. "Thank you."

"S'alright. The aloe vera should calm it down a bit," he said. "You'll need to get it looked at when we get out, though. Looks sore."

"What kind of hell-plant *was* that?" said Stella, spreading the goop further up her wrist. Her hand still hurt, but it was definitely helping.

"*Toxicodendron vernix*," said Magnus, "commonly known as thunderwood."

"*Thunder*wood?!"

He nodded. "It's mostly the sap that's a problem. You must have snapped a stem."

"It was growing right at my face!" said Stella. "What else was I meant to do?"

Magnus shrugged.

Stella scowled up at the observer cloud, hovering high overhead. It hadn't come any closer; hadn't moved to help. It just floated there impassively, watching.

"Is there anything *else* in here I should look out for?"

Magnus looked around and pursed his lips. "Aconite, pain tree, devil's thorn, deadly nightshade . . ." He counted them off on his fingers.

"So, all these plants basically want to kill us?"

"No!" protested Magnus. "Mostly they'll just give you a skin rash. And some of them are here to help us."

There was a sharp yelp from somewhere else in the cavern. One of the other teams had fallen into a similar trap. Stella couldn't tell who it was. The dense greenery hid everything.

"Can you grow a tree?" she said. "I mean, a proper tall tree?"

* * *

From up in the branches, they could see the whole cavern. The mouth of a tunnel yawned on the very far side, but it was a long way, through a dense tangle of unfriendly plants.

Stella leant out further. A pale path ran around one side of the cave, the plants on either side shrivelled by frost. "They're ahead of us! Bianca and Neve are way ahead of us!"

She swung down out of the branches, lithe as a monkey, and called Nimbus down.

We've got to speed this up, alright?

Stella gathered her fears and sent them all to the little cloud. *Getting left behind. Failing the trial. Toxic-blooming-thunderwood!*

The sharp stinging in her hand lent urgency to her wish and Nimbus let out a driving blast of hail. It began to batter a path through the plants ahead of them.

Magnus swung down from the lowest branch and his face contorted in horror. "You can't just kill them!"

"Maybe *you* can't, but I can," said Stella. "It's faster."

Magnus winced and covered his eyes. "Don't watch, Briar."

"Are you coming or what?"

* * *

Stella did her coat all the way up and leant forward into the wind. The tunnel out of the green cavern sloped up steeply, and the rock beneath their feet was shiny and smooth. She could see light at the far end, glowing like a promise. But about halfway up, a vicious wind had begun to blow – sharp, gusty, and unpredictable. First it drove them back, then turned, to knock them off balance. Stella put a hand against the tunnel wall to keep her feet.

Too strong for Nimbus, she thought, glancing down to reassure herself that he was still there, hugging the ground.

The wind buffeted her again and she skidded backwards into Magnus.

"Any bright ideas how we get up here?" said Magnus. Briar was crawling forward, leaving a patchy trail of lichen behind him, moving even slower than usual.

Stella squinted into the wind. The gusts were too erratic to snatch – she couldn't tell where the next one would come from.

"I might, but it's risky."

Magnus flinched as another gust whipped around them, full of searing flecks of ice. "Let's hear it then?"

"Take my arm," said Stella. "No, not that one, the other one." Stella stuck out her left arm and Magnus tentatively took hold of it. "Harder than that! You're going to be my anchor," said Stella "Do NOT let go!"

Magnus nodded and his grip tightened.

Stella glanced at Nimbus, trembling along at ground level. He usually helped her with this, but she didn't want to risk it. What if he got blown away?

She shook her head, telling him to stay put, then she brought her fingers to her mouth and whistled. Sharp and clean. Loud as a sheepdog trainer.

The tunnel filled with a pipe-organ moan. A moment later, every gust was howling towards her, like a pack of wolves. Stella held up her hand, ready.

She snatched the first gust out of the air and stuffed it into the bag at her side. Not fast enough! The next gust hit, and the next, driving the pair of them further down the slope.

Maybe this was a mistake.

Magnus bent lower and wrapped his arms tight round her waist. "Use both hands!" he yelled over the howling wind.

Stella snatched gusts out of the air and stuffed them into her bag; hand over fist, her eyes streaming and her cheeks burning with cold. They seemed to be endless. A constant battering stream of screaming gales.

Finally, the air began to calm.

She carried on, until there was just one last lonely breeze, circling the tunnel like a lost ghost. She let out a slow breath and wiped her eyes. "You can let go now."

Magnus hurriedly let go and stepped back awkwardly. "That was intense," he said.

Stella nodded. "I counted twenty. I've never caught that many before. And definitely not that fast." She went to take a step and nearly fell. Her feet were anchored to the ground – wrapped in a tight mat of roots and leaves. She yanked one foot free. "Was this *you*, Briar?"

The big cloud retreated down the slope nervously.

"Good thinking!" said Stella, grinning at him. "Now we're working like a team!"

Briar blushed apple-blossom pink and set off up the tunnel with a jaunty air, leaving little sunshine splashes of buttercups behind him. Magnus smiled.

* * *

"Careful!" Stella would have walked right off the edge, if Magnus hadn't stuck his arm out to stop her. They'd arrived on a ledge of ice, above a deep pool.

The walls of this cavern shone moonlight white, but the water beneath them was black as ink. A dark mirror. She didn't want to think about how deep it might be, nor what might live down there.

Stella swallowed hard and looked around. Stalactites and stalagmites, huge towers and elegant arches – all of them made out of ice. It was beautiful, but it looked dangerous too, the light gleaming and dazzling off a thousand blades and jagged edges.

From somewhere in the cave, the soft crunch of footsteps disturbed the frozen silence. *Bianca and Neve! We're catching up!*

Stella looked around. The echo made it hard to pinpoint the sound.

"There," said Magnus, pointing.

High above them to the left, a slender arch of ice stretched high above the pool. Its sides were crested with glistening icicles, like the spine of a sea monster. The Winter Twins had just climbed up to the near end. Stella glanced down at the bottomless pool below.

Heights AND deep water.

It was like Velda was here, in her head – *What are you afraid of, Stella?*

Thirty

ON THIN ICE

"COME on," said Magnus. "We can't let those two beat us."

"No, wait!" said Stella. "There's got to be another path."

"You'll be fine," said Magnus. "Just follow me."

Stella closed her eyes and took a deep breath to steady herself. There was no scent of herbs or salt in here. No smell at all.

A crackle broke the icy silence and Stella's eyes snapped open. The Winter Twins had reached the centre of the bridge and they seemed to be having an argument. Beneath them, a blue mosaic of cracks was spreading through the glassy structure.

It was obvious from here, but they couldn't see!

"Run!" she yelled.

Neve sprinted for the far end, but Bianca didn't move. She pointed at the bridge behind her and ice streamed out of one of her clouds.

A sharp crack split the air and the bridge fractured on the near side – a narrow blue gap, rapidly forking, spreading, widening. The first half of the bridge teetered for a moment, then it toppled and fell with a huge avalanche of sound – chunks of ice tumbling and shattering, bouncing and clattering, splashing into the dark water below.

High above, Bianca looked down at Stella and smiled.

She broke it! On purpose!

Bianca turned and walked away along the narrow rib of ice, leaving Arca floating alone.

He's going to escape again! thought Stella, with a little thrill of hope.

But Bianca darted back and picked something up. A fine silver chain, with a pendant dangling at the end of it. The ice beneath her feet groaned a warning and she scampered to the far side. Arca followed as though he'd been yanked.

Stella stared after them, her mind racing.

The pendant! That's what he was following. Not Bianca.

"We're going to have to turn back," said Magnus.

"Did you see that?" said Stella.

"Yeah! They sabotaged the bridge."

"No, not that!" said Stella, then remembered who she was talking to. "Never mind."

Maybe the council had seen though? She searched the ceiling of the ice cave for their observer cloud.

Perhaps that was the proof Farah needed? That moment, right there – when Bianca towed Arca away – it wasn't right. He definitely didn't *choose* to follow her.

Stella frowned. "Where's it gone?"

"Where's what gone?"

"The council's cloud. The observer. They're meant to stay with us, aren't they?"

The last time she'd seen it had been in the green cavern. Had it even made it through the tunnel? She hadn't thought to check.

Magnus joined her in searching for it. He turned and called down the wind tunnel. "Hellooooo, we're up here!"

"What are we supposed to do now?"

Magnus shrugged. "Carry on. We can't just hang about and wait for it. I guess it'll find us again." He pointed along the ledge to the right. "There's an opening here. Another tunnel. I vote we keep moving forwards."

Stella crouched and peered into the low tunnel. Its walls glowed a cool ethereal blue, the light shining through heavy slabs of ice.

The entrance was narrow; Trow sized. Was it even part of the course?

"What if we get hurt, or lost? They won't know where we are."

Magnus bent down and edged his way inside. "If we stay here, we lose," he said. "I don't want to prove my mum right. Do you?"

No. She didn't. And she had a lot more to lose than Magnus.

"Go on then, Nimbus." She ducked into the tunnel after him.

* * *

Leaving winter behind, thought Stella in relief. The last cave had felt like Velda's space – a cathedral of ice. She wasn't sorry to be moving away from it, though she glanced back often, hoping to see the observer cloud following.

The third time she looked back, the tunnel had changed shape. She stared at it. The change was subtle, but it was definitely different – oval, rather than circular.

Yet there hadn't been a sound. And she couldn't see it moving.

"Magnus . . ."

"What?"

"I think this tunnel might be shrinking."

Magnus turned back to look and his eyes widened. He whirled to look forward again. The tunnel ahead was narrowing too, moving at a glacial pace, but inexorably closing its grip.

"Ice trap!" said Magnus. "Where's your scarf? The one Farah gave you."

"*You* had it!" exclaimed Stella.

"Oh, yeah, right." Magnus pulled it out of his pocket, wrapped it twice round his hand and closed his eyes. It began to glow softly.

"More than that!" said Stella, watching the tunnel ahead, hoping to catch it in the act.

"I can't!" admitted Magnus. "I hate tight spaces."

"Then move!" said Stella, giving him a shove.

They both hurried forward, ducking and dodging around bulges of ice, their feet slipping on the treacherous blue.

At last, they stumbled out into a rocky cave and ran forward a few metres until they were well clear of the trap. Stella bent and put her hands on her knees, trying to calm her racing heart. Behind her, the ice walls flowed slowly together until barely a gap remained.

"We could have been crushed . . ." she breathed. "Frozen to death."

"I think it would have stopped before it killed us," said Magnus, but he didn't sound sure. He peered back through the narrow gap.

Stella straightened up and they both plodded on – nowhere to go, but forward.

* * *

A soft breeze rushed past them every now and again – it smelt brackish and damp, but it didn't build or howl – just kept its own steady rhythm, in and out, like a long slow breath.

Like a sleeping giant, thought Stella, then immediately wished she hadn't. Who knew what other surprises the council had in store for them?

They emerged onto a high rocky outcrop, halfway up the wall of a huge spherical cave. In the bottom, there was a surging pool of water. High overhead was a perfect circle of sky. *Daylight!*

Nimbus scooted up towards it.

"No, Nimbus! Stay with us!"

Nimbus stopped just beneath the opening and gave a low rumble.

"I know," she said. "Me too. But Magnus and I can't get up there." The walls of the cave were sheer and curved impossibly inwards. There was no way they could climb them.

Nimbus spiralled sulkily down towards her. As he did, Stella spotted a dark opening on the far side of the cave. She turned to tell Magnus, to find he was already picking his way gingerly along the top of the outcrop. It was very narrow in places, but it looked like it would take them all the way to the other side.

There was a sudden change in pressure and Stella's ears popped. She looked down to see the water in the pool disappearing with a sucking gurgle, like someone had pulled the plug. A moment later, it rushed in again, filling the pool even higher than it had been before.

A blow hole. Stella's heart contracted in fear. She knew about blow holes. Grandpa had told her about them, amongst his many dire warnings when she first arrived. Connected to the sea by an underwater tunnel, the hole overhead carved by waves rushing in. You did *not* go swimming in them. Not unless you wanted to drown.

"Magnus, wait! It's not safe."

Magnus stopped where he was, but made no move to come back and join her. "There's a way through," he said, pointing at the archway on the far side. "We have to try."

"This can't be the way," said Stella, watching anxiously as the water surged up towards them. "There isn't any weather. I think we're lost."

Magnus shook his head and continued climbing along the outcrop. "We're not lost. We've just taken a detour," he said stubbornly. "There's always more than one route through. Trust me. We've just got to get to the other side."

Did she trust him? *Yes.*

But she didn't trust that dark water, surging in the bottom of the cave.

There wasn't really any choice though. Where was the previous fork in the path? Probably all the way back in the green cavern. Locked behind a wall of ice.

She called back down the tunnel one last time. "Observer! We're going this way. Through the sea cave!" Then she began to pick her way swiftly along the rocky ledge towards Magnus. She did *not* want to be in here if a big wave came.

They'd made it almost halfway round, when all the water disappeared in a great rush.

Stella dived for the nearest boulder and wrapped her arms around it. "Magnus, hold on to something!"

Magnus glanced back, his face slack with fear. Then the water was around her, shockingly cold, lifting her feet from under her, then dragging her down. She emerged from the surface, coughing and spluttering, and wiped the stinging salt from her eyes.

The ledge ahead was empty.

"MAGNUS!"

She looked down into the dark seething water, but there was no trace of him. It had swallowed him whole.

"Nimbus, you've got to find him. Follow him. Get him help!"

But Nimbus didn't move. Just floated above the outcrop Magnus had fallen from.

"Please, Nimbus! Hurry!"

A soft moan drifted up from below. Stella scrambled along to where Nimbus waited and peered over the edge, her heart in her mouth.

He hadn't slipped far. Too far to reach, but not all the way to the bottom. He was lying in a crumpled heap about three metres below her. Beneath him, the water surged higher, frothing white.

"Magnus? Are you hurt?"

He *was* hurt. She could see. A thin trickle of blood ran down the side of his face.

"I'm alive . . ." called Magnus. "Briar?"

A misty waterfall of cloud fell down the rockface towards him.

"You should go on without me," said Magnus.

"Not a chance," said Stella. "We're in this together."

Magnus climbed cautiously to his feet and reached up towards her. Stella stretched her arms down, but their fingers didn't quite meet. Beneath him, the water rose hungrily and lapped around his ankles, before draining away again.

How long until the next big wave came?

Every seven. That's what Grandpa said on the boat. Waves came in sets. And every seventh wave was larger.

"Seriously," he said. "Leave me here. Just tell them where to find me."

"Urgh! Stop it!" said Stella, impatiently. "Start thinking like a weather weaver."

"No," said Magnus. "You were right. This isn't part of the trial. Which means it's for real. Climb back to the tunnel at least – you'll be safer there."

"I'm not leaving you." A second smaller wave surged into the cave below them and fear raced through her veins. They didn't have long.

Thirty-One

A SENSE OF
BELONGING

"HOW are we going to get you up from there?"

Magnus winced and touched the trickle of blood on his forehead. "I don't know."

"Come on," said Stella. "You must have some other tricks in your pockets?"

The flicker of an idea crossed Magnus's face and he felt around inside his coat. "Catch," he said, and launched the seeds towards her.

Some of them hit the rock wall. A handful landed with a soft patter next to Stella.

"What do I do with these?"

"Grow them."

A tremble of doubt settled in Stella's chest. "Can't you?"

"No. My head is thumping." Magnus slid down and sat, resting his head against the slick rock. "And I've never felt less like I belonged somewhere in my whole life."

Stella scraped all the seeds into a little pile and looked up at Nimbus. *Remember?* she thought. *How it felt before? Like we've got friends. Like we belong here.*

That afternoon in the practice field was so far from this dark and echoing cave, that it made her want to cry, but she closed her eyes and willed herself back there.

Tas's dancing, Grandpa's breakfasts, Mum and Dad's hugs.

Tamar's wildness, Farah's glow.

You and me, Nimbus, you and me.

Nimbus began to rain gently.

Narrow tendrils of green curled out of the seeds, thin as threads.

Magnus belongs too. Even if he can't feel it, right now. He's our friend.

Briar crept up over the edge as though Stella had called. She smiled at him and nodded. "You too, Briar. You're our friend, too."

Briar began to rain softly alongside Nimbus, and Stella closed her eyes.

We belong to each other.

We belong to our clouds.

We belong to the land.

We belong to the sky.

The fine tendrils grew, twisting and snaking with an urgent rustle, rapidly stretching into a tangled mat of fat vines. *Thank you! Thank you, both of you.*

Stella pushed the vines over the edge, so that they hung down the rock face. "It worked," she said. "Now hurry!"

Magnus looked up at her, his face pale and strained, and nodded. He grabbed two fistfuls and hauled himself up, with a grunt of determination. With a great tearing sound, the vines ripped free and Magnus tumbled back down.

"No!" Defeat flooded Stella's chest. "Sorry. I'm sorry. I *told* you I can't do this."

"It's not your fault," said Magnus, climbing cautiously to his feet again and rubbing his shoulder. "There's nothing for them to root into."

Stella looked at the spot where the vines had torn away. Magnus was right – nothing but smooth stone, backed by round, sea-polished boulders.

"Wait! I've got an idea." she said, looking at the largest rock. "Throw me an end."

A thick vine came whipping over the edge and she grabbed it before it could slither away. *Bowline – up the hole, round the tree, down the hole.*

"Try now!" she called.

The vine tightened and creaked under Magnus's weight, but the knot held. Stella turned to see Magnus pulling himself up over the edge.

He looked worse, close up. There was a massive bruise on his forehead and blood matted in his hair.

"Let's get out of here," she said.

* * *

"We're probably too late," said Magnus, wincing as he hobbled along the narrow passage. He'd done something bad to his ankle, but there wasn't time for sympathy.

"You don't know that," insisted Stella, towing him forward by the elbow. "And it's not much further. I can smell outside air." She was sure of it. The breeze in the tunnel carried the faintest promise of meadow flowers and herbs.

Magnus put his foot down and gritted his teeth. Stella looked away, so she didn't have to see him hurting. The way out was somewhere up ahead – they just had to make it that far.

"You should—" started Magnus.

"Don't even say it," said Stella. She looped his arm over her shoulder and they pressed on grimly.

* * *

There were voices now – snatches of excited conversation and clapping, daylight slipping around the curve of the tunnel. They were so close. But as they rounded the corner, Magnus pulled up short.

A storm cloud floated in the centre of the tunnel, its surface boiling with fractals of frost. Magnus stared at it wide-eyed. "Bianca's left it here to stop us! I bet Mum put her up to this."

Stella's heart raced. It seemed likely. But if so, where was Bianca? The tunnel didn't offer any hiding places.

She lifted Magnus's arm from her shoulder and crept closer, alert for any sudden change. Nimbus glided along just above her head, ready to transform into cloud cover if she needed it.

"Arca? Is that you?" she said, softly. "It's me, Tas's friend. You remember me?"

She fished in her pocket and pulled out the little lightning charm Tas had given her, up on the roof. *Storm sisters,* she thought and held it out in front of her. A peace offering.

The little cloud shuddered, dropping a wet splatter of sleet, and shifted from side to side.

"Be careful!" whispered Magnus. "You've seen what it can do . . ."

"You don't want to hurt us," continued Stella, edging closer. "We're friends. But we need to go past you. We need to get out. Okay?"

The cloud strained to one side, apparently trying to let her past, but then swung back suddenly, making Stella skip back in alarm.

It was like he was anchored in place. Stella glanced down. A fine silver chain with a small crystal pendant lay on the ground directly beneath the cloud.

Bianca's necklace! She must have left it behind, so Arca would block the exit. Stella crouched down and reached cautiously forward.

Arca contracted into a dark grey ball and Nimbus rumbled a warning. "Shh, shh, it's okay, I just want to . . . There." Stella hooked her fingers around the crystal and pulled it towards her. Arca lunged at her.

"Stop!"

The little cloud froze.

Stella scooted backwards on her bottom, keeping tight hold of the necklace.

"What did you do?" said Magnus, his eyes fixed on the little cloud.

It was uncanny, how still it was. Every whirling snowflake stopped in place, perfectly motionless; every feather of frost stilled. But she'd bet he was still dangerous. 'Blizzard class', Tas had said – capable of freezing someone solid in seconds.

"Arca, please can you move, so we can get past?"

The little cloud seemed to wake, whirling back into motion before pressing itself up against the wall.

"It let you catch it?" said Magnus, his face bright with admiration.

Stella twitched in revulsion. It hadn't *let* her do anything. It had no choice. It was being controlled. She curled the pendant tighter in her fist.

"Come on, let's go," she said. "We've still got to finish the course."

* * *

The mouth of the tunnel was in sight, when Stella spotted Bianca. She was waiting just by the entrance. *Waiting for our time to run out*, realised Stella, *before coming back for Arca*.

She hitched Magnus's arm higher across her shoulder and trudged forward. When Bianca spotted the pair of them, she sprinted into the tunnel, but stumbled to a halt a few metres ahead of them, her eyes locked on Arca, trailing close behind them.

"Give it back," she demanded, holding out her hand.

"No way," said Stella. She tugged Magnus's arm and they headed forwards.

"It's not yours!" hissed Bianca.

"It's not yours, either!" exclaimed Stella.

"Please! You have to!"

"I don't *have* to do anything," said Stella, pushing past her.

Stella and Magnus stumbled out of the tunnel, to see a crowd of the most senior weather weavers waiting for them.

Neve darted across to Velda and yanked her sleeve. Velda's eyes widened as she focused on the bedraggled trio of apprentices standing in the mouth of the tunnel.

Behind her, Ilana's arm was raised to strike the ship's bell, but it hadn't rung yet. They would have heard it.

We made it!

Ilana smiled at Stella and brought her arm down hard, setting the great bell clanging.

A great cheer rose from the assembled weavers then – it echoed around the huge cavern like a roar, battering the walls in celebration.

Velda hurried across to them, with Farah following close behind.

"Stella stole my pendant," blurted Bianca, as Velda came near.

"I didn't *steal* anything!" yelled Stella. "You stole Tas's cloud!"

Nimbus let out a throaty rumble.

The crowd quietened abruptly and the line at the front rippled as the nearest weather weavers edged away. Neve paled and slipped backwards into the crowd.

"What nonsense is this?" said Velda, impatiently. "Hand over whatever you've stolen from Bianca."

Bianca edged out of the tunnel to stand closer to Velda. She looked scared now, her eyes darting between Arca and Velda, as though willing Velda to make everything right.

"You realise that stealing would disqualify you from the trials?" said Velda quietly, her voice icy with threat. "Give it to Bianca."

"No!"

Nimbus let out a clap of thunder.

Farah hurried up behind Velda, her eyes on Nimbus, her hands raised to placate him. "Stella! Calm yourself. I'm sure we can sort all this out."

The crowd was silent now, focused on the unfolding argument, so Stella raised her voice. "Bianca stole my friend's cloud."

"No, I didn't!"

"She used this." Stella held the pendant above her head so everyone could see, but snatched it down again as Velda moved closer.

"Don't be ridiculous," said Velda. "Bianca caught that cloud herself. She told me all about how she captured him."

Bianca gave Velda a sideways glance, but Velda was getting into her stride now. "Bianca and her clouds have performed *admirably*," she said, her voice rising, "despite Stella's continued and *malicious* vendetta against them!"

Bianca nodded enthusiastically, but there was desperation in her eyes. Perhaps Velda didn't know about the pendant?

"Tell him to do something, then," Stella challenged Bianca. "Anything. Ask him to snow. That should be easy for an Ice Weaver?"

Bianca stared at Stella and then made a great show of frowning and pointing at Arca. "Stella's done something to him. He can't hear me!" she exclaimed, with a quaver in her voice. She was a good actress.

"He can't hear *anyone*, unless they've got *this*!" proclaimed Stella. "It's trapped him."

Velda let a great sigh. "Is that so? Then let's see you try!"

The confidence in Velda's voice rattled Stella and she looked anxiously up at Arca. *Arca? I need you to snow.*

The little cloud didn't move, just hung there as though awaiting orders.

Farah frowned in consternation and Stella swallowed.

"Arca, please! Snow!"

There was a breath of waiting, then fat flakes of snow began to tumble out of the little cloud. "You see? You see!" she said.

Thank you, Arca!

Velda stared up at the little cloud, wide-eyed, and shook her head. "Oh, Bianca, what have you done?" she said, her voice heavy with condemnation.

Bianca's mouth fell open. "What? No! You can't blame me!"

Two guards stepped forward and began to frog-march Bianca away. "It wasn't me. It's not mine!"

Velda's voice boomed loud, drowning out Bianca's protests. "Be assured, this will be investigated fully. We shall not rest until we discover *how* this cloud has been enslaved in such a way. We will discover *all* those responsible."

"*VELDA* gave it to me!" Bianca's wail cut across the silence.

Up on stage, Ilana held out an arm, commanding the guards to stop.

"She said I had to stop the Storm Weavers!"

Velda locked eyes with Bianca, her expression icy, but Bianca stared back at her, unrepentant. She wasn't going to take all the blame.

Farah stepped in front of Velda and looked towards the council. "I think perhaps it would be better if someone *else* investigates this time?"

Ilana nodded and Farah held out her hand. "Stella? The stone, please."

Stella clutched the pendant to her chest. The only person who should have it was Tas. But she wasn't here.

"Promise me, you'll find a way to free him?" she said.

"I swear by the rising of the sun," said Farah, and nodded solemnly.

Stella handed her the gem.

Thirty-Two

THE RECKONING

ILANA had so many wrinkles. Her face was like an ancient map of all the expressions she'd ever made. Stella couldn't read her at all.

"Tell us again how you came to suspect this?"

"The frost roses. It's Arca's party trick – Tas taught him how to do it before he got taken away. Is she on her way back?"

Ilana tapped her pen on the table in front of her. "She should be here any time now."

"You should ask her. She was the one that figured it out. I mean, we didn't know how . . . but then I saw Bianca drop her pendant in the Quest."

"We saw," said Ilana, nodding.

"Wait, how? We'd lost our observer cloud by then."

"One Ice Weaver remains true to the council," said Ilana. "He was tasked with watching Bianca." She smiled.

"Is Velda going to jail?"

Ilana steepled her hands together. She was clearly used to asking the questions, not answering them.

"She will have to answer for her actions, yes."

"And what about the other storm clouds? Are you going to let them all go?"

Farah put a warm hand on her shoulder. "The council have a great deal to discuss," she said. "But you can be certain that the Ice Weavers will no longer go unchecked."

Stella huffed. That wasn't a proper answer.

I'll set Tamar on them, she thought. Tamar wouldn't be so diplomatic.

"What about me and Nimbus? We're good, aren't we?"

Ilana smiled, her wrinkles folding into a well-worn expression of joy. "You two were nothing short of spectacular," she said.

Stella's heart swelled with pride. Beside her, Nimbus glimmered gold.

Ilana smiled, "But you'll have to wait until the Reckoning to hear the official result." She nodded at Farah. "That'll be all, for now."

Stella stood up, but paused behind her chair. "Um . . . there's one more thing?"

Ilana blinked slowly and raised her eyebrows. "Yes?" she said.

"Can my family come? To the Reckoning?"

"Of course," said Ilana. "I expect they'll be very proud."

"Only . . . they're stuck down at the jetty," said Stella. "The guards won't let them in."

"They're not weather weavers?" said Ilana, with a slight frown.

Stella shook her head.

Farah spread her hands. "If Stella is to be a weather weaver, her family will soon be part of our world," she said, reasonably.

"Fine! Fine," said Ilana flapping her hand at one of the guards by the door. "Peter, see to it."

Stella looked at him and her eyes widened. It was the guard who'd challenged them when they'd first arrived. He looked at her, stony faced, and nodded towards the door.

* * *

As they left the house, Peter's stiff march relaxed into a loping walk and his fierce expression softened. He snuck a sideways glance at Stella. "Have you heard?" he said.

"Heard what?"

"They're going to release the storm clouds! The ones that were taken."

Stella nodded. "I hope so."

Peter's eyes danced. "I couldn't say anything inside – not when I'm on duty. We're meant to be, you know . . . impartial. But it's the best news!"

Stella smiled in surprise.

"I can't wait to get home," he continued. "My little sister's face, when she gets her cloud back. It's going to be . . ."

Unable to find the words, he held out a large hand. Stella took it, expecting a brief handshake. Instead, the guard clasped it warmly. His eyes shone with happy tears. "I want to thank you," he said, earnestly. "This is all down to you."

"Well, it wasn't just me . . ." said Stella, glancing at Farah.

Peter shook his head, silencing her.

"Thank you," he said, firmly. "From me, and from all the other families who've had clouds stolen away. I don't think you've any idea how much good you've done today."

Stella felt the blush climb from her neck all the way to the roots of her hair. "You're welcome," she said.

"Now, let's go and round up that family of yours," he said. "Tell them what a little hero you are."

Stella's heart fluttered a warning. "Er . . . maybe don't tell them *everything*?" she said. "They're new to this."

Peter nodded his understanding.

* * *

The great hall was packed. All the chairs were filled. There was even a crowd of people standing at the back. Tamar was near the front, in the seats reserved for mentors. Stella was pretty sure she wasn't meant to be there, but nobody had stopped her.

Mum, Dad and Grandpa had managed to find themselves seats about six rows back. Dad caught her eye and gave her a wave. Stella didn't feel like it would be right to wave from the stage, with everybody looking, so she just gave him a tight little smile.

She, Magnus and Flynn were seated in a row on one side of the stage. It was no surprise that Bianca and Neve weren't here. But someone else was missing.

"Do you know if Chanchal's alright?" she whispered to Magnus. He was sitting very straight and his right knee bounced up and down.

"Yeah. She's fine. I saw her being brought out."

"Did she not make it through the caves?"

Magnus shook his head. "Got tangled up in the green cavern." His tone was clipped and he wouldn't look at her.

Stella could understand it, but it still hurt. They were a team. More than that, they were friends. It wasn't *her* fault his mum was, well . . . Velda.

Stella snuck a glance at the council. They were seated on the far side of the stage, in big fancy chairs, like thrones. There were far fewer of them now. Only eight – just one Ice Weaver remained – an elegant old man in a pale blue suit.

The only Ice Weaver loyal to the council.

If he was uncomfortable sitting alone, he didn't show it – his back was straight and his expression neutral. He exuded a cool self-contained calm.

There was a collective "Ahh!" from the crowd as vines spiralled up the columns at the back of the stage. Polite applause rippled through the audience and Ilana got to her feet and walked solemnly to the centre of the stage. The hall fell silent.

"There have been some changes, as you can see." She indicated the depleted council. "I'll tell you about our plans in due course. But first, we have three young weather weavers eager to hear the results of this year's trials!"

The hall burst into applause. Stella smiled at her family, clapping more enthusiastically than anyone else.

There was a scraping of chairs, and Stella glanced sideways to see Magnus and Flynn getting to their feet. She stood up quickly, almost knocking her chair over. Why did nobody tell her this stuff?

The old weather weaver held a hand out towards the apprentices.

"Three stand before us, but two will be bound."

Only two people were through! Stella crossed her fingers behind her back.

Me and Magnus! Let it be me and Magnus.

"Flynn, you may leave the stage."

Flynn's face filled with outrage. "I was first through! The first one!"

Ilana inclined her head. "Leaving your partner behind."

Stella shared a glance with Magnus and he gave her a slight smile. Stella's heart lifted. Maybe he didn't completely hate her?

"It's not my fault she couldn't keep up!" Flynn was angry now. One of the guards took a slight step forward – a quiet threat.

"Taking care of one another. It is part of the trial," said Ilana, blinking at him sadly.

There was no arguing with her. Stella saw the realisation sink in – Flynn's face hardened, then he turned and stomped down the steps at the side of the stage. Stella didn't envy him the long walk to the back of the hall.

"Stella, Magnus?"

Stella and Magnus stepped forward together.

"You took an unconventional route through the course!" said Ilana, with a smile.

"We had to," said Magnus. "The ice bridge was broken."

"Bianca broke it," added Stella.

The elderly Ice Weaver cleared his throat. "I can confirm that."

Ilana nodded, her face giving away nothing. "The council have conferred," she said, solemnly. "We concluded that you demonstrated determination and ingenuity in finding another route through. Furthermore, your courage and care for one another was exceptional."

Stella took Magnus's hand.

"I would like to be the first to offer my congratulations," said Ilana, breaking into a smile. "Magnus and Briar, Stella and Nimbus, you are hereby bound. I declare you: weather weavers!"

The hall erupted in cheers and clapping. At a nod from Ilana, flowers began to tumble from the ceiling like confetti.

Stella lifted Magnus's hand high in the air and grinned up at Nimbus and Briar. Relief washed through her, making her giddy as a summer breeze. Dad was on his feet now, whooping and cheering.

We did it!

Thirty-Three

A SMASHING TIME

STELLA wanted to go rushing straight back to Mum and Dad as soon as the ceremony ended. Instead, she and Magnus were shepherded back into the house.

"You'll see them soon enough," said Farah, back in organising mode. "We've got a few bits of official business to tidy up before you leave. You'll both need to pack up your belongings, too."

"Can we head out to the practice ground, first?" said Magnus. "I need a breather."

Farah nodded. "You can have a little while, yes. Maybe half an hour. But after that, I'll need you both back here. Yes?"

* * *

Stella followed Magnus outside. He jogged ahead and clambered down the boulders. She watched him go, with a slight pang. Maybe he just wanted to be alone?

But Nimbus and Briar were already playing chase, up and down the slope. And Nimbus wouldn't want to be dragged away. She climbed down to their spot on the boulders.

Magnus sat with his knees up to his chest, staring out at the water.

"Do you mind me being here?" asked Stella. "Or would you rather I go?"

Magnus shuffled across to make space for her.

Stella climbed down and sat next to him. They both gazed out at Whale Firth. Fitful gusts of wind pushed shadowy paw-prints across the water. The silence between them stretched wide and deep.

"I'm sorry about your mum," said Stella, finally.

Magnus shrugged and tilted his head forward, so his fringe hid his eyes.

Stella shifted uncomfortably and thought back to what Farah had told her.

"Perhaps she started off trying to protect everyone, but it got out of hand?"

Magnus sighed. "Doesn't matter really, does it? However it started, what she was doing was wrong. I just feel a bit stupid that

I didn't even *see* it. I mean even *Bianca* was in on it. Shows you how much my mum cares about me."

"Maybe she was protecting you, by *not* telling you?"

"Well, that worked out great. Now she's locked up, along with the rest of the Ice Weavers."

"What will you do?"

Magnus shrugged and leant forward to watch Briar, coaxing flowers up out of the grass. "For now?" he said. "I'm going to stay with Silvan, my mentor. I stayed with him during training, so it won't be much different."

Stella shook her head – she didn't know who that was.

"The tall green one on the council," said Magnus. "Big beard? Vines up the walls?"

"Oh! Him!"

"Mum doesn't like him – said he's trying to turn me into a 'second-rate botanist'. But he's not. He's great."

Stella grinned. "I think you've already proved you're not a second-rate anything. You're going to be a brilliant weather weaver."

Magnus smiled bashfully. "Thanks."

They sat in friendly silence for a moment. The sharp clink of tent pegs being hammered loose drifted up over the wall from beyond the practice ground – the market being dismantled. Strange to think that this time tomorrow, Wind House would be empty again – back to looking like a desolate ruin, haunted by Trows.

"What about you?" said Magnus. "Where will you go?"

"Back home, I guess – Grandpa's is just down the hill from Tamar's, which is easy. I suppose we might get a new house, now Mum and Dad are back, but hopefully it'll still be close to Grandpa's. You could come visit if you want? Hang out with me and Tamar?"

Magnus smiled. "I'd like that."

"You know Tamar was friends with your dad?" she said. "She mentored him."

Magnus looked at her in surprise. "Really?"

She nodded. "I bet she's got some good stories."

Stella turned back to look at the view and her heart began to dance: a small boat was nosing its way along the narrow channel, followed by two clouds trailing solid curtains of rain. She clambered to her feet, and shaded her eyes. Could it be? It was!

Tas!

"I've got to run," she said.

* * *

As she reached the Trowie mounds, she saw Farah waiting on the path, Arca floating perfectly still above her head. Tas was already racing up the hill towards them. Stella flew into her arms and spun her around, in a breathless whirl of celebration.

Tas squawked, laughing. "You rescued Arca! You superstar!"

She detached herself from Stella's hug and jumped up and down in front of the little cloud, waving excitedly. "Arca? It's me! I'm here."

Stella winced slightly and took her hand. "He can't hear you, Tas. He's not free yet. He's still trapped by that stupid stone."

"Trowie gem," corrected Farah, from behind her. "We thought it best to wait until you arrived to release him, Tassa."

Tas looked up at the little cloud and her face crumpled. "Well? Do it, then! I'm here, aren't I?"

"Patience," said Farah. "We'll need a little help."

Stella squeezed Tas's hand, then spotted Grandpa, puffing his way up the hill behind her.

"Good," said Farah. "*Now* we're ready."

Stella frowned at her in confusion.

"Your grandpa's forged quite a bond with the good folk. His work team have agreed to help us."

Stella stared at Grandpa in surprise and he gave a modest shrug.

"Now?" said Tas.

Grandpa narrowed his eyes at the sunset sky and nodded. "Yes. Should be late enough for them now," he said. "Let me go and see." He went over to the nearest grassy mound and crouched to knock on the door.

* * *

A tiny woman hustled even tinier children out of the kitchen as they went inside. The room was circular, with smooth walls, and a lingering earthy smell of peat smoke. It was about the right size for Stella and Tas, but Grandpa and Farah had to stoop to come inside.

Two little men stood by a stone-topped table – they were about as tall as Stella's shoulder. Their hair was long and straggly, and their grey clothes covered in stone dust, but they both stood straight and proud. One of them was broad shouldered as a bull, his neck almost as wide as his head. He wore a leather belt, strung with tools. The other was lean and wiry, his face narrow and his eyes furtive.

Grandpa nodded a solemn greeting. "Broonie, Karl. I'd like you to meet Farah, Tassa, and Stella, my granddaughter."

Tas just stared at them, wide-eyed, so Stella quickly nodded like Grandpa had. "Pleased to meet you," she said. She gave Tas a subtle nudge.

"Yeah," said Tas. "Me too." Her usual confidence seemed to have evaporated.

Not just me that's never met a Trow, then.

Broonie, the broader of the two, turned to Farah, a hint of challenge in his dark eyes. "You need our help," he stated.

Farah nodded. "We do. This child's cloud has been snared by one of your weather gems." She set the pendant on the table in front of them. Arca followed passively, then came to a stop, floating above the table like a lost dream.

Broonie lifted his chin at the little cloud. "You're not suggesting *we* trapped him?"

Grandpa looked at Farah in alarm, but Farah shook her head.

"We don't yet know who trapped it. We are still investigating."

"Perhaps you should ask your *own* people about that?" said Karl, his smile revealing crooked brown teeth.

Farah's face darkened. "Questions *are* being asked," she said. "In the meantime, we have come here to respectfully ask for your help."

"Please help!" blurted Tas. "You've got to set him free!"

Broonie looked at her and softened slightly. "Very well."

He turned and lifted a small metal frame from the shelf behind him, put the gem in the middle of it and turned a screw to clamp it tightly in place. Then, he selected a pointed hammer from the tools at his belt. "Be ready," he said to Tas. "He may be confused. And I *don't* want a storm in my kitchen."

He lined up the hammer, took a couple of practice swings, then struck it hard.

Clink!

The gem broke, releasing a wisp of cloud that rushed upwards. Above them, Arca turned darkest grey. A sheen of ice spread across the ceiling like an exploding star. Snow began to fly.

"Call him," said Farah, urgently.

"Arca!" Tas stared up at the growing blizzard with happy tears in her eyes. "It's me, Tas! I've missed you so much."

The little cloud shuddered and paled at the sound of her voice. The snow slowed, then flew back into the cloud as though it had inhaled.

Tas held up her arms and Arca dived, clothing her in cloud. Tas closed her eyes and wrapped her arms around herself, swaying gently as though to soothe them both.

At last, she opened her eyes and looked at Broonie. "Thank you," she said. "I owe you. Seriously, if you ever need *anything*, just ask."

Farah shot her a worried glance.

Broonie inclined his head.

* * *

Grandpa herded the girls and their clouds towards Mum and Dad's boat. "They've been itching to see you," he said. "That ceremony, the Reckoning – it was really something, wasn't it?"

"Oh! I wish I'd seen it!" said Tas, hooking her arm through Stella's. "I bet you stormed the Quest, didn't you?"

"She did, at that," said Grandpa, his voice warm with pride.

Tamar was down on the jetty, hoisting crates of jars and bundles of fabric up onto the deck. She seemed to have commandeered Mum and Dad's boat to transport all her larger purchases. "There you are!" she said to Grandpa impatiently. "Are you *going* to help, or not?"

"A 'please' would be nice," said Grandpa, stooping to lift one of the heavier crates.

Tamar pulled a face. "Please," she said.

Mum reached down to help Stella and Tas up into the cockpit. "Hot chocolate?" she said. Both girls nodded eagerly. "Make that *six* mugs," called Mum down the hatch.

"So, *you* defeated a sea witch?" said Dad to Stella.

"All by herself," said Tamar. "Remarkable, given she'd barely started her training."

"You dark horse," exclaimed Tas. "You didn't tell me *that* bit!"

Mum put her hands over her face and shook her head. But she had *said* she wanted to hear everything. And secretly, Stella was enjoying making Mum gasp in alarm. It made her feel she'd been brave, when, honestly, she'd been scared silly half the time.

Tas's mentor waved from the boat behind and Tas waved back. "I'll be there in a minute," she called.

"No!" protested Stella.

"We're meant to be home already – everyone will be wondering where I am." Tas heaved a short sigh. "You *are* coming back for the trials next year, though? To cheer me on?"

"Course I am!" said Stella. "Wouldn't miss it!"

Tas leant in and squeezed Stella in a tight hug. "Storm sisters!" she whispered.

"Forever," replied Stella.

Tas tapped Stella's shoulder and nodded quizzically at Mum and Dad.

They were having one of those silent parent conversations that involved hand gestures, raised eyebrows, and mouthed words. When they saw her watching, they both smiled.

"What?" said Stella.

Dad raised his eyebrows at Mum.

"We got you a present," said Mum. "It's traditional, apparently, when you pass the trials. Only, you don't have to wear it, if you don't like it, or if it doesn't fit, or—"

But Stella was already on her feet. "A present!" She beamed at them.

Dad sometimes brought back presents from his travels, but she hadn't been expecting one, this time. Just having them back felt like a present.

"We can always change it," said Mum, "if it's not right—"

"Hand it over, already!" said Dad.

Mum reached behind her and pulled out a parcel, wrapped in purple tissue paper. She handed it to Stella.

Stella grinned at both of them for a moment, then tore the paper off. There was a soft bundle of fabric inside. She shook it out and held it up. A long cloak, the colour of storm clouds – purple and grey.

"Look on the back!" said Dad.

Stella turned it around. A silver lightning bolt was embroidered from the neck to the hem. Mum and Dad watched her face anxiously.

"I love it!" Stella declared. She swept it around her shoulders and did a twirl in the middle of the cockpit.

"*Now* you look the part, Sparky!" said Tas. "What do you reckon, Nimbus?"

Nimbus circled Stella once, then settled around her shoulders.

Tamar looked Stella up and down and nodded in satisfaction. "It suits you well," she said, raising her mug of hot chocolate. "Here's to the newest Lightning Weaver."

The others all raised their mugs. "The Lightning Weaver!"

ACKNOWLEDGEMENTS

A whole Gathering of magical people helped shape this story; transforming it from early scribbles, to the book you now hold in your hands.

Heartfelt thanks to Lauren, wise beyond your years, for gently guiding the early drafts in the right direction. May the sun shine on you and your family.

Enormous respect to Hazel – you are a superwoman – stalwart and cheery, despite everything the past two years have thrown at us. I am so glad to have you captaining the ship.

Huge thanks to Tilda, my wonderful editor, for helping me find my way through the winding tunnels of multiple drafts – you are a perfect Quest partner. Thanks also to Jake for sensitivity reading – what a gift, to any author – to be able to borrow someone else's eyes for a while.

Big hugs to Becky – your enthusiasm and creativity are second to none. Thanks to David Dean for the amazing cover art – I am in awe – thank you so much for continuing this adventure with me. And to Hannah for the perfect chapter headers – I adore your attention to detail.

Antonia and Kat, you have taken a whisper and turned it into a roar – thank you for shouting from the rooftops on my behalf. May the wind lift your voices and carry these stories far and wide.

To all at UCLan – so many shining sparks amongst you,

there are too many to count. It was a joy to meet your publishing students, the rising stars of the future.

One of the true delights of this year has been new friendships with brilliant indie booksellers. They are the best kind of people – resourceful, hopeful and imaginative. Huge thanks to Tamsin (the other Tamsin) at Kenilworth books, for fulgent bookshop windows, emergency boxes of biscuits and friendly hedgehogs. You make the world a better place.

Big thanks to the Good Ship and all who sail in her – it's been a joy to navigate this journey with you – from blazing sunshine, through sudden squalls, you get it. To Sam and Jo – thank you for your sharp-eyed reading, incisive comments and solid cheerleading. And to the Bathstol Writers – what an excellent gang (shelf? library?) of writers you are. I'm looking forward to more coffee-shop writing sessions and book-signing flashmobs.

A Gathering Storm is all about friendship – finding where you belong and who lifts you up. Much love to Leonardo, Isabella and their friends, for putting up with all my random questions and telling me frequently to 'hurry up and write it'. In particular, thanks to Luana for letting me quiz you endlessly for the Romanian details that bring Tassa to life.

Love and thanks to Elizabeth and David, for the warmest possible welcome and for finding me the best editing hideaways on Bressay. Thanks too, to Linda and Mary – it was a joy to talk poetry, books, and myths with you. To Emily, Magnus, David and Hope – can't wait to see you all again soon.

To my besties, Cath and Catherine, for music, tears, and laughter, all essential in setting the world to rights. Here's to conjuring bright skies and weathering the rest.

A massive planet-sized marble in the jar to Cat. Up with intuition, playfulness and straight-talking. I don't know what I'd do without you. More Tamsin-ory coming soon. Keep on beetling . . .

To Callen – a word weaver of the highest order. Thank you for your endless generosity with plotting advice (complete with fully-deserved eye-rolls), constant encouragement and pep talks, but most of all, your friendship. I treasure it.

To my parents, Digger and Clare – for trumpeting unashamedly and delighting in every success.

And most of all, to Bernardo. Thank you for being my partner-in-adventure, for listening, hearing, supporting, and believing in me. I love you.

Have you read Stella's first adventure?

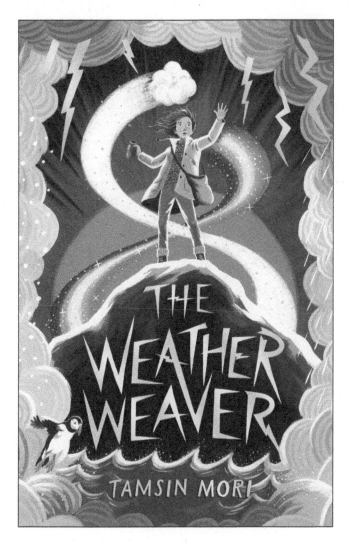

If you liked this, you'll love . . .

How far would you go to
save someone you love?

The
WIND
CHILD

Gabriela Houston